PERF

by

BECKY BELL

CHIMERA

Perfect Slave published by
Chimera Publishing Ltd
PO Box 152
Waterlooville
Hants
PO8 9FS

Printed and bound in Great Britain by
Omnia Books Ltd, Glasgow

PERFECT SLAVE

Becky Bell

This novel is fiction – in real life practice safe sex

Chapter One

The phallus-shaped gag filled Andrea's mouth completely, pressing her tongue down, tickling the back of her throat. Though made from rubber, the gag was rigid and unyielding. It was sealed into her mouth by a strap of thick black leather buckled tightly at the back of her head beneath her long blonde hair. The aroma of leather and rubber mixed together to create a pungent scent which she found intoxicating. Andrea inhaled deeply.

In contrast to the harshness of the gag, the blindfold was soft and silky – a mask of black satin cut to fit over the eyes and the bridge of the nose and padded on the inside so as to exclude even the faintest hint of light. The elasticated straps that held it in place were tight and the material pressed against her eyelids.

She was naked apart from a pair of white panties – tiny thong-cut panties, no more than a triangle of silk covering her mons and a thin gusset that had already buried itself between the slippery lips of her sex. And high heels of course. White patent leather shoes with an ankle strap and heels so high they forced her feet into an almost vertical stance. She couldn't have walked more than a few steps in them but, right now, walking was the last thing he had in mind for her.

She felt her arms being drawn behind her back. Her breasts were large and very round and this action lifted them and made them quiver. A coarse thick leather strap was being threaded under the top of her arms. She heard it being fed into a buckle. It was tugged tight, forcing her shoulders back and pushing her chest out. Her breasts quivered again. A surge of excitement made her moan. Her whole body was trembling. This was, after all, what she craved more than anything else.

Leather cuffs were being wound around her wrists. They were padded on the inside with something spongy and soft. She felt them tighten in turn and heard the two little buckles that held them in place being fastened. She listened intently to the sound of a snap-lock being fixed into a D-ring on the left-hand cuff, then it was pulled over to the right, effectively binding her wrists together. She loved all the little metallic noises, like the noise of bridles and tack being applied to a horse. It was the same thing after all: the horse being prepared for the rider – the slave being prepared for the master.

Now she heard the pulley being cranked down and she started as the cold metal ring attached to the overhead rope brushed against the small of her back. More clicks. Another snap-lock. Her wrists were pulled up slightly as the cuffs were locked into the metal ring.

He took two steps back. She imagined him looking at her, examining the way the bondage had transformed her body.

She sensed him kneeling in front of her. She felt padded leather cuffs being wrapped around her ankles. They were attached to a shiny metal bar. He had made her lay it on the floor in front of her before he'd applied the blindfold. In fact, she had been made to prepare all the equipment for him while he sat in a large upright chair and watched her every move.

The metal bar and the ankle cuffs made it impossible for her to close her legs. She was intensely aware of the gusset of the panties. It had worked its way right up against her clitoris, which was swollen and throbbing wildly.

She heard him walking over to the crank of the pulley. It clicked through the ratchet that controlled its movements. *Click. Click. Click.* Each sound drew the white nylon rope higher, forcing her wrists up into the air behind her back. As her wrists rose, the geometry of her body demanded that her head dip. *Click. Click. Click.* Her arms were being raised until they were almost vertical, her torso bent at right angles from her waist. The clicking stopped.

It was perfect. More perfect than anything she had imagined. And she had imagined this for so long it didn't seem possible that at last it was no longer just a cherished fantasy but a living breathing reality that was setting her whole body alight. There was pain, of course. She'd always known there would be pain. And so it had proved. But it was a pain like no other, a pain striated with a pleasure as intense as anything she'd ever felt in her life. The cramp in her shoulder muscles and her back was extreme. But it was indivisible from the pleasure that throbbed in her nipples and her clitoris and in the depths of her cunt.

There was worse to come, she knew. That was why he'd made her lay out all the equipment. She'd handled the nipple clips herself, seen their sharp, serrated jaws and felt the weight of the metal pendants that hung down from them. She had laid out the whip too.

He paused. He was looking at her again, she was sure, examining her new position. Her tight, apple-shaped buttocks were thrust upward. Her large, fleshy breasts hung down like inverted pyramids. She was sure he would be able to see that her labia, on either side of the thin creased gusset of her panties, were glistening with the sticky sap of her body. She had never been so wet.

She flinched as she felt his fingers touch her left breast. He weighed it in his hand, then pinched the nipple. She thought she heard the faintest of metallic tinkles as he picked up one of the nipple clips, the pendant clinking against the metal jaws. Almost immediately, something cold closed around the puckered flesh. She shivered. The little teeth in the spring-loaded jaws of the clip sank into her nipple and a hot, searing pain shot through her. The extraordinary thing was that it was accompanied by a wave of pleasure that was sharper than anything she could ever remember feeling before. The second clip followed, producing the same result. She was trembling all over, unable to control her body's reactions.

As she began to regain some semblance of control again she realised he must still be holding the tear-shaped weights attached to each clip. Now, very slowly, he lowered them, taking up the slack in the little chains until they were hanging free. The weights were heavy. They dragged her breasts down and cut the jaws of the clips deeper into her tender flesh, but she relished them. She shook her breasts from side to side, making the pendants swing so violently they knocked into each other, producing an almost overwhelming melange of pain and pleasure – a sensation she had already come to love.

She was coming. Her whole body was on fire. How many times had she lay on her bed trying to imagine what this would be like? How many times had she masturbated with her fingers plucking furiously at her clit, the handle of a hairbrush jammed into her vagina, a silk scarf tied over her eyes so she could concentrate on the blank screen of her mind? And how many times had she pictured herself lying bound and helpless in front of her master?

But the reality was a thousand times more arousing than anything she'd been able to imagine. By means of a few straps and chains he had removed her will. She belonged to him. She was his slave. It was that knowledge as much as the physical excitement that was producing her first orgasm. She strained every muscle against her bonds, wallowing in the feeling of total constriction. Then she came, her clitoris pulsing violently against the thin strap of white silk tautly bisecting her sex.

But that was only the beginning. She knew that she would come again and again. She simply could not stop herself. She had never felt so sexually alive. That was the point. The bondage, the gag, the blindfold meant that all her energy and feeling were concentrated on her sex. There was nothing else.

The nipple clips seemed to claw at her breasts like tiny hands, pulling them down, the whole breast stretched and tenderised. She heard him move. There was the lightest gust of air as he came up behind her. She smelt his musky aftershave mixed with the scent of rubber and leather. She knew what he was going to do now and she had never wanted anything more in her life. Her buttocks were tingling in anticipation.

The whip was long and tapering with a braided leather handle topped by a brass boss. He picked it up and ran the lash up her inner thigh. She moaned into the gag as it flicked against her labia.

'So needy,' he said. They were the first words he'd spoken since he'd ordered her to prepare the equipment. His voice sounded different, lower and more strained. 'You want it badly, don't you?'

She nodded her head.

'I knew from the moment I set eyes on you, Andrea. It's what you've always wanted.'

The whip pressed into her labia then sawed back and forth. If he did this for much longer she would come again. At the back, the panties were no more than a thin silk thong that rose from the cleft of her buttocks and joined the equally narrow strap that formed the waistband. He hooked the whip under the material and pulled it outward, forcing the gusset of the panties even more tightly into her sex. Then he pulled the whip from beneath the silk and the thong snapped back against her buttocks.

She could imagine him standing behind her in the heavy velvet robe, scarlet braided in gold thread. She could imagine him raising the whip.

Thwack! She screamed into the gag, pulling against her bonds. She had developed a complex masturbation scenario for herself. Being whipped was always part of it, but she had never been whipped in reality. She had never even been

9

spanked, and nothing had prepared her for the withering pain. Her whole body shuddered. The tear-shaped pendants hanging from her breasts knocked against each other, producing a second shock of sensation. Then pleasure, hot throbbing pleasure, simply overwhelmed her. Had she not been so firmly bound she would have fallen to her knees.

Thwack! This time, if anything, the pain was more intense. The whip had landed lower, closer to her sex. Perhaps for this reason the interval between the pain and the intense pleasure that followed was shorter and the excitement even more intense. She heard the rustle of the velvet robe as he raised the whip again. She could feel the two weals on her bottom throbbing as strongly as her clitoris, and at the same frequency. As the whip landed for a third time she came, the searing pain and the extraordinary pleasure it produced rooting itself directly to her clit. Her pelvis spasmed wildly. She was simply unable to control herself.

He'd seen what had happened. He let her orgasm run its course then smoothed his hand across her buttocks. His touch was so soft and tender, his hand so deliciously cool in contrast to the heat the whip had generated, that she almost came again.

'A secret slave,' he repeated quietly. 'You've wanted this for a long time, haven't you?'

She nodded. She had told him nothing about the fantasies that had obsessed her for so long, but he seemed to know.

She heard him moving in front of her.

'It might surprise you to learn how many women imagine they want to be a slave, to have a master and be totally in his control. But when they're faced with the reality, with the pain and discomfort, with the need to obey without question, they realise it is not what they want after all. There is a stark difference between dreams and reality. In reality, few women have the – let's call it the ability – to be a real slave.'

She heard his heavy robe drop to the floor. Her long blonde hair hung on either side of her face. He pulled it to one side, then began unstrapping the gag. 'You are one of the few, my child. I am sure of that now. Every slave must have a master to make them complete.'

The gag was pulled from her mouth. The rubber-covered phallus was covered with her saliva.

'You know that's true, don't you?'

'Yes, master.' She had never used that word before, though she had dreamt of saying it so many times its use made her shiver.

He gave a little giggle of delight. 'So it appears fortuitous that we met.'

It was indeed.

She had never imagined her sex dreams would come true. She thought of them as something she would keep forever secret, a fantasy which she used to excite herself when she masturbated, or to inspire herself when she found the act of sex failed to arouse. She had never imagined that the world she had created for herself actually existed. But here with Charles Darrington Hawksworth, in the specially equipped punishment room in his house, she realised she had found what she really wanted. Her dream was now a reality.

Charles Darrington Hawksworth was her master now.

It had started a week earlier, on Tuesday morning.

Andrea Hamilton worked for Silverton Communications, a small private company that designed the software necessary to communicate with orbiting telecommunication satellites. It was a very successful business and, during the two years Andrea had worked for the company, it had cornered a substantial chunk of the market.

Andrea was bright. She had graduated from Manchester University with a first in electronics and had been recruited by Silverton to work on their research and development programme. She liked the job and the people she worked for.

As usual, Andrea had travelled by tube from Islington to

the sleek and futuristic Silverton building in North London – a circular tower with black glass windows and a stainless steel revolving door. It looked as though it might be a set for a science-fiction film. Andrea's office was on the third floor.

'Good morning.'

Pam Mitchell was short and cute. She had frizzy black hair, a rather chubby figure and wore spiky high heels in a vain attempt to increase her height. 'Have you heard the news?'

'What news?'

'It was on the telly this morning.'

'What was, Pam?'

'Silverton have sold out to Darrington International.'

'What!' Andrea was astonished. Edward Highfield, the chairman and major shareholder, had always said he would never sell out. Silverton was his company and, so he had told his staff on numerous occasions, that was the way he wanted it to stay.

'He's obviously had an offer he can't refuse. There's a meeting downstairs at eleven. We're all supposed to be there. Apparently he's going to explain the situation.'

'Darrington. They're huge.' Andrea sat down at her desk. She had a sinking feeling. Any company taken over by a multi-national conglomerate was bound to suffer redundancies, and she was sure it would be a case of last in first out. With only two years experience, not only would she be first out but it would be hard for her to find another job in what was an extremely crowded field.

'You'll be all right,' Pam said, reading her thoughts.

At ten to eleven Pam and Andrea made their way down to the big conference room on the ground floor. As they trekked across the foyer with the other employees, all wondering what was likely to happen to them, Andrea glimpsed a black Mercedes stretch limousine drawing up at the front door. It had dark windows and Andrea could not see inside.

'Who's that?' Andrea said, nodding towards the car. Its

doors remained firmly closed.

'Big wig from Darrington, I guess,' Pam replied.

They trooped into the conference room, which was designed like a large lecture hall, with raked seating and a wooden rostrum. Edward Highfield was sitting on the rostrum behind a desk. He was making notes on a laptop computer, pointedly avoiding eye contact with the assembled audience. He looked, Andrea thought, decidedly sheepish.

At eleven precisely he got to his feet.

'Good morning, ladies and gentleman,' he began. 'I'm sure you've all heard the news. I'm sorry I wasn't able to communicate my intentions to you personally, but unfortunately the press got hold of the story. You all know what journalists are like.' This was intended to be a joke, but no one so much as tittered. 'As you know, I never wanted to part with this company, but I have been approached by Darrington International with an offer which I believe will enhance the prospects of all of us. The problem with a business like ours is the need for constant investment. We are at the cutting edge of technology and, unfortunately, in order to keep ahead of the game we are obliged to spend more and more on research and development. Darrington offers us the opportunity to do just that. In addition, I have a cast-iron assurance from the chairman of Darrington that all of your jobs will be protected.'

This was greeted by an exclamation of delight from most of the company and conversation immediately broke out. Everyone had shared Andrea's worries about possible redundancies.

Highfield raised his hands to calm the noise. 'What's more, I'm delighted to tell you that, as an indication of how seriously the chairman of Darrington takes this pledge, he has agreed to come here this morning and address you personally.' Highfield nodded to his secretary, who was standing by the main entrance. She opened the door and Charles Darrington Hawksworth strode into the room.

Whether it was Edward Highfield or Charles Hawksworth who had choreographed this dramatic entrance, Andrea did not know. She only knew that she couldn't take her eyes off the man who strode up to the rostrum and turned to face the rows of employees.

'Good morning.' His velvety voice was soft and cultured. 'Your chairman has explained the basic situation, I believe...'

He began to explain Darrington's plans to pump money into Silverton's new software and increase the marketing resources, but Andrea barely heard what he was saying. Instead, she found herself staring into his eyes. They were the deepest blue, she thought, that she had ever seen. What's more, though he was addressing his remarks to a room full of people, he seemed to be staring directly at her.

Andrea had no doubt that Charles Darrington Hawksworth was one of the most handsome men she had ever seen. His face was craggy, with a square jaw, a straight nose and a wide fleshy mouth. His thick curly black hair was greying over his temples, and he was tall and broad-chested. His clothes were immaculate; a beautifully tailored navy-blue suit, a white silk shirt and a matching yellow tie, and handmade shoes which shone like a mirror. Andrea was fascinated by his hands. He had long bony fingers and immaculately manicured fingernails. She wondered how it would feel to have those hands explore her flesh.

'...so, in conclusion, I have bought this company because of its talented workforce, and I have no intention of stripping its assets. I hope you will all continue to work for me and that together we will soon enjoy new success.'

Everyone applauded loudly, their enthusiasm no doubt based on relief that all jobs appeared to be secure.

Edward Highfield got to his feet. Andrea had never liked the man. Though he was moderately attractive and there was no doubt about his business acumen, she found him smarmy and insincere.

'Thank you, Charles,' he said.

Hawksworth bowed slightly, then strode out of the room with Highfield at his side.

Andrea was applauding too, though her eyes were still rooted to Hawksworth. As the applause died away, she noticed that Hawksworth had stopped in the doorway and was looking around. Once again she had the impression he was staring straight at her. She saw him speak to Highfield. Though she was too far away to hear what was being said, she thought he nodded in her direction. Then they were both gone.

'What a dish,' Pam said, as they filed out of the room. 'Jesus, Andrea, what I wouldn't give for a night with him. Did you see those eyes?'

Andrea nodded. She could still see them. It was as if she had stared straight into the sun and the light had burned her retinas.

'I wonder how often he's going to visit us. I want to be prepared next time. Throw myself under his car, something subtle like that,' Pam continued.

'I didn't really notice him,' Andrea lied, not wanting to discuss the real feelings Charles Hawksworth had aroused in her. 'Come on, let's get back,' she said. 'At least it looks as if our jobs are safe.'

It was a ritual. It had started as a routine but now every detail had become enshrined in significance, every moment was savoured, every detail added to the excitement. But tonight there was an urgency she had rarely felt before.

She had begun to strip off her clothes as soon as she got home. She abandoned her jacket on the sofa in her small living room and headed straight for the bedroom. Everything was kept in the bottom drawer of a large pine chest. She took it all out and laid it carefully on her double bed, reminding herself not to hurry, that the anticipation was as much a part of the ritual as the performance.

Unbuttoning her blouse, she went into the small en suite bathroom. She adjusted the mixer taps until she got an even flow of warm water, then took off her blouse and her skirt. She was wearing a black lace bra that strained to hold her fleshy breasts, tan-coloured tights and small bikini briefs. As she reached behind her back to unhook the bra she looked at herself in the mirror on the wall. She stared into her eyes and there, gazing back at her, she could see the face of Charles Darrington Hawksworth, those deep blue eyes perfectly still, the expression on his face betraying no emotion.

She allowed the bra to drop away. Her breasts trembled. She had large nipples surrounded by a narrow band of dark brown areolae, which was pimpled with little papillae. Her nipples were already erect. They had been like that since the meeting. In fact they were so hard and knotted they had turned a deep red, standing out from the orb of flesh like cherries on a cake. Tentatively she tweaked the left one between her thumb and finger and felt a surge of sensation. She looked into the mirror. Charles's eyes were disapproving and she knew why. She was not allowed to touch her nipples this early in the proceedings. Everything had its place.

She turned the water off, scented it with bath oil, then stripped off her tights and panties and climbed in. She lay with the back of her head against the edge of the bath and closed her eyes. On the blank screen of her mind, Charles Hawksworth appeared again, his expression unchanged, those eyes looking at her critically.

She could feel her clitoris pulsing. The temptation to open her legs and run her finger down to manipulate it was strong, but she resisted it. Everything had its place. She usually spent longer luxuriating in the water, enjoying the prospect of what was to come, but tonight her needs were altogether too urgent. She stood up, soaped herself down, then washed the lather away with a big sponge. As it cascaded off her body the water channelled down between her legs. In the mirror it looked as if she were peeing.

Climbing out of the water, she picked up a big fluffy towel and rubbed herself dry, ignoring the sexual feelings this aroused as the towel brushed her breasts and her sex. She threw the towel aside and then walked into the bedroom. She felt little butterflies of excitement beginning to flutter in her stomach.

The corset was made from black leather. It was tight, at least one size too small for her, and narrow, no more than a wide belt of material that cinched around her waist. Andrea pulled it into place, the leather cold against her warm body. She struggled with the hooks and eyes that held it in place, sucking her breath in to get it to do up. The constriction excited her.

Dangling from its hem were four black leather suspenders. Andrea sat on the bed. She had laid out a pair of sheer black stockings. She picked one up and inserted her foot into the nylon, rolling it up over her leg. The nylon was woven with Lycra to give it a shiny, almost wet look, and Andrea loved the way it transformed her flesh, making it smooth and silky, clinging to the contours of her calves and thighs. She clipped it into the suspenders at the front and the side of her thigh, then repeated the process with the second stocking.

She stood up. The black patent leather high heels were on the floor by her wardrobe. She climbed into them. The heels were so high it was impossible to walk for more than a few steps, but the shoes tightened the muscles in her calves and deepened the gluteal fold where her thighs tucked into her buttocks. She had installed a floor-length mirror on the bedroom wall opposite the foot of the bed, and she stood in front of it to admire herself. Over her shoulder she could see Charles Hawksworth admiring her too. She looked like a whore. The thought made her clitoris throb.

She allowed her hands to run down over her flat smooth belly, framed as it was by the leather corset at the top, the long suspenders at the sides, and the opaque black stocking-tops underneath. She had very short, soft pubic hair, oddly shaped in an inverted narrow triangle, but between her legs she was virtually hairless with nothing to mask her thick pouting labia. She could see the first inch of them now, pursed at the base of her mons.

Slowly, walking with tiny steps because of the shoes, she bent and reached down at the foot of the bed. The ropes were permanently tied around the wooden legs but tucked away under a valance, out of sight of casual visitors. She pulled the first one out and set it down on top of the mattress, then tottered around the bed and did the same with the other three. Knotted to the end of each was a metal snap-lock.

The shoes were already making her feet and the muscles of her calves ache, but the pain was mixed with a peculiar pleasure.

Four black leather cuffs lay on the bed. Putting her left foot up on the mattress Andrea wrapped one of them around the silky nylon that sheathed her ankle, and buckled it tight. She did the same with her right foot, then sat on the bed again. Being right-handed, it was comparatively easy to buckle the cuff around her left wrist by holding it tightly against her body, but the right wrist was more awkward. She had practised the manoeuvre so many times, however, that it didn't take long.

The feeling of each cuff circling her limbs increased her excitement markedly. She looked in the mirror again. Her body was banded by black; the tight leather corset biting into her waist, and the leather cuffs and the bands of the black stocking-tops around her thighs. In contrast to these tight black rings, her exposed flesh – particularly her large round breasts and the tops of her slender thighs – seemed incredibly creamy and soft. She could see Charles Hawksworth's eyes looking at her, examining every detail of her body.

Andrea picked up the final item of her equipment. It was a narrow black leather belt. She pulled it around her waist and buckled it tight. Another, much wider piece of leather was attached to the back of this belt, hanging down loosely between her legs. Projecting from this was a small but stout dildo made from cream-coloured plastic.

Sitting on the bed, Andrea scrambled over to the middle of the mattress, then opened her legs. Leaning forward she secured the snap-locks attached to each rope at the bottom corners of the bed to a shiny metal D-ring at the side of the ankle cuffs. She lay back, feeling a surge of excitement. She tried to close her legs but couldn't, the bondage preventing anything but the slightest inward movement.

For a moment she did nothing, wallowing in the sensations that were coursing through her body. The dildo was sticking up vertically between her legs and she could push herself down on it so her labia were crushed against its shaft. Her clitoris was throbbing so wildly she thought she might come before her preparations were complete. But she managed to wrestle herself back from the edge.

Sitting up again, she took hold of the dildo and directed it down to the mouth of her vagina. In the past, before this ritual had become so complicated, she had merely jammed the handle of her hairbrush into her sex while she strummed her fingers against her clit and dreamt of being bound and helpless. Now she had evolved greater refinements.

Bracing herself, she slid the tip of the dildo into her vagina. At once a wave of sensation made her shudder. Her sex was wet and the dildo slid home effortlessly. She pushed it all the way in, then folded the leather it was attached to up over her belly. It buckled tightly into the front of the belt around her waist, pressing down against her labia and holding the dildo firmly in place.

Lying back again changed the angle of her sex, pushing the dildo into new areas of sensitivity. She moaned. Again she struggled with herself, as exquisite sensation rolled over her. She didn't want to come yet – not until she was ready.

The next manoeuvre required a bit of contortion. Stretching

herself up the bed, pulling until the ankle cuffs bit into her flesh, she reached over with both hands to the snap-lock at the top left-hand corner. She managed to clip it into the D-ring on the cuff around her left wrist. Then she rolled on to her back and stretched her right arm up to the rope lying on the mattress at the top right-hand corner.

Andrea was no fool. She did not want to tie herself in bondage so tight that she couldn't escape. Maybe she could have managed to open the snap-lock with the fingers of her right hand and insert it into the D-ring on her right wrist, but even if she could there was no guarantee she could get it open again. She had practised it several times and had managed to get herself free on every occasion, but she was still not prepared to risk it. What she had done therefore, to give herself the impression of being bound and spread-eagled, was to knock the locking mechanism out of the snap-lock, leaving instead a hook-like projection. It was easy enough to get the D-ring onto this hook and equally easy to unhook it again. Then, as long as she was careful not to move her right arm around too much, she could struggle and tug against it as if she were really bound.

With her head twisted around so she could see what she was doing, she managed to slip the D-ring over the hook. She immediately pulled her arm down so the rope was taut and the hook wouldn't come free. She pulled on all her limbs, wanting to feel the constriction. It wasn't perfect. Somewhere in the back of her mind she knew the bondage was a sham, that she could merely flick her right arm up and undo herself, but it was as near to the real thing as she was prepared to risk.

She closed her eyes. She was acutely aware of her bondage, the way the leather cuffs pulled at her wrists and ankles, stretching the muscles and sinews of her body. She loved the feeling of the tight sleek stockings and the even tighter leather corset. The suspenders were so restricting they cut channels into the flesh on the tops of her thighs.

Normally she would lie like this, spread-eagled across the bed, for a long time, savouring every feeling, teasing herself by rolling her hips from side to side very slowly so the base of the dildo rubbed against her clit, bringing herself closer and closer to the brink of orgasm but never quite over it.

But tonight was different. Tonight Charles Darrington Hawksworth was standing by the side of the bed looking down at her, his eyes unblinking, his expression varying between indulgence and stark disapproval. Tonight she was rolling her hips wildly, rocking the whole bed, her clitoris responding with sharp tweaks of exquisite pleasure. She clenched her vagina around the phallus, feeling the juices that were running over it.

Those deep blue eyes burnt into her. She could see him examining her tits. She thrust them up towards him.

'Do they please you, master?'

The phantom said nothing. His eyes moved to her belly. Andrea tried to spread her legs further apart. Then she felt her vagina convulse reflexively around the dildo. It did it twice in quick succession, and she whimpered. She pushed her buttocks up clear of the bed. She was coming now and she knew there wasn't a thing she could do to stop herself.

She opened her mouth, arched her head back against the pillow until it was almost at right angles to her spine.

'Master...!' she screamed as she came, her orgasm locking every muscle and sinew in her body.

It was a long time before she opened her eyes again. When she did Charles Darrington Hawksworth had gone.

Chapter Two

'Ms Hamilton?'

'Yes.'

'This is for you.' Three days later Andrea opened the door of her flat to a tall, extremely broad, blond-haired man in a grey chauffeur's uniform. He was holding a white envelope in his hand.

'For me? I don't understand.'

'I'm to wait for a reply.'

'Oh. You'd better come in.'

Andrea was wearing a tracksuit. It was seven o'clock and she was just thinking about what to wear tonight for dinner with Greg Anders, her current boyfriend.

'Thank you, madam,' the chauffeur said. He took off his cap, tucked it under his arm, and stepped inside.

Andrea was puzzled. She didn't know anyone who had a chauffeur. She tore open the envelope and took out a white deckled-edged card. The writing was neat and italicised:

Dear Ms Hamilton,

I hope you will not think of this as an impertinence, but I wonder if you would care to have dinner with me on Saturday. I think you know the reason why. If you do not, simply return this invitation to George. If, as I suspect, you do, then he will return for you at seven on Saturday evening.

Whatever your decision I will always remain

Yours faithfully

Charles Hawksworth.

Andrea stared at the note. She read it again. She felt herself blush. She hadn't the faintest idea that Charles Hawksworth had any interest in her. Of course, she remembered how he had paused at the door and seemed to indicate her to Edward Highfield, but she had convinced herself that his interest existed only in her imagination. He could have been pointing out any one of a hundred people. Now it appeared that her first impression had been right.

'You work for Mr Hawksworth?'

'As I understand it, we both do, madam.'

She smiled. 'Yes. That's right, we do. But I've only been working for him since Tuesday.'

'Indeed. May I ask you for your reply, madam?'

Andrea caught her breath. She didn't think that an hour had gone by since last Tuesday when she hadn't thought of Hawksworth, hadn't pictured his deep blue eyes and, what's more, hadn't had some wild sexual fantasy about what he might do to her. She hadn't the faintest idea why the briefest of meetings – indeed, it could hardly be called a meeting at all – had produced such an extraordinary response in her, but there was no denying that it had. Now it appeared that this short encounter had also made an impact on him.

'Tell Mr Hawksworth I shall be delighted to dine with him on Saturday.'

'Very good, madam. I'll pick you up at seven.'

'Are we going to a restaurant?'

'I'm sorry, madam, I don't know Mr Hawksworth's plans.'

For some reason Andrea didn't believe him, though she had no idea why.

The chauffeur put on his cap and let himself out without another word.

Andrea went to the fridge and poured herself a glass of white wine. She needed it. She slumped down on her sofa, sipped the wine and read the note again. *I think you know the reason why.* What did that mean? The only thing that had happened between them had been an exchange of glances. But she had the weirdest feeling that Hawksworth had looked deep inside her and learnt her deepest secret –

and that he knew what she had been imagining over the last three days.

No one at Silverton could have given him that information. Not even Pam, her closest friend in the company, knew anything about her sexual fantasies. So how had Hawksworth found out? Perhaps that was not what the phrase meant at all. Perhaps it merely referred to a mutual attraction which was clear from the way Andrea had stared at him. He was an attractive man, after all, and was probably used to women gazing at him with thinly disguised lust. That's what it must be.

The chime of the doorbell startled her. She looked at her watch. She realised she had been sitting on the sofa day-dreaming about Charles Hawksworth for half-an-hour, and now Greg was outside waiting to pick her up.

She quickly stuffed the note into the pocket of her tracksuit, ran to the door and picked up the answerphone. Greg usually waited at the front door of the building for her to come downstairs.

'Sorry, I'm running late. Can you come up?'

'Sure,' his distorted voice said cheerily.

Two minutes later he was sitting on the sofa with a glass of wine in one hand and the bottle on the low table in front of him.

'Sorry about this. It won't take me long to get changed.'

'No hurry. I thought we'd go to that Thai place. No need to book.'

Greg was short and a little bit on the tubby side, with a pleasant round face and mousy-coloured hair.

She waltzed into the bedroom. She had already taken a bath, put on her make-up and laid out a blouse and skirt. She pulled the slightly crumpled note from her pocket and carefully put it away in her bedside table. She stripped off the tracksuit and stood naked in front of the tall mirror. The thought of Charles Hawksworth had stiffened her nipples, and she was sure she could feel a slick of wetness on her

24

labia. Experimentally, she ran a hand down between her legs. Her sex wasn't just wet, it was soaking. As her fingers glided between her labia her clitoris throbbed strongly, crying out for attention.

She ignored it and took a pair of white satin panties and a matching bra from the chest of drawers. As she drew the panties up over her thighs they brushed against her sex and her clit throbbed once more. She tried to calm it by running her hand over the silky material and pressing it against her labia, but this only made matters worse. The touch of the cool satin of her bra against her breasts was making her nipples tingle. As she adjusted her breasts, lifting them slightly to allow them to sit more comfortably in the cups, this movement too produced strong waves of feeling.

The thought of going out to dinner was not appealing. In fact it was the last thing she wanted to do. She glanced into the mirror again. Over her shoulder she could once more see Charles Darrington Hawksworth's knowing blue eyes.

Calmly she opened the top drawer in the pine chest and rummaged inside. It was where she kept her stockings and tights. She found what she was looking for, a pair of glossy white hold-up stockings with lace welts. Sitting on the bed she pulled them on, smoothing the nylon over her legs. Then she stripped the counterpane from the double bed and lay back on the crisp white sheet. She stretched her legs apart, and the white satin gusset of her panties pulled tautly across the delta of her sex.

'Greg!' she shouted.

'Yeah?'

'Why don't you come in here?'

She wished she had the courage to put on the leather cuffs and tie herself to the bed first, to let him see what she really wanted. But she didn't.

Greg opened the bedroom door tentatively. His eyes widened as he saw her lying there.

'You look great,' he said breathlessly.

'Do I?'

He walked up to the bed and gazed down at her, his eyes roaming over her body. 'You know you do. Those stockings are really sexy.'

'So what are you going to do about it?' she goaded.

She arched her buttocks off the bed, angling her sex up towards him. She'd had sex with Greg a couple of times, but she'd never done anything like this. She raised her foot and dug it into his thigh, moving it up until she could feel his rapidly stiffening cock beneath her toes.

'What's got into you?' he said. There was a strange hint of disapproval in his voice.

'You have,' she lied.

He stripped off his jacket and began to unbutton his shirt as she rubbed her toes against his cock. The nylon rasped against the material of his trousers. Andrea stretched her arms above her head and spread them apart, imagining they were about to be bound.

Greg threw his shirt aside and pushed her foot away to enable him to unzip his trousers. His cock had escaped the fly of his boxer-shorts and sprung out from the opened zip, fully erect. He hopped inelegantly from one foot to the other as he pulled his shoes and socks off, almost losing his balance, then slipped off his trousers and pants.

Andrea could feel her pussy throbbing. She snaked one hand down to her belly and ran it under the white satin of her panties.

'Do you want to watch?' she invited.

Her fingers distended the taut white satin as she pressed one finger, then two, into the mouth of her vagina. Greg's eyes were locked on her sex.

'You've never done that before,' he said quietly.

'There's a lot of things I haven't done,' she said. She slid her fingers deep into her cunt. She moaned loudly. With her free hand she pulled the gusset of the panties aside so he could see exactly what she was doing. 'I'm very wet,' she whispered, sawing her two fingers back and forth. She was sure he could see and hear that for himself. Her fingers were glistening with her juices.

She used the middle finger of her left hand to find her clit. It was hard and swollen. Immediately, she began pushing it from side to side with little subtlety. She wasn't in the mood for subtlety. Each movement produced a huge wave of sensation. She had never done anything like this before with any man, and the novelty was exciting. But she knew it was really the thought of Charles Hawksworth's invitation that was driving her on. *I think you know the reason why.* Did he really know all her secrets?

Greg was staring down at her, his circumcised cock sticking out at right angles from his belly.

'Is there anything you've ever fantasised about, Greg? Ever wanted to do something and never had the courage to ask?'

He hesitated. She saw him tear his eyes from her sex and look up to her face. 'What do you mean?'

'There is something, isn't there?' She could see it in his eyes. For a moment they had dulled and turned inward, accessing some secret thought. 'Come on, tell me. I'll do whatever you want.' The idea that Greg had a secret fantasy, like hers, was terribly arousing.

'Really?' he said. She saw his cock twitch.

'Come on, Greg, can't you see the state I'm in?'

'Turn over.' His voice was suddenly flat and unemotional.

Andrea looked at him steadily, then she pulled her fingers out of her sex and rolled over. 'Like this?' she asked.

Greg did not reply. He climbed onto the bed and knelt at her side. His eyes were focused on her arse, the white satin panties stretched tautly across her pert cheeks. He took hold of the waistband of the panties and pulled them down until they banded the top of her thighs, leaving her bottom bare.

'This is what I've always wanted to do.' He sounded angry, as though he was cross with himself for allowing this fantasy to escape.

Andrea sensed what he was going to do a fraction of a second before he brought the palm of his hand down with a resounding smack on her left buttock. Almost immediately he raised his hand again and delivered an even more stinging stroke to the right.

'Lovely red arse,' he said through gritted teeth.

His hand struck again, twice in quick succession, left buttock first and then the right. Andrea gasped. Each slap was a symphony of sensations. Her clitoris and her vagina throbbed violently as she felt the tingling heat from her bottom radiate inward. Though she had never been spanked before she had often tried to imagine how it would feel. Now she knew. It felt wonderful. She closed her eyes so she could concentrate on the feeling and, lying in wait for her in the secret chamber of her mind, was Charles Hawksworth. He was smiling indulgently.

'Oh yes,' Andrea moaned, wriggling her bottom to encourage Greg to spank it again.

Thwack! The sound of flesh on flesh reverberated around the room. Andrea knew she was going to come. She thrust her hand under her body, into the panties and down between her legs, forcing her finger between her labia and onto her clit.

Thwack! Thwack! Each stroke increased the excitement. There was pain, sharp prickling pain, but it was overwhelmed by the fierceness of the pleasure the spanking created. Andrea felt her whole body tense, the physical stimulation matched by the mental as Greg exposed one of the deepest currents of her sexuality.

He lifted his hand again and Andrea felt the stinging slap on her already tender buttock. The pain and pleasure travelled straight to her clit and, this time, her sex exploded in orgasm, making her cry out loud as every nerve in her body responded. In the middle time of this cacophony of feeling, she heard Greg make an odd coughing sound, almost like a sob, and felt a warm liquid spatter over her buttocks and her back.

She was too involved in her own climax to do more than register, almost subliminally, that he had come too.

The stinging turned to wonderful tingling sensations. Her body melted, her muscles relaxed.

'That was incredible,' she enthused dreamily, rolling onto her side. She ran a hand over her back and massaged in the thick, gooey juice he had deposited there.

Greg had climbed off the bed and was looking for his clothes, his rapidly deflating cock still dripping with spunk.

'What are you doing?' Andrea said.

'I think I'd better go.'

'Why? That was great, Greg. Really sexy. Don't you want to do it again?'

'No, I do not,' he said with real venom. He found his trousers and pulled them on.

'And here was me thinking you enjoyed it,' she said, astonished by his reaction.

'I didn't know you were into all that.'

'I didn't know you were either. Does it matter? We can just enjoy it, can't we?'

'I should never have...' His voice trailed off. He threw on his shirt, put his socks into his jacket pocket, and levered his feet into his shoes.

'Aren't we at least going to have dinner?'

'No. I want to go now.'

And that's exactly what he did. He ran out of the bedroom and, a few seconds later, Andrea heard her front door slam.

She lay back on the bed. The contact of the sheet with her buttocks made them tingle anew. It was delicious. She couldn't understand Greg's reaction. Obviously he'd let his inhibitions down in an unguarded moment, and had instantly regretted it. She doubted he would want to see her again. If he were ashamed of his guilty secret, he wouldn't want to see the only woman who knew what he was capable of again.

Andrea supposed it was no great loss. They had dated three or four times and she had never felt anything more than a vague liking for the man. She had certainly never cherished the idea that it might develop into something more significant.

Pulling off her crumpled panties, Andrea spread her legs. She could see her labia in the tall mirror on the opposite wall. They seemed to be smiling at her – a vertical smile. She spread her thighs wider and her vagina winked open, its dark scarlet flesh glistening with its own sticky sap. Very slowly, Andrea reached over to the bedside table. She took out a thick rubber dildo and directed it to her sex.

The next twenty-four hours until her date with Charles Hawksworth were going to seem like a lifetime, she knew that. She would just have to find ways to amuse herself until then.

'I'm waiting, master,' she said aloud. The word set her nerves on edge.

'Where are we going?'

'Battersea, madam.'

'Battersea?'

The large black Mercedes had arrived at ten minutes to seven, double-parking just outside her front door. The terraced house had been converted into two flats, and Andrea occupied the upper floor. She had been ready for half-an-hour and stood at the window, hiding behind the curtains, keeping watch. At exactly seven o'clock the barrel-chested chauffeur had rung the bell.

'Yes, madam. The heliport.'

'We're going in a helicopter?' She tried to keep her astonishment out of her voice.

'You are, madam. It's quicker.'

Andrea hadn't been expecting that. Though she hadn't the faintest idea where Charles Hawksworth lived, she'd assumed she would be driven there.

'Where does Mr Hawksworth live then?' she asked.

'He has an estate in Wiltshire.'

Andrea digested this information. Her anticipation was growing by the second.

'There's champagne in the refrigerator, madam, if you would care for a glass.'

The interior of the stretch Mercedes was vast and had every luxury; a television, a video recorder, and two telephones. A cocktail cabinet was set into the bulkhead that divided the passenger compartment from the driver. Opening the highly polished walnut doors, Andrea saw that half the cabinet contained glasses and square decanters of spirits, while the other half was a small refrigerator. Inside were four half bottles of champagne. She opened one and poured the bubbling wine into a long flute glass. This was definitely the way to travel.

'Are there going to be any other guests?' she asked as she sipped.

'I've no idea, madam,' the chauffeur replied.

Andrea sat back in the comfortable leather seat and watched the world go by. The traffic was heavy as the big car travelled down to the embankment and along the river towards Battersea. Andrea had been determined to look her best, and wore an expensive new dress; a black number with a single shoulder-strap and an asymmetrical neckline that revealed a great deal of shadowy cleavage. The material clung to Andrea's narrow waist and shapely buttocks, its hem cut to just above the knee, and the skirt split on one side to reveal a glimpse of thigh. Glossy black nylon sheathed her legs, accompanied by strappy black high heels. She had applied a little more make-up than usual to emphasise her blue eyes, and had twisted her long hair up into an elegant French plait that left her neck and shoulders bare.

It took thirty-five minutes to drive to Battersea Bridge, in which time Andrea drank two glasses of champagne. The wine took the edge off her nervousness. Since she'd set eyes on him, she'd spent every moment of every hour thinking about Charles Darrington Hawksworth. All sorts of rumours circulated the office about him and the vast fortune he had built up, but no one knew anything about his private life, not even whether he was married.

Andrea was still unable to work out why he'd had such a hypnotic effect on her. Since he'd invited her to dinner she could only assume that the attraction was mutual. He had picked her out of a room full of employees, after all. But that didn't explain her strange feeling that Charles Hawksworth knew her deepest secrets. Of course, that was absurd. Other than the way she looked and what was in her personnel file – if he had bothered to ask to see it – he knew absolutely nothing about her.

She wondered what sort of dinner this was going to be. She imagined a huge house with glittering chandeliers and expensive antiques, but whether they were to dine alone or with other guests she had no idea. Now she had discovered she was being flown all the way to Wiltshire, she was convinced they would not be alone. She was convinced she had been invited to a country house party, and she had to confess that the idea of not having Charles Hawksworth to herself was more than a little disappointing.

She had been thinking about Greg Anders, too. Her feelings towards him were confused. He hadn't spoken to her since he'd spanked her bottom, though she'd left more than one message on his answerphone. From his reaction she guessed he was not only ashamed of what he had done, but that he regarded her as a slut for encouraging him and for having the temerity to enjoy it. But what he had done to her had been thrilling. She could still feel the way he made her bottom tingle and how that had excited her. The effect had lasted most of the next day; every time she sat down little prickles of sensation reminded her of what had happened. From Greg's explosive reaction there was no doubt in her mind that he had harboured his fantasy for a long long time – perhaps as long as she had harboured hers. Unlike her, however, he obviously felt guilty about it and did not want to admit to himself or anybody else exactly how powerful his urges really were.

She could understand that. She'd also had a great deal of difficulty coming to terms with her own needs. She'd never been able to work out where her desire to be dominated had come from. It seemed to have arrived out of the blue, like a seed blown on the wind, taking root on fertile ground. And, like a seed, it had germinated rapidly and grown into a plant that dominated her sexual psyche.

She remembered the precise moment the seed had taken root. Andrea had always liked sex, but it had never been more than pleasantly stimulating and, until three years ago, she had never had a proper orgasm. Despite the fact that she had picked lovers who were capable and unselfish, their lovemaking never produced anything more than a gentle crescendo of feeling – certainly nothing like the explosions of breathtaking ecstasy all her friends seemed to experience.

Then, when she was nineteen, she met Steve Matthews, a university lecturer. He was a shy and retiring sort of man, never been seen in anything other than jeans and a check shirt, but Andrea was attracted to him. One evening he'd asked her to go for a drink with him. They had ended up at his flat.

On returning from the loo, Andrea had knocked into a shelf of books in the hall. One of them had fallen to the floor and, when she picked it up, she was amazed by the graphic photograph on the cover. It showed a girl in a tight leather corset, black stockings and high heels, spread-eagled across a bed, her wrists and ankles bound by coils of white rope. Standing by the side of the bed was a man, his face deliberately obscured by the photographer. He wore nothing but a pair of tight leather trousers. On the girl's face was an expression Andrea could not forget; a look of unbelievable excitement, mixed with fear. Later she realised she was reading her own emotions into what was probably nothing more than a blank stare, imagining how it would feel to be tied, bound and helpless like that, completely vulnerable and exposed.

She hadn't asked Steve about the book. She was too embarrassed by the feelings it generated in her. But when she got into bed with him, the cover still vivid in her mind, she'd been unable to control herself. She'd come almost before he entered her, and not with one of her usual pusillanimous climaxes, but a five star rip-roaring orgasm that tore through every nerve in her body. Then she came again and again, the photograph printed indelibly in her mind, as though it had been branded there. Those were her first *real* orgasms.

The next day Andrea rushed to a bookshop and found the book. She read it from cover to cover, the images of domination and bondage intoxicating her. She had no idea that people indulged in such practices. She'd masturbated several times before she'd got to the end, coming in seconds.

She could not work out why the photograph had touched her so deeply or what traits in her psychological make-up inspired such desires. At first the power of her need frightened her and, like Greg, she would admit it to no one, not even herself. Gradually she had to accept it and explore its intoxicating possibilities. Whether tonight would be part of that exploration she did not know.

The helicopter ride seemed to take no time at all. She sat back in the plush leather seats and watched the lights of civilisation twinkle far below her. Soon they were descending and Andrea could see a black Range Rover waiting next to the helipad below. As she alighted, a woman stepped forward with her hand extended to greet her.

'I'm Laurie Angelis, Mr Hawksworth's major-domo.'

'Pleased to meet you.' Andrea shook her hand, and couldn't help but notice the strong grip of the woman.

Laurie Angelis opened the door of the Range Rover and Andrea climbed inside. It was a relief to get out of the wind created by the helicopter's rotors. As Laurie put the car into gear, the helicopter's engines roared and it lifted off. Andrea guessed they were going to collect other guests.

'Did you have a good trip?'

'Wonderful. I'd never been in a helicopter before.'

'Mr Hawksworth is waiting for you.'

Andrea thought that Laurie must be one of the most beautiful women she'd ever seen. Her long black hair shone around an oval face with a straight nose, high cheekbones and the darkest of brown eyes. She reminded Andrea of a thoroughbred racehorse. Her one-piece catsuit clung to the contours of her sleek, svelte body. Andrea's eyes were drawn to the jutting cleavage in her V-neck and the impossibly long legs encased in high-heeled black boots.

'This is a beautiful place.'

'It is.' The last two words were said in a tone that did not encourage further conversation.

As the Range Rover approached the brick wall Andrea had noticed from the air, Laurie operated a small switch on the dashboard and the two wooden gates in front of them swung open, closing again the moment they had passed through. The brunette drove along a wooded drive to the porticoed entrance of a large country house, wheeling the car around so that Andrea was closest to the panelled front door. It opened as the car smoothed to a halt.

'My dear, how nice of you to come.' Charles Darrington Hawksworth opened the passenger door. He was wearing a dark suit, a white shirt and a yellow silk tie, and held his hand out to help her down from her seat.

'It was nice of you to invite me,' she said.

She stood on the gravel drive facing him, her hand still clasped in his. He brought it to his lips and kissed it so gently it made her shiver. He looked at her intently. She had never been so close to him before and the power of his gaze was totally compelling. For a moment she was transfixed, like a rabbit caught in the headlights of a car. He made no attempt to move or release her hand.

'How rude of me,' he said suddenly. 'Please come inside.'

He led her through the front door. The house was huge and immaculately decorated. Obviously no expense had been spared with either the furniture or the décor. As Charles Hawksworth ushered her into a large sitting room Andrea noticed the collection of blue-chip paintings on the wall, a Matisse, and a Gauguin among them. A log fire smouldered in the large stone fireplace. There appeared to be no other guests. At least, not yet.

'I've opened a rather nice Perrier Jouet Belle Époque,' he said, indicating a green bottle sitting in a silver Georgian wine-cooler. 'Would you care for a glass?'

'That would be lovely.'

He turned and picked up the bottle. 'I must say, you look wonderful,' he said over his shoulder. 'That dress is perfect on you.'

'Thank you.' Andrea blushed a little at the compliment.

Charles poured the wine into crystal champagne flutes and handed one to her.

'Your health,' he said. 'Here's to bravery.'

'Bravery?' she queried.

'I think it was very brave of you to accept my invitation. You have no idea what might lie in store for you.'

Andrea laughed lightly. 'That's precisely why I came.'

'Good.' They touched their glasses together, then sipped.

'So, why did you ask me here?' Andrea asked.

'How very direct. I like that. I asked you here because I think you are an exceptionally beautiful woman.'

'The world is full of beautiful women,' she said coolly.

It was his turn to laugh. 'Perfectly true.' He stared at her for a few long seconds, and then changed the subject. 'Perhaps we should go into dinner.'

'Am I the only guest?'

'Of course,' he said.

Andrea felt her heart thumping. She had been convinced she would be one of many guests, and this dramatically increased her excitement.

He led her into a small dining room with scarlet walls and a circular table covered with a crisp white linen cloth. The table was laid with crystal glasses, solid Georgian silver and a candelabrum that held four tall white candles. A maid with curly auburn hair stood by a set of doors that clearly led into the kitchen. She was wearing an extremely abbreviated black dress that revealed most of her shapely legs, black fishnet tights and a little white lace apron. Her shoes were also black, with remarkably high heels, which struck Andrea as odd considering she was going to have to work in them. But the heels were not the strangest thing about her attire. Around her throat she wore a stainless steel collar, about an inch thick. Attached to the front of the collar was a small steel ring.

'Tell chef we're ready,' Hawksworth said.

'Yes, sir,' the girl replied, turning at once for the kitchen.

'I hope you like French food.'

The meal was delicious, and Charles Hawksworth was totally charming and totally attentive. He asked her about her work, about Silverton, and told her, in turn, why he believed in the future of the company.

It was not until coffee was served that Andrea, emboldened perhaps by the fine wine that had been served with the meal, returned to the subject that was her chief concern.

'You didn't answer my question,' she said.

'What question was that?'

'Why did you invite me, rather than any one of a hundred other beautiful women I'm sure you know?'

He smiled. 'Would you like a brandy?'

'No, thank you.'

'I hope you don't mind if I do.' He gestured to the maid, who was still standing by the kitchen door. She vanished at once. 'May I be perfectly frank with you?'

'Please.'

'I am a rich man, Andrea. I have been a rich man for

quite a long while. And the biggest advantage of being rich is that it means I can get whatever I want. My slightest desire, my smallest whim, can be catered for.'

'I can understand that,' Andrea said.

'Good.' He paused, bringing those deep blue eyes to bear on her again. For a moment the world stood still. 'My wealth, naturally enough, has allowed me to develop certain... tastes.'

Andrea's pulse was racing. The palms of her hands were perspiring and she was having trouble breathing.

'I also have, it seems, an intuitive ability to know whether a woman shares these tastes. That, in a nutshell, is why I asked you to come here.'

'You've only seen me once before,' Andrea said, trying to keep the emotion out of her voice.

'Perfectly true. And of course I may be wrong about you. Absolutely and totally wrong. In that case we'll have had a pleasant and enjoyable evening together, and that will be that.'

'And if you're right?'

'Then, I hope, we will have a great deal more to share with each other.'

The auburn-haired maid came back into the room with a silver tray, a crystal decanter, and two balloon glasses. She set the tray down on the dining table.

'Are you sure you won't change your mind?'

Andrea needed a drink to calm her nerves. 'Perhaps I will... thank you.'

The maid poured the brandy. It was the colour of autumn leaves. She put the stopper back in the decanter and returned to her place by the door.

'I think you should get to the point,' Andrea said bravely. So far everything she had suspected about Charles Hawksworth was true. She was sure he somehow knew all her secrets.

He smiled. 'You are aware of the expression that a picture

is worth a thousand words?'

'Yes, of course.'

'Are you easily shocked?'

'I… I don't think so.'

'Good. Then perhaps I should give you a little demonstration.' He beckoned to the maid. 'Julia, how would you rate your performance tonight?'

'I spilled a little of the wine, sir.' During the main course the maid had indeed spilled three or four drops of the wine on the tablecloth.

'As you know,' he continued addressing the pretty girl, 'Laurie would normally correct such small errors, but tonight I would like to show my guest how we deal with these matters.'

'Yes, sir.' The girl bowed her head.

'You know what to do?'

'In here, sir?'

'No, in the sitting room. We'll bring our own glasses.'

Julia immediately walked out of the room, not by the kitchen door this time, but into the hall.

'Julia has been with us now for three months. All things considered, she has worked out very well.'

Andrea's heart was beating so fast she could hear it in her eardrums. 'What are you going to do?' she asked.

'You'll see.'

Charles got up and came around to the back of Andrea's chair. For a moment she thought he was going to put his hand on her shoulder, but instead he pulled her chair out from the table.

They walked together into the sitting room.

At first Andrea did not see the maid. She was hidden by the bulk of the large cream sofa. But then, as they drew closer, she came clearly into view and Andrea stopped dead in her tracks. She felt the blood rush to her cheeks. What she saw confirmed everything she had suspected. Charles Hawksworth knew her probably better than she knew herself!

39

Julia was bending over in front of the large fireplace, her legs spread wide apart and her hands gripping her ankles. She had pulled the tight dress up over her hips so it was bunched around her waist. The fishnet tights were down around her thighs, leaving her buttocks naked but for a pair of tiny black panties. The gusset of the panties was drawn into a tight string that cut deeply between her labia and the cleft of her meaty buttocks. Andrea could see the thick curly auburn hair of her cunt.

Charles walked up to her and put his hand on her back. The girl started slightly. Then he turned and looked straight at Andrea, those searching eyes drilling right into hers.

'I see I have made my point,' he said quietly. Without a word he moved to the side of the fireplace. Andrea couldn't imagine how she hadn't noticed them before, but there, in a china umbrella stand, was a selection of leather whips. Charles extracted a short riding-crop and returned to Julia.

'Three, I think.'

Without looking at Andrea he raised the whip, paused for a second with it above his head, then swept it down firmly onto Julia's buttocks. Her flesh trembled and she gave a little coughing sound, her fingers turning white as she gripped her ankles more firmly.

'Thank you, sir,' she whispered huskily. 'May I have another?'

'Of course you may.'

Hawksworth raised the whip again. The second cut was lower, almost on her thighs, but clearly more painful as the girl reared up and cried out loudly, before gathering herself and grasping her ankles again.

'Thank you, sir. May I have another?' she intoned through gritted teeth.

The riding-crop had a thick leather loop at one end. Hawksworth wriggled this under the gusset of her panties, then he yanked the whip upward, making the gusset bite even more cruelly into her sex. Julia moaned.

Two bright red stripes had appeared on her smooth buttocks. Hawksworth pulled the whip away from under the panties, then raised it again. The instrument whistled as it fell. This was the hardest blow of all and the girl cried out in pain.

'T-thank you, s-sir...' she hissed.

'Very good, Julia. You may go now.' He held out the whip.

Andrea sat on the sofa as the maid pulled the tight skirt down over her buttocks, took the whip from Hawksworth's hand, and replaced it in the umbrella stand. Then she left the room.

Hawksworth sat down in a large leather wing-chair, immediately opposite Andrea.

'That is what you want, isn't it?' he said.

Andrea sipped her brandy. Her hand was trembling. Every stroke of the whip had affected her quite as much as it had affected the maid. Her own bottom was tingling, her nipples were so hard they felt like little pebbles, and her sex was alive, squirming internally as if a tiny snake had crawled inside her. There was no point denying it. 'How did you know?'

'I told you, by instinct. It is something of a gift.'

'Do a lot of women respond in this way?'

'Not many. A select few, shall we say.' He smiled again.

Andrea was trying to think clearly, but her emotions were in a spin. Though she had suspected Hawksworth had invited her to dinner precisely because he had in some way detected her innermost needs, she had not thought any further than that. Now she was completely exposed. He seemed to know everything there was to know about her desires, and she hadn't the faintest idea what was going to happen next. Was she supposed to tear all her clothes off, kneel at his feet and beg him to whip her?

He seemed to sense her unease. 'Don't worry. It takes some getting used to,' he said quietly.

'What do you want from me?' she asked meekly.

'The precise reverse of what you want from me. You've never had a master, have you, Andrea?'

It was the first time he'd used her name.

'No. I only… I've only had dreams, fantasies…'

'Of course. The question is, do you want those fantasies to come true? Only you can answer that. I have, how shall we put it, trained several women. You are very attractive and I would enjoy training you. I can arrange for you to be released from your work for a period of four weeks, and you would come here, to this house. There are only two conditions. First, you must obey without question. If you don't, you will be sent away. If you do, at the end of the four weeks I will give you a choice.'

'What kind of a choice?'

'That will depend on your performance.'

'And the second condition?'

Hawksworth sipped his brandy, his long fingers elegantly cradling the sparkling crystal balloon. 'A simple test. There's a stark difference between fantasy and reality. It is simply a waste of my time if the reality proves too… difficult for you.'

'It won't,' Andrea said decisively. The tendrils of excitement were wrapping themselves around her heart. What she had wanted for so long was actually going to happen. She had found a real master.

'Good. Then shall we go?'

She finished the brandy and got to her feet. Without a word, Hawksworth led her through to the back of the house. They arrived at a small door at the end of a long corridor. He opened it.

'Go inside. Take off all your clothes, apart from your panties. What size shoe do you take?'

'Um… five.'

'Good. I'll be back in a few minutes.'

The room was bare, apart from a metal frame single bed. Quickly, not allowing herself to think too much about what she was doing, Andrea took her dress off and laid it neatly

42

on the bed. She removed her shoes, tights, and her black strapless bra, then sat on the bed with her hands on her knees. She didn't think she had ever felt so excited in her entire life.

The door opened. 'Please take your watch off too,' Hawksworth said. He had changed into a velvet robe of scarlet, braided with gold thread. Andrea obeyed his command. He barely glanced at her almost naked body.

'Now follow me.'

The room next door was the same size but quite different. It was carpeted in heavy black cord, which had also been used to line the walls and ceiling, and even the doors. Hanging from the three wooden beams that traversed the ceiling were a selection of pulleys, chains, and leather straps. In one corner stood a metal frame about the size of a double bed, and on one wall were a number of metal rings clearly used to spread-eagle a victim in the standing position. But most frightening of all, was a rack of instruments of flagellation, containing every conceivable type of weapon, from riding-crops and tawses to paddles and cat-o'nine-tails. Next to this rack was a large wooden cupboard, its double doors firmly closed.

'Put on those shoes.'

A pair of white patent leather high heels were waiting in the middle of the floor, and Andrea stepped into them. The heels were so high they pushed her feet into an almost vertical position.

'In the cupboard you will find all the equipment I intend to use.' Hawksworth's voice was calm, but had a cruel edge to it. 'I want you to fetch it. Do you understand?'

'Y-yes,' Andrea said weakly.

'Excellent. Then we'll start with a gag...'

Chapter Three

'So what happened?'

It had been a mistake to tell Pam that she was having dinner with Charles Darrington Hawksworth.

'Well, he offered me a job.'

'A job?'

After the excesses of Saturday night, Hawksworth had cut her down from her bondage. He'd left her alone while she got dressed in the room next door, then ushered her back into the sitting room. He'd told her to go into the office on Monday morning, hand over any important work and tell everyone, including her immediate boss, that she was being assigned to his personal staff for a trial period of one month. It was almost the truth, after all.

'He wants me to sort out his computers.'

'God. And I thought it was going to be something a hell of a lot more romantic.'

'Don't be silly, Pam.' It was a great effort for Andrea to suppress the excited tension that was threatening to bubble to the surface and give her away.

'So how long will you be gone?'

'About month.' She tried to sound vague, as though it was no big deal.

'He's very dishy. I suppose, if you're going to be working with him personally, you might get to know him a lot better.' Pam stuck her tongue out and wriggled it about obscenely.

'I doubt it,' Andrea lied. 'Listen, I'd better go. I must see Gordon before I leave.'

'See you in a month then. And if you can't be good, be careful.' Pam held up two fingers and mimed rolling a condom over them.

'Pam! You're incorrigible!' Andrea feigned indignation.

'Ask him if he wants another assistant. I could show him a good time.'

But would you be prepared to be bound and whipped by him? Andrea thought. Pam's sex life, as far as she knew, was extensive but conventional.

After ten minutes with Gordon Plait, her boss, Andrea left the building. She supposed she should have asked Charles if she could think things over before she made up her mind, but what would have been the point? The events of Saturday night had completely changed her life. This was an opportunity she intended to grab with both hands.

He had arranged for the car to pick her up at four thirty. His instructions had been very specific. She was to wear a plain dress with no underwear or tights, and a pair of flat-heeled shoes. She was not to wear make-up or jewellery or a watch. The only possessions she was allowed to bring with her were the keys to her flat. Someone would be assigned to look after it while she was away.

So, standing in a plain shirt-waister in front of her bedroom window, acutely aware that she was wearing neither panties nor a bra, she had watched the large black Mercedes pull up at the kerb at twenty minutes past the hour. At four thirty precisely, the blond chauffeur got out and rang the doorbell.

Andrea took a last look around, double-locked her flat door, and ran down the stairs.

The chauffeur opened the rear passenger door for her, but did not smile or say a word as she climbed in.

'Good afternoon.'

The voice startled Andrea. Sitting in the back of the car, with her long legs crossed, was Laurie Angelis. She was wearing a wrap-over white silk blouse, a knee-length black leather skirt, shiny gunmetal grey nylons, and calf-length boots with a stiletto heel. Her long jet-black hair was pinned into a tight chignon, which showed off the graceful curve of her neck. Andrea noticed that her fingernails were painted with a deep blue varnish.

As Andrea sat next to her, the chauffeur closed the door and got behind the wheel.

'I thought…'

'From now on, don't think,' Laurie interrupted sternly as the car pulled away. The glass divider between the passengers and the driver was open. Laurie pressed a button and it glided up with an electric whirr. 'That's better,' she said. 'Now we have our privacy. Mr Hawksworth likes me to prepare all his little…' she appeared to be searching for the right word '…chicks, personally. Just so there are no misunderstandings. Give me your keys.'

Andrea hadn't factored Laurie into the equation. But she suddenly remembered what Hawksworth had said over dinner, that Laurie was responsible for enforcing discipline. If the 'training' Charles had talked about was conducted at the manor, it looked as though Laurie would be on hand to supervise. Andrea handed her the keys, and the brunette put them into a small black handbag at the side of her seat.

'What are you wearing?'

'Just this dress and the shoes,' Andrea said. 'That's what I was told to wear.'

'Take them off.'

'What?'

'You heard me. Get down on your knees and take them off.'

'But… can't I wait until we get to the house?'

'Andrea, I thought it had been explained to you.' Laurie remained calm and authoritative. 'You are here to obey. That's all. If you do not wish to do as you're told, I'll get George to turn around and take you home. It's as simple as that. Now, I won't ask you again.'

In Andrea's mind she had seen herself alone with Charles Hawksworth, alone as they had been on Saturday night. But clearly Laurie was acting on his orders, and if she wanted to see him again she had little choice but to obey. She looked at the driver through the tinted glass partition. He was paying no attention to her, but there was little doubt he would be able to see everything in the rear-view mirror.

Andrea slid to her knees.

The spacious floor of the limousine was covered in thick wool carpet. She unbuttoned the dress and reluctantly pulled it off, her breasts quivering. The car came to a halt at a set of traffic-lights and she saw people on the pavement peering in, probably trying to see if the opaque black windows concealed some notable celebrity. Fortunately, Andrea knew, all they would be able to see was a reflection of their own faces.

The car pulled off again.

'Now your shoes,' Laurie said, her voice betraying no emotion.

Andrea slipped her shoes off.

'I want you to kneel on all fours, facing the front.'

Again Andrea saw no alternative but to obey.

'Open your knees, girl. I want to take a good look at you.'

This was not what Andrea had imagined her journey would be like. She'd pictured herself sitting in the luxurious car, drinking champagne and savouring what Charles Hawksworth would do to her when she got to the manor. She had not expected to be kneeling naked at the feet of Laurie Angelis, being made to obey her every command.

But, as she eased her knees apart, intensely aware that in this position her sex was completely exposed, Andrea felt a stab of excitement deep in her tummy.

The car had stopped again. This time Andrea could see the chauffeur's eyes looking at her in the rear-view mirror. She wondered how many times he had seen such a spectacle.

'Do you shave?' Laurie asked.

'No.'

'In future, you will address me as Ms Angelis.'

'Yes, Ms Angelis.' For some reason that litany produced

another sharp pang of arousal. She felt her nipples stiffening.

'You've not much hair.'

Andrea heard the rasp of nylon as Laurie uncrossed her legs. Slowly she extended her foot. The black leather toe of her boot ran up the inside of Andrea's thighs until it touched her labia. Andrea shuddered. A woman had never touched her so intimately before.

'Turn around,' The foot dropped away.

Andrea shuffled round as the car pulled away from another set of traffic-lights.

'I can see why he wants you,' Laurie said thoughtfully. She reached forward with her right hand and cupped Andrea's breast. Her dark blue fingernails tweaked the nipple. 'Have you ever been with a woman?'

Andrea blushed at the frankness of the question. 'N-no,' she whispered.

'No what?' Laurie snapped.

'No... Ms Angelis.'

'You haven't... how interesting,' Laurie purred with a mischievous glint in her eyes, the corners of her rouged lips turning up slightly in a knowing smile. 'Mr Hawksworth likes to watch, did you know that? He likes me to entertain him. I think I shall enjoy entertaining him – with you.'

Andrea closed her eyes and groaned softly.

'Oh dear, hadn't you thought about that? After all, obedience is obedience, my dear Andrea. Whilst with us you have to do as you're told... whatever that may be.' She smiled again, revealing perfect white teeth.

Andrea said nothing, but her mind was spinning. Laurie was quite right of course. Hawksworth had made it absolutely plain to her that she had to obey his every whim. But she'd never imagined that would involve having sex with another woman. The idea shocked her, but it was not a shock of revulsion. No, quite the reverse. She felt a sickly sweet excitement enveloping her and her clitoris pulsed strongly.

Laurie seemed to sense this reaction. Her smile broadened.

'That turns you on, doesn't it? Well, I'm sorry to disappoint you, but you're going to have to wait. Since you are, how shall we put it, a *virgin* in that department, Mr Hawksworth will want to watch your initiation. Now, come closer.'

There was a large nylon holdall on the floor by Laurie's feet. She reached into it and took out a stainless steel collar, hinged at the side with a small steel ring. It was identical to the one Andrea had seen the maid wearing on Saturday night. Laurie leant forward and hooked it around Andrea's throat. There was a loud click as the locking mechanism engaged at the back of her neck.

The brunette delved into the bag again. 'Put this on.' She dropped a red satin basque onto the thick carpet in front of Andrea. 'Red is good with your blonde hair,' she added.

Andrea picked it up. The garment was beautifully made, the satin soft to the touch, with black lacing decorating the front panel. It didn't have a full bra; the small semi-circular cups were obviously intended to fit under rather than over the breasts. Andrea wrapped the corset around her body. It was a little too small for her and she couldn't manage to fit the eyes into the hooks at the back, however hard she tried.

'That's not a very good start,' Laurie sighed, clicking her tongue in disapproval. 'You'd better lie down.'

Andrea obeyed, the interior of the car easily big enough for her to lie flat on her stomach. Laurie knelt beside her.

'Breath in.'

Gradually Andrea felt the corset gripping her body as Laurie worked her way down the long row of fastenings, each one cinching the basque more tightly and making breathing more difficult. It was boned around the waist to give the wearer an hourglass figure.

'I imagine you can manage to put these on for yourself.' Laurie sat back on the seat and pulled a cellophane packet of stockings out of the bag. They were a light champagne colour. 'You can sit up here.' She patted the seat beside her.

Andrea sat on the black leather. It felt cold against her

naked buttocks. The quarter-bra cups of the basque thrust her full breasts up, making them stand out brazenly. She took the stockings out of their packet and rolled them slowly up her legs.

'They have a seam, make sure it's straight,' Laurie ordered.

As best she could, Andrea tried to get the seam running in a vertical line up the back of her legs. The stockings were very sheer. They had a fully-fashioned heel and the seam ran right up to the wide welts that banded her thighs. Andrea clipped them into the long satin suspenders and felt a familiar buzz of anticipation. Her body knew how to respond to this treatment. In her masturbation ritual, donning a corset and stockings was always a precursor to orgasm.

'Now kneel again, in front of me.'

This time Laurie pulled out a coil of thick silky white nylon rope. She threaded one end through the ring in the steel collar.

'Put your hands together, in front of your chin,' she ordered.

Andrea did as she was told and the brunette quickly looped the rope around her captive's wrists, tying her hands together tightly and making it impossible for her to lower them.

For only the second time in her life, Andrea's bondage was real.

Andrea tried to pull her hands away from the steel collar but the bonds gave not an inch. The feeling thrilled her. When she pleasured herself, though she could secure three of her limbs as she lay spread-eagled across her bed, the fourth had always been at liberty. She'd had the impression of being tightly bound, but not the reality. She could always free herself. Now she did not have that option.

Laurie had taken another item from the bag; a black leather helmet with a criss-cross of laces at the back. She quickly wound Andrea's hair into a simple ponytail, then pulled the helmet down over her head, looping the hair through a hole just above where the lacing began. A narrow hole in the front of the helmet fitted over the nostrils, and there were three larger ovals for the eyes and the mouth. The brunette began to pull the laces tight, until Andrea could feel the soft leather moulding itself to the contours of her face like a second skin.

'Sit back up here,' Laurie commanded, patting the seat.

Andrea moved to obey. Without thinking, she tried to extend her hands to balance herself and, when her bonds held them firmly in place, her spiral of excitement took another turn. She managed to squirm up onto the leather seat, but without her arms for support could not prevent herself from falling against it heavily. She was *very* excited. As she wriggled her bare buttocks against the leather, she could feel a slick of wetness on her labia.

She glanced out of the window and realised that the car had taken a different route from the last time. It was not going south to the embankment, but west along the Euston road.

'Where are we going?' she asked, forgetting herself for a moment.

'You will learn not to speak until you're spoken to,' Laurie snapped. She slapped her hand down hard on Andrea's thigh, making her yelp. The noise attracted the driver's attention. She saw his eyes examining her in the rear-view mirror.

Laurie took a pair of red leather high heels from the holdall. She bent forward and fitted them onto Andrea's feet. They had an ankle strap which she buckled tightly.

'Nearly done,' she said. She turned to look at Andrea, bringing herself to within an inch of her face. 'You love it, don't you?'

There was no point in lying. Andrea's whole body was throbbing with familiar sensations, intensified by a whole set of new ones. 'Yes, Ms Angelis,' she said softly. Their mouths were so close she couldn't help imagining how it would feel to kiss those full lips and feel that pliant mouth crushed against hers. The thought created another jolt of pleasure.

Laurie raised her hand and stroked Andrea's leather-covered cheek. 'Close your eyes,' she whispered.

Andrea did as she was told. She heard the noise of two zips being closed and felt a tightness over her eyelids. The oval holes in the leather over her eyes had been zipped up. She opened her eyes tentatively, but the inky darkness was complete.

She felt Laurie moving slightly on the seat next to her. She heard a clink of a glass. Then the weight beside her shifted again. Laurie was having a drink. They seemed to have escaped the worst of the traffic now and the car's forward progress was less halting. Its smooth suspension and quiet engine were soporific. Andrea inhaled the pungent smell of leather. It reminded her of last Saturday night. That experience had been the most exciting of her life, but that was only the beginning. What had happened to her today was already so far beyond anything that she could have imagined that it left her in little doubt that Charles Hawksworth's 'training' was going to be a voyage of self-discovery.

In the blackness behind the blindfold she could picture herself, sitting with her hands tied in an attitude of prayer, her forearms resting against her breasts, the tight red basque cinched around her body, the suspenders pulling the stocking tops into peaks on her thighs.

Laurie had effectively robbed her of her will. And that was the point, after all. She was no longer allowed to think or do even the simplest thing for herself, and that was what was so exciting for her. She was glad she had been dressed so provocatively. She wanted to look her best when she met her master again. He was all that mattered now.

'Out.'

She must have fallen asleep because she woke with a start. A hand was pulling her up.

For a moment she forgot about her bound hands and got a jolt as she tried to use them to move forward. The rope and the steel collar soon reminded her she was not free to make such instinctive movements.

'Come on.' The voice was Laurie's.

Hands were pulling at her body. She stumbled forward onto the soft carpeting and was virtually dragged out of the car. The air was cold and fresh. She was sure they had arrived at the manor.

'Take her inside.' Laurie's voice again.

She tottered forward on the high patent leather shoes. Hands grasped her by the shoulders and pushed her forward. She could hear the gravel crunching under her feet. Then the hands lifted her slightly and the texture of the ground underfoot changed. She had been expecting the carpet of the hall, imagining she was being taken into the house through the front door, but this felt and sounded like wooden boards.

The hands guided her to the right. After twenty or thirty of her diminutive steps, they pulled her to the left and brought her to a halt. The hands dropped from her shoulders.

'Open your legs.' This voice was female too – but it wasn't Laurie.

Andrea obeyed. She felt a hand brush between her legs, then something rubbed against her thigh above the stocking tops. It moved higher.

'Shift her forward.' Another female voice, but a different one this time. It was coming from behind her.

A hand on Andrea's arm guided her forward two or three steps.

'That's it.'

Andrea gasped. Whatever had been glancing against her thigh was suddenly pulled tight right up between her legs, burrowing between her labia. Andrea had no idea what it was, but it felt like a rope.

There were noises she couldn't identify. The rope altered

position slightly, being pulled up sharply between her buttocks and at the front of her mons. The latter brought it in direct contact with her clitoris, and Andrea gasped again.

'Sensitive little flower, isn't she?'

'Is that tied off?'

'Yes.'

'Come on then.'

Andrea heard footsteps on the wooden floor and then a door was slammed. A key grated in a lock.

She stood stock-still trying to hear whether there was anyone else in the room. The tight leather helmet over her ears muffled most sounds and she doubted she would be able to hear breathing. She imagined Charles Hawksworth sitting in a leather wing-chair with his legs crossed, looking at her with that mixture of disdain and appreciation, his eyes roaming her body. She thrust her shoulders back and raised her head, wanting him to see that she was proud to be his slave. But after three or minutes she became convinced she was alone.

Tentatively she tried to take a step forward but the rope, or whatever it was between her legs, wouldn't budge, only jamming itself more tightly into her sex and making her clitoris zing. She moved back slightly but, though she could take two or three steps in this direction, it only had the effect of forcing the rope deeper into her sex.

The short journey from the car, bound and blindfolded, had created huge waves of excitement within her. The idea of being dressed like a whore, with her breasts and buttocks and sex exposed, being manhandled by strangers she didn't know and couldn't see, thrilled her like nothing else ever had. Why it should have such an effect on her she simply did not know, but there was no denying it. She could feel her nipples were as hard as pebbles again, and there were little pulses of feeling deep in her vagina that she always got when she was wet. She was sure she could feel her juices leaking out over the rope.

She tried to relax and calm herself down, but with the rope buried deep in her sex, that was impossible. Every time she made the slightest movement she felt it jerk against her clitoris and the sensitive flesh at the mouth of her vagina.

With her forearms she crushed her breasts back against her chest, feeling the hard nipples embedded in the malleable flesh. She rubbed them from side to side and little ripples of pleasure cascaded through her body. Almost imperceptibly, she began to wriggle her hips from side to side, making the rope brush across her clitoris. By moving her arms and her hips at the same tempo, she was able to co-ordinate the two sensations.

In the darkness of the leather helmet the images came thick and fast. She saw herself tied helplessly in the punishment room last Saturday. She saw Laurie's eyes inches from her face, and her rich, kissable mouth. And, in her imagination, she saw herself being pulled from the car, bound and helpless while nameless and numberless strangers looked on. Suddenly she was coming. Her whole body was trembling. She jerked on the ropes that held her hands so tightly, not because she wanted to get free, but because the feeling of being bound increased her excitement so much.

'Master,' she moaned aloud.

If she'd had any lingering doubt that she wanted to be there, wanted to be subjected to whatever Charles Hawksworth had in mind for her, it had vanished. This was so much better than any of her fantasies. She had never been so excited in her life.

She pushed herself forward, crushing the rope against her clitoris, making herself come. As she orgasmed, the word 'Master' was on her lips, elongated to a long, attenuated whisper.

'Quite a performance.'

Andrea instinctively twisted her head towards the sound of Laurie's voice. The door had opened so quietly that Andrea wasn't sure how long the woman had been standing there watching her.

The brunette's footsteps crossed the room.

'Close your eyes tight,' she said.

Andrea felt the zips over her eyelids being opened.

'You can open them now.'

After so long in the dark, the light in the room was blinding. It took some minutes before Andrea could open her eyes fully. She found herself in a narrow rectangular room with bare white-plastered walls and no windows. The floor was indeed wooden, and the only furniture was a single bed with a thin, uncovered mattress.

The rope between Andrea's legs was thick and white. The two girls who had brought her in had strung it from metal rings set in the walls. There were other rings positioned on the walls and a pulley fixed to the ceiling. The wooden frame of the bed, Andrea noticed, had leather cuffs attached to each of its corners.

'Mr Hawksworth is waiting,' Laurie said. She had changed into a silver cocktail dress with a short skirt and a draped neck, her longs legs clad in nylon so sheer it was almost transparent. The heels of her shoes were spiky and finished in shiny metal.

The mention of Hawksworth's name made Andrea's heart leap.

Laurie untied the rope from the metal ring and allowed it to drop to the floor. It had become so deeply embedded in Andrea's sex that Laurie had to ease it out, making Andrea whimper.

'Follow me.'

Laurie strode out of the door and Andrea obeyed, disorientated by her comparative freedom. Her sex felt sore from contact with the rope and her labia prickled as she walked. But none of that mattered. All that mattered now was that she was about to see her master.

The corridor was long, with high arched windows along

its length that looked out onto a cobbled courtyard. Andrea guessed they were in the stable block she'd seen from the air as she'd arrived on Saturday. A series of doors ran along the left-hand side, doubtless concealing rooms similar to the one in which she had been confined.

'In here.'

Laurie turned into the last door at the end of the corridor, and Andrea followed.

The room was identical in shape to the one Andrea had occupied but, instead of a bed, it contained a large dressing table and two chairs. Every conceivable type of cosmetic was laid out, as well as make-up brushes, bottles of perfume and a large jar of cotton balls. In one of the chairs sat a chunky woman of about fifty, wearing a plain black dress.

'She's required in ten minutes,' Laurie said to the woman as she came up to Andrea and began to untie her hands. Andrea felt an uncomfortable rush of blood to her arms as she lowered them. The rope had left marks on her wrists.

'Nice figure,' the woman commented. 'Is she the new one?'

'Yes, she is,' Laurie confirmed sharply.

'Mr Hawksworth has good taste… as ever.'

'Just get her ready.'

Laurie marched out of the room, leaving the door open.

'Sit down,' said the woman.

Andrea did as she was told. The woman unlaced the leather hood. She pulled it off Andrea's head, then picked up a hairbrush and began brushing out her hair. When she was satisfied she sat in the second chair and began to apply make-up to Andrea's face.

There was no mirror, so Andrea could not see what the woman was doing, but she was using colours that Andrea would ever have chosen herself. She varnished Andrea's fingernails a deep scarlet. From now on, Andrea realised, even the control of her own make-up was going to be taken away from her.

'Is she ready?' Laurie had walked back into the room.

'Just the lipstick.' The woman applied a shade that matched the nail varnish.

The enigmatic brunette scrutinised Andrea's face. 'She'll do.'

Laurie opened one of the drawers in the dressing table and took out a pair of metal handcuffs. 'Up,' she commanded. 'Hands behind your back.'

Andrea obeyed and the cold metal was snapped around her wrists.

'Follow.'

This time Laurie opened the larger door at the end of the corridor. It led out into the garden. A flagstone path bordered by a honeysuckle-draped wooden trellis led to the back of the main house.

The women's high heels clacked on the stone. It was almost dark now and a chill breeze had sprung up. If Andrea's nipples were not already knotted by excitement then they would certainly be so now.

The house was warm. Just inside the back door Andrea noticed a small rack of brass hooks with metal chains hanging from them, like dog leads. Laurie unhooked a leash and clipped the snap-lock at one end into the ring on Laurie's collar. Then she led her forward.

They walked under the stairs and into the sitting room where Andrea had been on Saturday night. The room was deserted but she could hear voices, men's voices, coming from the dining room.

'Wait here,' Laurie said. A fire blazed in the grate of the large fireplace, and Andrea was left to stand by it as Laurie went into the dining room, closing the door behind her. Andrea looked around. She noticed the china umbrella stand with the leather whips, and remembered how the maid had been beaten, bending over exactly where she now stood.

The dining room door opened and Laurie came out. She took hold of the chain leash again and led Andrea forward. 'Remember,' she said, 'you are not to speak unless you are asked a direct question.'

'Y-yes… Ms Angelis,' Andrea responded quietly, her emotions a swirling cocktail of excitement and trepidation.

Charles Hawksworth sat at the dining table with two other people; a man and a woman. Both the men wore black tie and evening dress while the woman, a short bleached-blonde in her early forties, wore a slinky white silk slip-dress with spaghetti straps. The front of the dress was decorated with little glass beads and she wore a heavy gold necklace.

'Good evening, my dear.' Hawksworth welcomed Andrea with a flashing smile. 'I hope you had a pleasant trip. I'm sorry I could not be there to greet you personally but, as you see, I had guests.' Those deep blue eyes held Andrea's for a moment. Each time she saw him she never failed to be astonished by their power. She was shocked by the presence of the two strangers – but excited too. This must be another test, like the outfit she'd been made to wear and the tarty make-up; a demonstration that it no longer mattered what she thought or wanted. She had gifted all that to her master.

'Come closer,' Hawksworth urged, and then looked at the statuesque brunette. 'You may leave her with us, thank you Laurie.'

Laurie unclipped the leash from the collar and left the room without a word.

'What do you think, Donald?' Hawksworth turned to his male guest.

'Astonishing,' the other man said. He was short and chubby with a receding hairline and a small button nose. His beady eyes were riveted to Andrea's mouthwatering chest. 'I don't know how you find them, Charles.'

'I told you, old chap, it's an instinct. There's a submissive streak in a lot of women.'

'Not in me,' the woman said at once. 'No man's ever going to truss me up like a chicken.' Her accent was American.

'But you enjoy being dominant, don't you Erica.' It was a statement from Hawksworth, rather than a question.

59

'I like dishing it out, sure.'

'Well, I think that's a very similar impulse, in a sense.'

'If you don't mind me saying so, Charles, that's bullshit,' the woman sneered.

'A lot of people believe that sadism and masochism are just different sides of the same coin.'

'Well you're not going to get me on the other side.'

'Where did you find this one?' the man asked, clearly trying to change the subject.

'She works for Silverton.' There were cups of coffee and large brandy balloons in front of each of them. Hawksworth picked up his glass and sipped the rich amber contents.

'May I touch?' the man asked, dabbing his sweating forehead with a large cotton napkin.

'But of course,' Hawksworth acquiesced, with a warm smile.

'You lay one finger on her and I'll cut it off,' Erica snapped. She got to her feet. 'I do all the touching for the both of us.' She moved behind Andrea, her silk dress rustling and brushing the tied girl's back. She caressed Andrea's buttocks. 'Nice tight butt,' she said approvingly. Her arms wrapped around Andrea's body and she encased her erect nipples with her palms.

'What are you going to do with her?' she asked her host, as though Andrea wasn't there.

'The usual training,' said Hawksworth, thoughtfully swirling his brandy as he watched the woman's greedy hands mauling Andrea's soft breasts.

'And then?'

'That's entirely up to her.'

'If she's going into The System we'd be extremely interested. Wouldn't we, Donald?'

The man leered and licked his teeth. 'We most certainly would, my dear,' he drooled.

Andrea didn't understand what they were talking about. Once again all her expectations had been dashed. She'd expected Charles Hawksworth to be alone. She'd imagined he would want to take her up to his bedroom and seduce her, though she'd been sure the sex would be far from conventional. But she hadn't expected anything like this.

'God, she's making me horny,' the man announced hoarsely, reaching beneath the crisp tablecloth to surreptitiously rearrange his straining trousers. 'Just look at those lovely tits.'

'He's always been a tit man,' Erica said, heightening her husband's discomfort and frustration by increasing the teasing of the lovely soft flesh in her hands. She pinched Andrea's stiff nipples between thumb and forefinger, then pulled her breasts up until the flesh was stretched taut. Andrea moaned and closed her eyes. 'Would you like to see more?' she goaded cruelly.

'More?' the man wheezed, now dabbing his cheeks and chin.

Hawksworth got to his feet. He crossed the room and pressed a button in a console panel of wood near the kitchen door. Immediately the panel slid back to reveal a large television and video recorder. Charles touched two more buttons on the console and the television screen crackled into life.

Andrea saw the picture resolve into a shot of a tall girl in a tight red satin basque, her head entirely covered by a black leather helmet, and a long white rope pulled up between her legs. It took a while for her to realise that the trussed girl was her.

'Look at that!' the plump man enthused, leaning forward in his chair, his beady eyes bulging.

Erica sat down next to him and stared at the screen. The girl on the screen squirmed against the rope, her hips grinding from side to side, her large breasts trembling. She was making little gasps and moans of pleasure as she moved. The camera zoomed in on her pubis, the cords of the rope buried in her almost hairless cunt. Then the lens travelled up over the red satin basque to her nipples, the dark red flesh puckered and tight.

'She's bringing herself off,' Erica said quietly, almost to herself. The American's hand had slipped into her husband's lap and was tugging on the fly of his trousers, where a large bulge distended the material.

Andrea was fascinated by watching herself on the screen. It seemed as if her whole body was focused on her sex, every movement sawing the rope between her labia. The extraordinary thing was that, just as her clitoris had throbbed wildly then, it was throbbing with almost as much energy now, as she watched herself. She could already feel a trickle of wetness leaking over her thighs.

'Do – do you do this to all of them?' the man asked Hawksworth.

'No,' Hawksworth said, with no further explanation.

On screen Andrea's whole body was trembling. She watched the fingers of her bound hands under her chin stretch out as if trying to catch a ball, her wrists pulling at the rope that secured them to the steel collar. Her breasts were quivering. She stepped forward, the rope biting even deeper. 'Master,' the captive girl on the screen sighed, then repeated the word in one long whisper.

The television screen flickered, and then went blank.

Hawksworth turned and walked back to the table. His eyes were staring straight at Andrea again, and he looked as if he were angry with her. She had been so engrossed in watching herself she had not noticed Hawksworth's reaction to her performance. For some reason he was obviously not pleased.

'I have some things to do,' he said, turning his attention to Donald and Erica. 'Would you excuse me?'

'Sure thing,' said Erica, her hand moving inside her husband's trousers, and then she looked hungrily at Andrea. 'And what about her?'

'Just leave her where she is,' he said. The tone of his voice cut her to the quick. It was one of complete indifference. 'I'll see you both for breakfast in the morning.' Without another word he walked from the room and closed the door, leaving his guests staring silently and avariciously at his latest plaything.

'Put it on again,' Donald said immediately. 'The video – put it on.'

'What for?' exclaimed his wife. 'We've got the real thing.'

'We're not allowed to have her, you know that. She's not had any training yet.'

'There's many a way to skin a cat, Don,' countered his wife, with a smug leer and a lick of her thick lips as her eyes devoured the submissive and shapely source of her desire.

She removed her fingers from where they'd been working in her husband's lap, got to her feet, and glanced around the room, as if searching for something. Her eyes lighted on the thick candles that flickered in the candelabra. She blew one out and prised it from the silver holder.

'Open your legs,' she said, moving slowly towards Andrea.

Andrea didn't know what to do. She didn't like the lecherous couple, but for some reason she had offended her master, and she didn't want to make the same mistake again. She could only assume that if he'd left her there with these people he meant her to obey their commands. So she took a deep breath and hesitantly did as she was told, and shuffled her feet apart.

Erica dragged one of the dining chairs behind her. 'Now, bend right over,' she instructed. 'Rest your forehead on the seat.'

Andrea obeyed, well aware that in this position her sex was fully exposed.

'Legs wider apart.'

She spread her legs further. She could feel her labia parting. They would be able to see how wet she was.

Erica's hand touched the small of her back. She felt something cylindrical being inserted into the mouth of her vagina. Erica was pushing the candle into her body!

'Look at that,' Donald said under his breath.

The candle skewered deeper. It had not the girth of an erect penis, but it was longer. It burrowed inside her, right up to the neck of her womb. She felt her clitoris pulse strongly against it.

'Now hold it there,' Erica ordered. 'Grip it tight. If it falls out I'll tell Hawksworth you refused to co-operate. You know what that would mean.'

Andrea didn't want to think about that. Instead she used her vaginal muscles to grip the candle. The effort produced a huge wave of sensation. She gasped.

'Light it,' Donald suggested, sniggering.

'Light it?'

'The candle,' he urged, sitting forward on his chair. 'Light the candle.'

Erica sniggered too. 'Now that *is* a good idea.'

Andrea heard the striking of a match.

'Now, what are we going to do with this?' Erica moved away again, knelt between her husband's feet, and again reached inside his open trousers. She fished out his turgid cock. It was short and stubby and gnarled with veins. She rolled back his foreskin, and without further ado, she leaned down to suck the pulsing column into her loose mouth.

Suddenly Andrea flinched as something hot touched her tender labia. Hot wax from the top of the candle had dribbled down. She gasped and squirmed.

Erica released her husband's cock, and it sprang back to the vertical as she licked her wet lips and chin. 'Can't do that for long,' she drooled, looking up at him. 'You're *much* too excited.'

She scrambled to her feet, bent over the table at Andrea's side, and pulled the white silk dress up over her waist. She was wearing silky white panties and champagne-coloured hold-ups, their elasticated welts digging channels in her thighs.

He got up too, his erection spearing out from the opened trousers. He slipped his bracers of his shoulders, pushed his trousers down to his knees, and stood behind his wife. Taking hold of the panties, he pulled them to one side. Andrea caught a glimpse of a mass of dark pubic hair, before he grabbed Erica by the hips and drove his cock straight into her sex.

'Oh, *God*.' Erica shuddered. 'You're so hard…'

'And you're so fucking wet!' he grunted triumphantly.

There was no subtlety. He hammered into her, holding her hips and pulling her back onto his erection as he drove forward, his belly slapping loudly and rhythmically against her quivering buttocks.

'She's… really… got… to you…' Erica snorted, each word punctuated by his inward thrusts.

The feeling was mutual. Andrea had never experienced anything like this. She had never seen another couple having sex right before her eyes. But then she had never been bound before, or had a lighted candle jammed deep into her sex. She tried to concentrate on keeping the candle in place but, with her cunt as wet as it had ever been, that was not easy. If she gripped too hard the candle would be squeezed out, but if she didn't grip hard enough it would start to topple over. The constant adjustments she had to make with the muscles of her vagina were provoking her just as much as the spectacle in front of her eyes. And the wax dribbling torturously down onto her sex was like the pain from the whip; hot tingling pain that rooted itself right to her core, translating itself into intense pleasure.

Erica was coming. She threw her head back and cried out loud, her whole body trembling as she thrust herself back against the hard phallus that was reaming into her. She looked around at Andrea, as if to give herself a final push into orgasm, then came, her eyes shut tight in ecstasy.

'Please…' Andrea whispered. 'Please…' She had no idea what she was pleading for. She didn't want to come again. She suddenly realised that was why her master had been angry with her. She should have saved herself for him. She should have resisted the temptation of the rope just as she should have resisted what was happening to her now. But she couldn't. She adjusted her grip on the candle for the hundredth time, tightening her muscles slightly, and felt a huge wave of sensation pulse through her just at the moment the largest splash of wax oozed against her sex. She saw the man's cock slide almost all the way out of his wife's sex, the thick shaft wet with the sticky juices of her body, then slam back in again. This time he held himself deep inside her and groaned almost incoherently that he was coming. At that exact moment Andrea came too, her sex clenching reflexively around the candle, the hot pain from the melting wax only adding to her intense excitement.

The breathless and red-faced man pulled out of his wife. 'Come on,' he panted to her, 'let's go upstairs.'

His wife straightened up. Her dress fell back around her thighs. 'Pity we can't take her with us.' She blew the candle out and pulled it from Andrea's clutching vagina.

He pulled up and refastened his trousers, and they walked out of the room hand in hand.

Andrea straightened up and hovered by the chair, not at all sure what she should do now. She hoped there wasn't another video camera recording what had just happened. If there was her master would know she had come again. She was convinced that was the reason he had looked at her with such disapproval. She knew she should have saved herself for him. And now she had been provoked again. Perhaps, as it was his guests who had caused it, this time he would be more understanding. He had left her alone with them, after all.

She longed to be taken to him. She longed to be alone with him. She wouldn't mind if he wanted to punish her for what she'd done. She deserved it. She would welcome it.

The door to the kitchen suddenly swung open and two maids emerged. Both of them were wearing the short black dresses and lace aprons Andrea had seen Julia wearing on Saturday night. They completely ignored Andrea and began clearing away the table. One was short with a round doll-like face and very short brown hair, while the other was as tall as Andrea, with wavy red hair.

'What am I supposed to do now?' she asked them.

'Be quiet!' the redhead snapped. 'You're not allowed to talk!'

It took several trips back into the kitchen to clear the table completely. As soon as it was done, Andrea was left alone again.

She was intensely aware of between her thighs. The candle wax had solidified and seemed to be pulling at her sensitive flesh. But it was not an unpleasant sensation. She looked down at her body, her breasts thrust out by the shelf-like bra of the basque, her nipples still knotted into tight corrugated buttons.

Her body ached from the tightness of the corset and from her bondage, the metal handcuffs chafing against her wrists. But she didn't care. All she cared about was seeing her master again. The evening had gone wrong and it was all her fault. She stood where she was without moving, not daring to sit down in case that too was held against her.

It was an hour or more before the sitting room door opened again.

'Follow me.' Laurie's expression was one of disinterest. If Hawksworth had told her how displeased he was with Andrea, it did not show on her face.

They walked out into the grand reception hall. Andrea felt her pulse quicken as Laurie led her up the wide carpeted staircase to the first floor. Was she being taken to see her master?

The answer was clearly no. They passed the double doors that looked as if they belonged to the main bedroom and headed up a second, much narrower staircase to the floor above. Here Laurie opened a door and shepherded Andrea into a small bedroom. Prettily decorated with a flowery print wallpaper, it contained the usual bedroom furniture, including a wardrobe, bedside tables, and a small double bed. Another door led into a small white-tiled bathroom.

Laurie caught hold of Andrea's wrists and unlocked the handcuffs.

'Strip off,' she said.

'What's going to happen to me?'

'Don't speak until you're spoken to. How many times do I have to tell you?'

'Sorry, Ms Angelis. But...' Andrea knew better than to go on. She quickly unhooked the basque, then sat on the bed to pull off her shoes and stockings. It looked as if Hawksworth had no intention of seeing her again that night.

'You can use the bathroom but don't remove your make-up.'

Laurie picked up the discarded clothes, turned on her heel and strode out of the room. Andrea heard the door being locked from the outside.

This, she knew, was her punishment. Being left up there on her own was a thousand times worse than being bound and whipped. Even if Hawksworth had instructed Laurie to do it, that would at least mean he had thought about his new slave. But to be shut up in the small room, naked and alone, was an indication of his indifference.

He had not called her up to his room, so perhaps he was with one of the maids? Andrea had noted the way Julia looked at him. She was obviously in training too. And the other maids she had seen in the dining room might well be there for the same reason. There were lots of rooms in the stable block. Did each contain a beautiful woman waiting, like her, for the privilege of serving her master? That thought depressed her even more.

There was a glimmer of hope, though. Laurie had told her to keep her make-up on. Could that mean that Hawksworth might still call for her?

She realised then that her whole life had changed completely. In the space of a few hours she had gone from being an individual with a relatively normal life, to being totally and absolutely dependent on one man. But, however much she wished it could have begun differently, she did not regret the change for one moment. When her master gave her the chance, she would be a perfect slave.

Chapter Four

Andrea had fallen asleep, but was stirred by the noise of the key turning in the lock and someone coming into the room. Light from the landing filtered in, but it was still fairly dark and without her watch she had no idea what time it was. She squinted up and tried to protect her eyes with a forearm.

Laurie loomed over her. She was wearing a pair of glossy black Lycra leggings over a figure-hugging body in the same material, with black high heels but no make-up. It looked as though she had been roused from her sleep.

'You're required,' she said, with a hint of disapproval. In her left hand she held a leather harness, in her right a black silk slip.

Andrea scrambled to her feet, her heart thumping from a rush of adrenaline.

'Turn around.'

Andrea obeyed, turning her back on the brunette. Laurie dropped the slip on the bed, then held up the harness. It consisted of a thick leather collar with a short strap attached to it. Two leather cuffs were firmly secured to the strap, one above the other. She wrapped the collar round Andrea's neck, over the steel collar she already wore, and buckled it in place. The strap hung down between her shoulder-blades.

'Put the slip on.'

Andrea picked it up. It was made from the finest silk and had the narrowest of spaghetti straps. She pulled it over her head. The material felt deliciously soft against her skin.

'Hands behind your back,' Laurie ordered.

As Andrea obeyed, Laurie took hold of her left wrist and twisted it up to the top cuff. She wrapped the cuff around it and buckled it tight, then secured Andrea's right wrist into the lower cuff. The bondage was awkward and uncomfortable, straining the muscles in her arms and shoulders and making her elbows stick out to her sides like chicken wings.

Laurie opened a drawer in one of the bedside tables. She took out a brush and quickly tidied Andrea's long blonde hair. 'Follow me,' she said, when she was satisfied.

The bondage had created an immediate surge of arousal in Andrea, but she could not separate that from the excitement she felt at the thought of being taken to her master.

They walked down the narrow staircase and along to the pair of panelled double doors. Laurie knocked, then turned and headed off down the landing without another word. Andrea watched as she disappeared into one of the other bedrooms.

The house was silent. Nothing moved. She listened intently for any noise from inside what she guessed must be Hawksworth's bedroom, but could hear nothing. She had been given a second chance. Hawksworth had changed his mind. Now it was up to her to show him that it had all been a mistake and that she could be a perfect slave.

It was at least ten minutes before the door opened. To her immense surprise, and disappointment, it was opened by Julia. She was wearing only a lacy black suspender belt, tan stockings and black high heels. She had small round breasts, the size and shape of tennis balls, which sat high on her chest. The thick auburn pubic hair that covered her mons had been trimmed into a neat triangle.

'Bring her in.' It was Hawksworth's voice.

Julia caught hold of Andrea's elbow and pulled her inside, closing the door behind them. Her eyes flashed at her briefly, and in them Andrea saw anger. She was clearly not happy that Andrea was there.

'Good evening, my dear,' Hawksworth said.

The bedroom was large and luxurious, decorated in shades of cream and white. Hawksworth was lying on a large double

71

bed with his head propped up on three or four pillows. He was wearing a dark blue silk robe.

'Come here.'

Andrea walked over to the bed. It was quite a distance from the door, and she could see Hawksworth following her every step. As she neared he looked up at her face. Again she felt the strange hypnotic power of his eyes.

'Get her the shoes,' he said.

Julia brought over a pair of black patent leather high heels. She placed them by Andrea's feet.

'Put them on,' Hawksworth ordered quietly.

It was a little difficult with her arms secured behind her back, but Andrea managed to step into the shoes without overbalancing. They increased her height by a good four inches.

'Now tell me, Andrea. I want to know.'

Andrea didn't know what to say. 'I'm sorry, you want to know what?'

He tutted. 'Don't you know by now that you must call me master?'

Andrea blushed and lowered her eyes. 'I'm sorry... master.'

He smiled confidently. 'We'll let it go this time. But I do seem to have to make a lot of allowances for you, Andrea.'

Julia had moved round to the other side of the bed and Hawksworth patted the mattress next to him. She climbed up and knelt by his side.

'I'm waiting,' he said, with an exaggerated sigh.

'I didn't know, master. I was just too excited. Ms Angelis blindfolded me and I... everything was so confusing. The bondage affected me too, and that rope...' It all came tumbling out. She knew she wasn't making a lot of sense. 'I just couldn't help myself...' she finished quietly.

'Did you imagine that rope was put there for your pleasure?'

'No, master.' She lowered her face, suddenly feeling

72

ashamed of herself.

'It was a test, Andrea. Your pleasure, your needs are no longer an issue. I wanted to see if you understood that. Sadly, you disappointed me. I can see that I'm going to have to teach you control.'

'Yes, master. I'll do anything.'

'Of course you will. And I think you should have to start your lessons right now, don't you?'

'Yes, master.'

'Are you right-handed?'

'Yes, master, I am.'

Hawksworth nodded to Julia. She scrambled across the bed, took hold of Andrea's hips and turned her around. Quickly she unbuckled Andrea's right wrist from the leather harness.

'Kneel here, on the bed.' Hawksworth was lying in the middle of the huge mattress; it was so large there was plenty of space on either side of him.

Andrea did as she was told, her heart pounding. She didn't care what he did to her now, she was just happy he had not left her locked in that room alone.

'Come closer.' He beckoned her with a perfectly manicured finger.

Andrea shuffled forward on her knees.

'Closer still.'

She could smell his musky cologne.

'That's better. Julia, I want you behind her.' The girl immediately scrambled over the bed to obey. 'Good. Now lift your slip.'

Andrea used her free hand to lift the hem of the delicate garment.

'Open your legs a little more.'

Andrea squirmed her knees apart, conscious that Hawksworth's eyes were staring at her sex.

'Now, I want you to lean forward and raise your arse.' He reached out and hooked his hand under Andrea's long hair

73

and around her neck, pulling down until her forehead was resting on his chest. His other hand undid the knotted belt of his robe and pushed the garment aside. His circumcised cock was still flaccid, nestling in a bed of wiry hair.

'Go ahead…'

Andrea's vision was severely restricted. But, as she felt him holding her down more securely, Julia lifted the hem of the black slip at the back and lay it over Andrea's hips. She caressed the neat round curves of Andrea's bottom, lulling her gently, and then suddenly and violently slapped Andrea's left buttock.

'Very *good*,' Hawksworth said smoothly as Andrea yelped and bucked and he had to hold her even tighter. 'Give her five more.'

Thwack! Julia's hand landed on Andrea's right cheek, even more powerfully this time. Andrea gasped, her hot breath forced out against Hawksworth silk robe. From the corner of her eye she could see his cock beginning to engorge, like a serpent awakening.

Thwack! The next blow landed on her left buttock again. Already tenderised by the first slap, the flesh was lit with a wave of pain, like a thousand hot needles being driven into her at the same time. But almost before the pain could register, it had turned into a pulsing throb of delight that made her vagina clench. She moaned softly.

'Three more. Harder!'

Thwack! Thwack! Thwack! The blows fell in quick succession, each one harder than the last. The girl apparently enjoyed her work, for Andrea could feel the sticky sap of Julia's sex leaking over her thigh. Hawksworth's cock was fully erect now, and he was wanking it gently with his hand. Andrea hoped above hope that he would use it on her, that he would order her to straddle his body and sink down on that long hard shaft. She wanted that more than she'd ever wanted anything.

'Now lick her arse,' Hawksworth ordered.

Andrea felt Julia's tongue moving across her bottom, just the tip, the wetness of it cooling the superheated flesh. She was unable to contain a gasp of pleasure. No woman had ever touched her so intimately but she felt no revulsion, only a rapid rise in her level of arousal.

'Is she wet?' Hawksworth asked.

Unceremoniously, Julia thrust two fingers into the mouth of Andrea's cunt. 'Soaking, master,' she reported.

The master's hand let go of her neck. 'I want to see you touch yourself. You are not to come. Do you understand that? I want to see you exercise some control for a change. Discipline and control.'

'Yes, master,' Andrea said.

Immediately she ran her hand down between her legs. Her clitoris was swollen and hard. She rubbed her finger over the top of it and felt an explosion of feeling so violent she snatched her finger away. Two or three seconds of that and she would definitely orgasm.

But Hawksworth missed nothing. 'Do as I say,' he insisted.

'But, master—'

'Do you not know better than to answer back?'

Andrea prodded her finger against her clitoris again. It throbbed wildly. She didn't know what she was going to do. She had never been so turned on in her whole life. Everything that had happened to her that day – being stripped in the car, the bondage and the blindfold, the rope between her legs, and the sight of Donald fucking his wife while she was made to watch – all conspired to arouse her in a way she had never been aroused before. How could she be expected to stop herself from coming?

'Julia,' Hawksworth said. 'Help her along.'

The girl scrambled up to him, kneeling alongside Andrea. She stroked one hand down Andrea's back, briefly caressing her still-stinging buttocks, then she pushed it down between her legs. Two fingers, then three, thrust into Andrea's wet vagina.

'*No...*' Andrea cried, as a whole new set of sensations lanced through her body. She felt her sex clench tightly around the girl's fingers. Julia's other hand played with her breasts, circling the nipples so the silky material was rubbing against them. 'Oh no, no, please,' Andrea moaned, her whole body shuddering.

'Yes, Andrea,' Hawksworth said insistently.

Andrea was desperate. The orgasms she had experienced in the stables and in the dining room were nothing compared to what she was feeling now. Every nerve and sinew in her body was crying out for relief, a huge wave of sensation building up behind the flimsy dam of her self-control. She knew if she came now Hawksworth would almost certainly send her away. What she had already seen on the estate was beyond her wildest dreams, a living reality that made her fantasies pale into insignificance. But unless she could hold herself back she would never be able to explore that living reality.

Hawksworth made a gesture to Julia. Andrea felt the girl's fingers slipping out of the hungry mouth of her cunt. Julia's other hand also left Andrea's breasts. Then the girl bent forward over the master's body. She opened her mouth and Hawksworth fed his large erection into it. Julia gobbled it up greedily, squirming her buttocks from side to side, her small round tits hanging down over his belly.

'Mmm...' she hummed enthusiastically, as if to emphasise it was she and not Andrea who was being given the ultimate privilege.

But the sight of the girl eagerly bobbing her head up and down and Hawksworth's cock glistening with her saliva only made Andrea's state of excitement more intense. She surreptitiously lessened the pressure of her fingertips on her sensitive nub, but it made no difference at all. The tempo of her body was far too fevered. She would come now even if she lay back and did nothing.

She tried to adopt another approach. She pressed her

fingers against her clit so hard she hoped it would hurt and the pain would wipe the pleasure away. But that didn't work either. There was pain as she crushed the little button, but there seemed to be a mechanism in her body that turned pain to intense, throbbing pleasure. She gasped, reflexively pulling on her left arm, the jolt of the bondage that held it so awkwardly up between her shoulder-blades only adding to her excitement. She tried to concentrate on the master. He was still looking at her, watching her fingers move across her labia, but those deep blue eyes were glazed. Julia had one hand wrapped around the shaft of his cock, the other cupping his balls, moulding them reverently between her fingers.

Hawksworth's mouth opened slightly and his eyes closed. Almost immediately his cock jerked visibly and Julia sank her mouth down onto it, until her stretched lips and button nose were grazing his pubic hair. Her cheeks hollowed as she sucked avidly. He moaned loudly, then opened his eyes again, looking straight at Andrea. 'I give you permission,' he whispered.

As she watched his back arch up off the bed, Andrea's orgasm exploded, the relief as great as the need. Her body shuddered and for a moment she thought she would pass out as a scarlet wave of passion broke over her. She closed her eyes in surrender.

When she opened them again Julia was pulling away from Hawksworth's spent erection. Andrea watched her swallow deeply and shudder, a pearl of spunk trickling slowly down her chin.

It was difficult to sleep. That was partly because her hands were bound together by padded leather cuffs secured to a metal ring in the stone wall at the top of the narrow cot. But it was mostly because Andrea could not stop her mind from working.

It had been two days since she had seen Charles

Hawksworth. Two days and two nights. After her session with Julia, she had been stripped of the slip and returned to the small upstairs bedroom for the rest of the night. In the morning, Laurie had taken her back to the stable block where she had been led into one of the narrow rooms and given breakfast. There she had been left, naked and alone. Meals had been brought to her twice a day, and twice a day she had been taken to the bathroom facilities at the far end of the block, where she had been allowed to shower and use the toilet.

The only other break in the monotony of the day had been the arrival of the woman in the black dress. She had made-up Andrea's face, attended to her hair, varnished her finger and toenails, and applied rouge to her nipples. The first time this had happened, Andrea had been convinced it was a prelude to being taken to Hawksworth. But it was not. The door remained locked and no one came.

At night, though she had no idea of the time, Laurie had come into the room, placed Andrea's wrists in the leather cuffs, and secured them to the metal ring. All without a word. Then the heavy wooden door had been locked and the lights turned out.

The second day had followed exactly the same pattern. Laurie entered her room and bound her hands above her head and left without comment.

Andrea had a list of questions she wanted to ask her, but dared not say a word. She knew she was being punished. With nothing to do but sit and think about what had happened, she was sure that the master's neglect was a much worse punishment than being bound and whipped. Making her watch Julia giving him pleasure was a punishment too.

She supposed she had imagined that she and the master would be alone together and that his 'training' would be on a one-to-one basis. But, now she came to think about it, she realised that she should never have made that assumption. Whipping Julia in front of her the previous Saturday had been a clear indication that there were other women, other slaves, at the manor. Andrea was just one of many.

The idea did not depress her. She knew, given the opportunity, that she could show Charles Hawksworth as absolute a devotion to submission and obedience as any of the other girls. She could be the perfect slave. All she wanted now was another chance to prove herself to her master. Over and over again she kicked herself for not realising that the way she had been bound on that first night was a trick, a way of getting her own emotions to betray her. If only she had thought about it. If only she had realised what was going on, she might well have replaced Julia in the master's bedroom and spent the night with him. Instead, her overweening sexuality, the shock of being in a world where all her deepest fantasies could come true, had been too much for her to cope with. If she were honest with herself she guessed that, even if Laurie had told her the truth, her arousal would have made it impossible not to have an orgasm. Too much had happened to provoke and arouse her, and the fact that she had been blindfolded had turned her mind inwards, further increasing the effect of the bondage and the tight corset.

Fortunately, in Hawksworth's bedroom, she had just managed to hang on, but it had been a very close thing. If he had not given her permission she would have been totally unable to stop herself from coming. Hawksworth had tapped into a current in her sexuality that ran deeper than even she had realised.

And then there was the effect the other woman had had on her. She could still feel the way Julia's fingers had invaded her body. There was no denying that the girl's touch had amplified and accelerated everything she had felt, but she put it down to the overwhelming excitement of the moment rather than any deep-seated homosexual impulse on her part.

The position of her arms pulled her pectorals taut and made her shoulders ache. She had tossed and turned herself into every position to get comfortable, but the pain would not go away. In the mood of depression she was in now, she welcomed it.

'Comfortable?'

The door of the narrow room opened, flooding it with light from the corridor. Laurie walked in carrying another nylon holdall. She put the light on and closed the door.

'I asked you a question,' she said, sitting on the edge of the cot.

'No, Ms Angelis.'

'Good.' The brunette was wearing a tight-fitting catsuit of silky yellow with a low V-neck, against which her generous cleavage strained. The material clung to the contours of her body like a second skin, the crotch so tight it had creased into the folds of her labia. Her high-heeled calf-length boots were brown leather.

Laurie reached forward. The central link on Andrea's leather cuffs was attached to the metal ring in the wall by a small padlock. Laurie fitted a key in the lock and allowed it to spring free.

'You may lower your arms.'

Andrea did so. A thousand nerves tingled in protest at their confinement in the same position for so long. Her muscles spasmed too.

'Put this on.' She dropped a black corset onto Andrea's supine body. 'And make it quick.' Laurie took hold of the leather cuff on her right wrist and unbuckled it.

Andrea got to her feet. The corset was made from black lace and had a three-quarter cup bra. As she fitted it around her body she realised it was quite as tight as the one she had been made to wear in the car, and required the same sort of manoeuvres before it could be done up.

Laurie took stockings and ankle boots from the bag. The stockings were sheer and black, the ankle boots black too, with a narrow high heel.

Andrea's pulse was racing. Being dressed like this could

surely only mean one thing: she was being taken to see her master. As quickly as she could, she rolled the stockings up her long legs and clipped them into the suspenders, making sure the seam was straight. The suspenders needed adjusting to hold the stockings more tightly, pulling them into peaks on her thighs. She smoothed the nylon with her palms, eliminating every wrinkle.

'You seem to be learning,' Laurie said when Andrea had finished.

'Thank you, Ms Angelis.'

'Now sit on the bed, I have to do your hair.'

Laurie began to brush and pin Andrea's hair up into a French plait. It took about ten minutes.

'Now stand and put your hands behind your back.'

Again Andrea did as she was told without question.

The brunette re-fastened the leather cuff on her right wrist, then stooped elegantly and took an identical pair from the bag. These she wrapped around Andrea's arms just above the elbow, forcing her arms together, making her throw back her shoulders and thrust out her chest.

'There, that's much better.'

'Are you taking me to see the master?' The question had slipped out before Andrea could stop herself. She was just too anxious to know.

'I've told you about speaking without permission,' Laurie warned immediately.

'I'm sorry, Ms Angelis.'

'So you should be.' Laurie looked genuinely angry. 'Now, for that you can bend over. Rest your forehead on the cot.'

Andrea did as she was told immediately. She could feel Laurie's eyes burning into at her buttocks, the lips of her sex pursed between them. She sensed the dominant woman was a little uncertain about what to do next.

'No,' Laurie eventually said, her voice a little strained. 'We'd better let the master punish you instead. Come on, follow me.'

Oh God, Andrea thought. She was going to see the master, and the first thing Laurie would tell him was that she'd committed yet another misdemeanour. She wanted to plead with the woman not to say anything, but she knew that would only make matters worse. How could she have been so stupid as to speak without permission?

Laurie walked along the corridor and out into the covered pathway, with Andrea following behind. It was dark and there were stars sparkling in a moonless sky.

Once inside the main house Laurie led the way upstairs. She stopped outside the double doors to Hawksworth's bedroom and knocked. While they waited in tense silence she inspected Andrea critically.

'Come in,' Hawksworth finally called from within.

Laurie opened the door, then took hold of Andrea's arm and guided her into the room.

'Good evening,' Hawksworth said. He was sitting in an oatmeal armchair by the main window, the thick curtains drawn across it, his feet up on a matching upholstered stool. He was wearing the dark blue silk robe and had a glass of brandy in this hand. There was a file in his lap. 'Bring her here, Laurie, if you would.'

Laurie marched Andrea right up to the chair. Andrea held her breath, waiting for her to inform on her.

Forsaking any niceties, Hawksworth idly ran his free hand up the outside of Andrea's nearest thigh to the top of her stockings. 'Very pretty,' he said pensively. 'Open your legs, girl.'

Andrea did so without hesitation, keen to please him and keep Laurie from telling on her.

Hawksworth's icy eyes looked levelly at her sex. 'Have you masturbated since I last saw you?' he asked, as casually as if he were asking if she'd had a cup of tea.

'No, master,' Andrea said with total conviction.

'Good.' He ran his hand higher, until it was an inch away from her sex. There was a hollow there at the top of her thigh and his fingers traced around it. 'Do you know that your labia are already wet?'

'Yes, master,' she said meekly, 'I do.' She hoped that wouldn't be another black mark against her. Surely he didn't expect her to be able to control herself to that extent?

'What has caused that?'

'The thought of seeing you, master,' she said at once, feeling it was the right answer.

He smiled. 'How perfectly charming. Get me another brandy, would you Laurie?' He raised his glass and the woman took it from him. She poured a generous measure of the rich amber liquid from a tantalus sitting on a bow-fronted mahogany chest.

'Laurie was a slave too, you know,' Hawksworth said to Andrea while he awaited his refill. 'Not a very good slave, as it happens. She's very beautiful though, isn't she?'

'Yes, master, she is,' Andrea responded truthfully.

Laurie gracefully handed Hawksworth the brandy.

'Why don't you show Andrea just how beautiful you are, Laurie?'

The woman smiled knowingly. The catsuit had a long zip from the apex of the V-neck to the crotch. She held the tongue of the zip between elegant finger and thumb, and slowly pulled it down. She eased off the ankle boots, then pushed the silky material off her shoulders and wriggled it down her legs. Under the catsuit she was wearing a plunge-fronted strapless bustier of white satin, its long body cutting right down to her waist. A matching suspender belt was clipped to white stockings with lacy welts, and beneath these she wore thong-cut panties. She had large breasts that ballooned out against the restraint of the bra, but her stomach was neatly flat and her waist incredibly narrow. Her long legs were contoured by muscle, and her skin was deeply tanned and smooth. She pirouetted a little, and Andrea saw she had a small tattoo of a blue butterfly on her left buttock.

Beside Hawksworth's chair was a pair of white high-heeled

satin slippers, their toes decorated with a tuft of boa feather. Laurie slipped her feet into them.

Andrea saw a look pass between her and Hawksworth, and he nodded. Nothing else needed to be said.

Laurie walked to the chest of drawers beside the bed. As she stooped to open the top drawer, the tiny triangle of satin at the back of the panties was stretched tightly over her two oval buttocks. She took something out of the drawer, and Andrea caught a glimpse of a thin metal chain.

The brunette drifted up behind Andrea, her heady perfume wafting around the motionless girl.

'Begin,' Hawksworth said.

Laurie's hands crept around Andrea's body. Carefully they folded down the lacy bra cups that covered her breasts, tucking them under the silky mounds of soft flesh so they were still supported. Laurie's fingers tweaked her nipples. They were already jutting out prominently.

'Let me,' Hawksworth said, his voice betraying a little emotion for once.

'Kneel,' Laurie ordered firmly, pressing down on Andrea's shoulders.

Unable to use her arms, Andrea sank to her knees a little awkwardly. Her whole body was trembling and her excitement extreme. For whatever reason, Laurie had not told the master about her transgression, and now she could concentrate on showing him exactly how devoted she was to her submission.

'Keep your legs apart,' Hawksworth chided, looking down at her from his chair.

Andrea immediately adjusted her position.

Laurie took his brandy glass and the file from his lap and handed him the chain she had taken from the bedside unit. At each end was an odd-looking oval, made from flat metal with two circular pads of hard plastic pressed tightly together. On either side of each oval were two raised metal flanges.

'Laurie's favourite toy,' Hawksworth said, the hint of a

smile dancing across his lips.

He leant forward, pushing the footstool away. With his right hand he cupped Andrea's right breast while the fingers of his left pressed the two metal flanges on one of the ovals. As he pressed, a series of spring-loaded levers opened the two little pads. Andrea could see that their inner surfaces were covered with tiny raised bumps.

Hawksworth fitted the pads over Andrea's vulnerable nipple, then released the pressure on the flanges, allowing the jaws to close. As the pads bit into her tender flesh, Andrea felt a lance of intense pain quite unlike anything she had felt before. Through lowered lashes she saw Hawksworth staring at her, intent on observing her reaction. Tears welled up, blurring her vision, and she whimpered pitifully. But then, incredibly, the pain transmuted itself into a simmering wave of pleasure that turned her whimper into a moan of delight.

Hawksworth picked up the second clip. He positioned it over her left nipple and allowed the little pads to sink into the puckered flesh. This time the pain was combined with pleasure right from the word go. Andrea tossed her head back and gasped.

'Look into my eyes,' Hawksworth ordered, his tone hypnotic.

Andrea's head rolled forward and she gazed into those glistening pools of aquamarine. For the first time she thought she saw a glimmer of real excitement in them as he reached forward and took hold of the chain that was now looped down between her breasts. Slowly he lifted it. The weight of her breasts pulled the nipple clips tighter and, for a moment, the pleasure was overridden by discomfort again. He pulled the chain up until her breasts were pointing up to the ceiling, her usually dark red nipples blanched white by the tightness of the clips. Then he allowed the chain to fall through his fingers. As it dropped, her breasts fell back too, the luscious flesh quivering, the movement provoking a whole set of new sensations in her nipples. The feelings routed themselves straight to her sex and her clitoris began to pulse urgently.

'Stand,' Hawksworth ordered, his tone now stern, confusing the poor girl.

With her arms so securely bound behind her back it was even more difficult to stand than it had been to kneel, but Andrea managed it without any assistance being offered. Her tethered breasts quivered deliciously as she moved, the chain clinking and her nipples prickling with pain-laced pleasure.

'I've been very disappointed in you, Andrea,' Hawksworth said when she was again standing still before him, her shapely form covered in a delicate sheen of perspiration and glowing in the subdued lighting. 'Now I hope you have learnt your lesson. If not, then this experiment is over. We will see. Normally I would leave this treatment until later in your training, but you have left me no choice. You understand that you must obey Laurie as if she were me?'

'Yes, master, I understand.' Andrea felt as though she was in a bizarre dream.

'Good.' Hawksworth rose from the chair and moved away. The large bed had been stripped back to a white linen sheet, and he lay on one side of it. He propped himself comfortably against the pillows. 'Begin,' he said for the second time that night.

Laurie smiled. It was the cruel smile Andrea had seen in the car. She took Andrea's hand and led her over to the bed.

'Lie on your back,' she ordered.

Andrea lay down, the lacy basque rasping against the white linen. With her arms bound behind her back so securely her body was arched like a bow. Her sex was throbbing as rhythmically as her heart was beating.

Laurie knelt on the bed bedside her. She reached behind her back and began to undo the four or five hooks that held her bustier bra in place. As she cast it to one side her breasts trembled. They were large and pendulous and as tanned as the rest of her body. Her nipples were pierced with gold rings.

'Have you ever kissed a woman before, my dear?' she breathed.

'No, Ms Angelis.'

'Good…' She lcant forward until their mouths were no more than a few inches apart. 'Kiss me now.'

With a little hesitation, but determined to show her master that she could be totally obedient, Andrea raised her head and cushioned her lips against the brunette's. Strangely, she felt no revulsion. Laurie's mouth was quite different from a man's, soft and pliant and wet. Andrea slipped her tongue between the other woman's lips, and Laurie sucked it deep into her mouth.

As they kissed, Laurie's hands travelled over Andrea's breasts to the clips on her nipples. She jerked them up forcefully, making Andrea gasp into her mouth. Then their tongues were fencing, entwined against each other like snakes.

Andrea felt her pulse quicken. It wouldn't have mattered if she had found the whole experience disgusting. After two days in the wilderness she would have done anything to please her master. But far from disgust, Laurie's lips and tongue were producing sharp pangs of delight deep in Andrea's tummy. Andrea felt an urgent desire to press the whole length of her body against the sexy woman, to feel those pliant breasts and that flat belly crushing into hers.

But that was not what Laurie had in mind. She broke away from the kiss and straightened up. That cruel smile was playing on her moist lips once more. She opened her legs and straddled Andrea's body, with her face towards the girl's feet. Then she shuffled backwards until Andrea was staring up at the broad plain of her succulent sex, covered by the white satin panties. The damp gusset of the panties was lodged in the crease of her sex.

Laurie took hold of the thin strip of material between her

legs and pulled the gusset aside, completely exposing her cunt. To Andrea's astonishment it was not sparsely haired like her own, but carefully depilated with every detail of her labia clearly visible. She had never looked so closely at a woman's sex before. The inner labia surrounding the mouth of her vagina were thin and delicate, while the outer lips, which enclosed them, were much fatter and rougher in texture. Laurie's cunt was wide open and Andrea could see the dark scarlet flesh of the interior glistening with the sticky juices of her excitement.

'Lick me,' Laurie purred, moving her sex down until it was an inch or so from Andrea's mouth.

Andrea could still smell the expensive scent she wore, but now it was mixed with a much more primitive odour. She peered to her side and saw Hawksworth watching intently, his whole attention focused on her. There was nothing she could do but obey.

Tentatively, she raised her head and insinuated her tongue between the hot wet flesh of Laurie's cunt lips. She tasted sweet. Andrea wasn't sure what she should do. She tried to remember what she liked men to do to her. Moving her tongue along the slit of Laurie's sex she searched for her clit. It was not difficult to find. Her tongue butted up against it. She felt a frisson of sensation run through Laurie's body as she lapped the little knot of nerves and, strangely, her own body reacted in exactly the same way. With the tip of her tongue she circled Laurie's clit, then began to push it from side to side. She felt the tiny button throb.

'Is she doing it properly?' Hawksworth asked, his voice a little muffled by the warm flesh swamping Andrea's head.

'Mmm… she's a natural talent,' Laurie cooed, her voice husky and deep.

'Excellent.'

Andrea felt her own excitement mounting. She was performing for her master, her submission total. She could see herself as if from above, her body clad in the tight black basque, her arms bound tightly behind her back, with Laurie squatting above her. Lying on her arms like this was producing a new and excruciating pain which only seemed to feed her arousal. But it wasn't just the bondage that was exciting her. The feel and taste of Laurie's sex was incredibly arousing too. She had never imagined that she could get pleasure out of doing such a thing to another woman, but she'd been wrong. Of course, there was the excitement of breaking a taboo, of doing something she had never done before, but there were other much more physical sensations that were driving her wild. There seemed to be a direct connection between Laurie's sex and her own. She could feel what Laurie was feeling, her clitoris pulsing at the same frequency as the brunette's. She wished her hands were free. She would have loved to push her fingers into Laurie's cunt and feel that velvety soft flesh close around them.

She tried to see what Hawksworth was doing, but now her view was totally obscured by Laurie's squirming thighs. She thought she heard him removing the silk robe.

'Open your legs, now.' It was him! Was he going to join in?

Andrea obeyed, spreading her legs apart, the nylon stockings rasping against the sheet. She felt a hand, she was sure it was Hawksworth's, caressing her thigh above the stocking top.

Then Laurie's body moved. For a second her sex lifted away from Andrea's hungry mouth, but as it settled back again at a slightly different angle, Andrea felt an entirely new sensation. Laurie's mouth was now pressing against her sex, her wicked tongue delving into Andrea's vagina, then moving up to her clit. As Laurie found the swollen button and teased it expertly, Andrea felt a jolt of sensation so strong that, for a moment, she thought she was going to orgasm instantly. Laurie's mouth was so soft and pliable it seemed to mould itself to Andrea's sex, sucking it to create a pool of melting flesh, alive with new and breathtaking sensations.

Andrea knew she must not come. She fought against her bonds, hoping the pain would distract her, and tried to concentrate on giving Laurie more pleasure. She forced her face hard up against the other's sex, pressing on her clitoris with her tongue. But that only seemed to make matters worse. The pain from her bondage twisted into fiery pleasure while the feelings from her own clitoris seemed to arc, like an electric current, up to Laurie's. They were joined, the connection complete. What Andrea had felt earlier was nothing compared to what she felt now.

Andrea could feel every ripple of sensation in Laurie's body, each matched by an exact equivalent in her own as the brunette licked her clit. The nipple clips, crushed by Laurie's weight, bit even deeper into her breasts, and the feel of Laurie's soft tits pressing into her belly created more provocation. Andrea knew she must not come but she simply didn't know how she was going to stop herself. All the different sensations in her body, the aching pain from the bondage, the nipple clips, the squirming tongue against her clit, and the feeling of another woman's sex crushed for the first time against her own mouth, were combining into one glorious sensuous rhythm that could not be denied. She wanted to wallow in it, to allow herself to be carried away by the feeling of a woman's mouth doing such wonderful things to her, but she knew she dare not. She did not want to incur Hawksworth's wrath again. Somehow she had to stop herself from coming.

What made it worse was that she could feel the orgasm mounting in Laurie's body. Her clitoris was pulsing wildly against Andrea's tongue and her vagina, Andrea was sure, was as wet and needy as her own. Laurie's whole body was undulating subtly, her buttocks pushing back against Andrea's face.

'Yes... yes...' Laurie breathed, the words pronounced against Andrea's sex, the movement of her lips and her hot breath producing new paroxysms of pleasure in the blonde.

Suddenly Laurie went rigid. She raised her head and cried out loud, her thighs crushing Andrea's head, her sex pressed down on her mouth and nose so tightly that Andrea could hardly breath. She seemed to stay like that for minutes, her body locked around the central core of feeling that had created her orgasm. Then Andrea felt her melt, her body relaxing, every muscle and nerve softening. This was the most provoking sensation so far. Laurie's mouth was still pressed to her sex, but now it was kissing tenderly, and Andrea was able to feel it even more acutely than before. She had to have her own orgasm… she just had to.

Now Laurie was climbing off her. Andrea lay on the bed, her body arched tautly, the black basque cinched tightly around her body, the black stockings stretched smoothly over her legs. Her lips and chin glistened with the liberal evidence of Laurie's pleasure. She was panting with the effort of holding herself back. She saw Hawksworth kneeling beside her, his large erection in his fist.

He smiled. It seemed like the first time he'd ever smiled at her. Perhaps it was; she couldn't remember clearly now.

Laurie appeared behind him. She reached down and replaced his hand, and began masturbating him in her tight fist, an inscrutable smile playing on her own glistening lips.

Hawksworth reached forward, seemingly oblivious to the skilful hand that was pumping in his lap. He held the metal chain that was looped between Andrea's nipple clips and slowly pulled it up. The biting pain had numbed her nipples, but now a whole new myriad of sensations invaded her flesh as he lifted the chain higher, pulling Andrea's breasts taut.

Andrea whimpered, the pain – so like intense pleasure it was indistinguishable – forcing her to wince and squeeze her eyes tightly shut. She simply could not resist this new goad. She was going to come now, and there was nothing she could do to stop herself. She had failed her master.

But, as her clitoris throbbed and the overwhelming

sensations rippled through her body, she felt something warm and viscous splattering over her tortured breasts. She opened her eyes to see another offering of Hawksworth's seed arcing from his purple and bursting cock, and splash audibly onto the black basque as Laurie skilfully milked every last drop from the swollen stalk cocooned in her delicate fist.

'I now give you permission, Andrea,' he sighed, as he breathed languidly and filled his lungs.

Andrea whimpered with relief and gratitude. She scissored her legs together to trap her clitoris between her labia, fighting the bonds that constrained her, every nerve in her body singing with relief as she allowed the orgasm to overwhelm her. As her body rocked and rolled the chain that held her breasts was yanked from Hawksworth's hand, causing another tumultuous jolt of sensation.

Eventually, it was over. Andrea felt his spunk running thickly down her breasts and into the cups of the basque. She could taste Laurie's juices on her lips. Then pain began to take over, the cramp in her arms and shoulders now so acute and the nipple clips excruciating. But she didn't mind. It had all been worthwhile. She had redeemed herself. She had been the perfect slave.

Chapter Five

'Get up.'

Andrea had been day-dreaming, and hadn't really heard the door open.

'I said, get up.' Laurie stood in the doorway. She threw a leather garment onto the cot. 'I'll be back in five minutes.'

The door shut again and was locked.

Andrea got to her feet. When Laurie had brought her back to the stable block she had stripped off all her bonds and the tight lingerie, but had not used the leather cuffs to bind her to the cot, so for the first time at the manor she had spent the night unfettered. The woman in black had already taken her down to the bathroom, watched while she showered and used the toilet, then given her some breakfast.

The leather was black and supple. It was a one-piece garment like the catsuit Laurie had worn last night, but with a much higher collar and full sleeves. Quickly Andrea pulled it on, putting her feet into the legs first, then pulling on the upper half, the fit so tight she had to struggle. When finally in place it fitted like a second skin, stretched tightly over her curves, the front pressing and rounding her breasts against her chest. Attached to each side of the garment were two straps, one above the other, the lower one level with her hips. The leather shimmered exotically where it moulded itself to the dips and swells of her shapely form.

Andrea was feeling buoyant. Her nipples were bruised and sore and her arms and shoulders ached from the previous night's confinement, but she welcomed the pain. It was a sign that she had passed a test and come through with flying colours. Laurie's arrival could only mean one thing: she was being taken to see her master again. It proved that, after last night, he was pleased with her. She was back in his good graces and she planned to stay there.

The experience with Laurie, the first full-blown lesbian encounter of her life, had left her wondering if she had always had homosexual urges but had hidden them from herself. It seemed odd that her response should have been so strong if she didn't harbour a latent desire. And, thinking of it now and remembering exactly what they had done together only a few hours before, produced a sharp reaction. Quite frankly, she couldn't wait to repeat the experience.

Of course, it was possible that what had really turned her on was her submission. She had, after all, been ordered by Hawksworth to have sex with Laurie. And she'd been securely bound. They were the two elements in her sexuality that had brought her to this house. It was possible that her arousal came not from what she had done with Laurie, but from the fact that Hawksworth had ordered her to do it.

Whatever the reason, it was not something she was likely to forget. She could still see Laurie's hairless sex poised above her face, and she could still taste her juices.

The door opened again. Laurie strode into the room and closed the door behind her. She inspected Andrea's outfit critically. She was wearing a tightly cut pair of black leather trousers and a black silk blouse.

'Don't think last night is going to get you any favours.'

'No, Ms Angelis.'

There were two diagonal zips in the front of the catsuit, one over each breast. Laurie unzipped one and Andrea's breast thrust through the opening.

'Are your nipples sore?'

'Yes, Ms Angelis, they are.'

Laurie flicked the dark red nipple with her pristine fingernail. Andrea winced. She caught Laurie's eye. There was a look that Andrea could not mistake: it was a look laden with lust.

Apparently putting her feelings to one side, Laurie did

the zip of the catsuit back up. She pulled Andrea's left arm down to her side and buckled it into the leather strap attached to the side of the suit. The second strap fitted just above the elbow. She repeated the process with the other arm.

'Follow me.'

The procedure was the same as the first night at the house. The woman in the black dress made her up and brushed out her hair. If anything emphasised Andrea's slave status, this did. Every aspect of her appearance was under her master's control.

It took about fifteen minutes for the woman to finish her work. Laurie fitted the chain leash to the ring on the steel collar, then led Andrea to the house.

She heard voices the moment they entered the austere building... male voices.

Laurie led her along towards the sitting room, but at the bottom of the staircase she turned in a new direction. They came to a halt in front of a large panelled oak door. This was clearly where the voices were coming from.

'Remember, you must obey everything demanded of you,' Laurie whispered. 'You must obey everything without question.'

'Yes, Ms Angelis.' It was clear that the master had company. Of course she'd hoped he would be alone, that he would give her his undivided attention, but that was up to him. This was another opportunity to prove herself to him, and she felt the now-familiar excitement at the prospect.

Laurie knocked on the door.

'Enter.'

She opened it.

Andrea looked into a spacious room. At its centre was an oval mahogany table surrounded by at least thirty chairs. The large fireplace matched the one in the sitting room, and she noted several more impressionist paintings on the walls. Five men sat at one end of the table with Charles Darrington Hawksworth. What's more, Andrea recognised one of them.

Her spirits plummeted and her knees turned to jelly. It was Edward Highfield, the chairman of Silverton Communications!

Laurie led Andrea into the room by the leash, then let it go so it hung between the girl's breasts, nestled in her deep cleavage. Laurie then left the room without a word.

There was a tense silence, disturbed only by the large clock ticking relentlessly on the mantelpiece. Andrea closed her eyes and waited, her mouth suddenly dry.

'Why, she's gorgeous,' one of the men eventually enthused.

'Stunning.'

'I don't know how you do it, Charles.' That was Highfield. Andrea opened her eyes and peered at him. He gave no sign of recognising her, though they had often met to discuss work-related matters in the past.

'She's not yet fully trained, you say?' asked one of the men of their host, his eyes crawling over Andrea's leather encased body as he leaned forward over the table.

'She's only been here for four days,' Hawksworth confirmed. 'But her training has already begun. Hasn't it, Andrea?'

'Yes, master,' she said quietly, bowing her head respectfully.

'And what does this training consist of?' This came from the smallest of the men, a round, chubby character with thin strands of hair brushed from one side of his shiny pate to the other in a ludicrous and futile attempt to hide his baldness. He picked up the coffee cup before him and slurped its contents, his hand clearly trembling with excitement, and the cup giving him away further by chinking against its saucer as he replaced it. Andrea realised that Julia was in attendance. She'd have served their coffees, and was now standing silently in one corner, slightly behind Andrea.

'Andrea is required to perform a number of tasks,' Hawksworth responded to the question. 'If she does not perform them to my satisfaction she has to be punished. The punishment can take many forms.'

'And she agrees to this?' Highfield asked, sounding astonished.

'Naturally,' Hawksworth said confidently. 'Shall we proceed? Or is anyone in a hurry to leave?'

None of the men moved. Their eyes were riveted to Andrea's mouthwatering form.

'Very well,' Hawksworth continued, having quickly studied the men sitting with him. 'You all understand the rules?'

The men nodded, without averting their stares from the leather-encased beauty standing submissively before them, almost within reach of their sweating palms.

Hawksworth beckoned Julia to his side. Andrea saw she was carrying two small velvet bags with drawstrings. She handed one to her master, then moved around the table with the other, pausing while each man dipped his hand inside and drew out a numbered black ball.

'I'm feeling lucky today,' the bald man said, extracting the number three.

'We're all feeling lucky, Andy,' Highfield said, taking out number five.

The other men drew numbers too. Julia returned to Hawksworth's side and deposited the empty bag on the polished table in front of him. 'And now I think it's only fair to let Andrea choose her partner,' he said.

It had been obvious to Andrea what had been going on, but this confirmed it: the men were drawing lots for her. She was to be given to them like a prize in a raffle, and was not expected to express her preferences. But, however horrified she felt at the idea, she realised this was just another test of her obedience. Two of the men were physically unattractive, and the other three weren't much better, and she would never have gone to bed with any of them in normal circumstances. But these were not normal circumstances. As with everything else, she had gifted her ability to choose to Hawksworth, and the idea that he would stretch her

97

obedience to such limits secretly excited her. And she thanked God that it did.

Hawksworth handed the second bag back to Julia. With tiny steps in her remarkably high heels and flirtatious swings of her hips, she moved over to Andrea. Pulling open the drawstring she lifted the bag over Andrea's right hand, strapped as it was to her side.

'Pick a ball, my dear,' Hawksworth instructed, somewhat unnecessarily.

Andrea grasped one of the black spheres. Julia pulled the bag away, took the ball from her fingers, and carried it back to the master.

He looked at it and held a theatrical pause for some seconds, savouring the hungry looks of expectancy and reddening complexions of the men around him. 'Number five!' he at last declared.

Edward Highfield exhaled and grinned broadly. He accepted the congratulations of the others, who reached across the table to shake his hand and tell him he was a lucky dog. He was a large man, tall and big-boned, but he was marginally slimmer than any of the others. Perhaps, thought Andrea, he was the most attractive of a pretty sorry bunch, with a craggy open face and large green eyes. His hair was wiry and unkempt, and was beginning to turn grey at the temples.

'You'd better claim your prize, old man,' urged Hawksworth.

'I knew there was a good reason for selling out to you,' Highfield said, taking a deep breath.

Andrea remembered how Highfield had always said he would never sell out. Had the opportunities the manor offered been the reason he'd changed his mind?

Highfield got to his feet. He moved around the table, picked up the leash, and led Andrea to the door. 'I hope you all have a very pleasant afternoon,' he said to his friends.

He closed the door behind them and led her down the

corridor. He appeared to know his way around. Andrea remembered where they were. It was the part of the house where Hawksworth had taken her the previous Saturday, though now it seemed more like a lifetime ago. He opened the door to the small square room where Andrea had been so helplessly bound.

'Well, that's more comfortable,' he said, closing the door after them and bolting it. 'I must say I didn't expect you to be here, Andrea. It's quite a surprise. It's all right, you can cut all the speak-until-you're-spoken-to crap with me.'

Andrea was astonished. Highfield certainly hadn't given the slightest clue that he'd recognised her.

He laughed. 'So this is your idea of sorting out Hawksworth's computers, is it?'

'Is this the reason you sold out?' she asked warily, avoiding his mocking question.

'Of course. It's part of the deal. You know what my wife's like, Andrea. Her idea of sex is three minutes in the missionary position. If I take longer than that she complains and tells me to go and finish myself off in the bathroom.' Highfield paused and licked his lips as he slowly devoured her with his eyes. 'I suppose, as you still work for me, this could be considered sexual harassment.' He took the diagonal zip across Andrea's right breast and pulled it down. Her soft flesh burst out, her nipple already hard. 'Now look at that lovely thing,' he drooled. 'I've always fancied you, Andrea. Did you know that?'

Before she could answer he undid the other zip, pinched her nipples, making her wince and sigh softly, and pulled so more of her breasts became visible. Then he cupped and caressed both generous handfuls. 'Isn't this fun?' he breathed. 'I can't imagine anyone else I'd rather have as my slave. That's what you are, isn't it? My slave?'

'Yes,' she whispered, 'I'm your slave.'

He sniggered. 'Oh, my dear girl. I'm *really* going to enjoy this.'

He turned her round and stroked her buttocks through the skin-tight leather.

'The question is, what are we going to do with you? I've been quite lucky at these little raffles. I had a very nice little piece in here a couple of weeks ago. She was really into pain. So, let's see now.'

He walked to the rack of whips and picked up a riding-crop. He came back and flicked the leather loop at the end against Andrea's nipples. She felt a stab of pain. Instinctively she bent forward, trying to protect herself.

'Stand up straight,' he snapped.

She did as she was told.

He raised the whip, then brought it down forcefully onto her right breast. She flinched and cried out aloud. But the pain was short-lived. She felt the familiar pulses of pleasure setting her nerves alight.

Thwack! The whip landed on her left breast, cutting across her nipple. Again the pain transmuted into intense pleasure. She looked down at her chest, the breasts squeezed out obscenely through the tight leather, the metal zips digging into the flesh, two red stripes already beginning to appear.

'Look at me,' Highfield ordered firmly.

She looked up, watching him with wide eyes as he raised the whip again. It cut down across her right breast again. Her flesh quivered. She felt a huge surge of excitement in the depths of her cunt.

Thwack! The next blow fell on her left breast, each tit being given equal treatment.

'Now bend over,' he said. The smile had been wiped from his face. It had been replaced by a lust that glazed his eyes and made his mouth hang loose.

Andrea bent over the table. She felt his hand smoothing the leather on her buttocks again.

'What's this?' he asked. His hand had found another zip. This one ran from the middle of her arse, down between her legs and right round to her navel. He found the tongue of

100

the zip and pulled it all the way. The leather peeled open, revealing Andrea's sex.

'I always wondered what your pussy looked like. Now I know.' She felt his fingers prodding her labia. One, then two, thrust clumsily into her vagina. 'I see the whip makes you randy, too,' he said hoarsely, her wetness obviously betraying her feelings, as his voice betrayed his.

Highfield stood back. She heard a rustle of clothing. He took off his shirt and jacket and hung them on the back of the door, then pulled off his shoes and socks. Quickly he got out of his trousers and pants.

'Just too, too good to miss,' he said quietly, almost to himself.

He took her by the hips and pulled her back against himself. She felt his turgid cock slide between her labia.

'Christ,' he panted, 'I wonder if I can get some of the other girls from the office to volunteer. What about that friend of yours – Pam, isn't it? I'd love to get her in here too. Perhaps I could have the two of you together.'

He thrust forward. Andrea felt his cock plunge deep into her vagina. She was wet – very wet, the bondage and the whip having the usual consequences. Being used like this by her old boss was a new low in humiliation, but it was precisely that, she realised, that made it so exciting. Her total submission, her obedience, was being tested to the limit. She knew why Hawksworth had selected her, instead of Julia or one of the other girls, to be the 'prize'. She even wondered if the draw had been rigged so she was sure to end up with Highfield. It was all a test. If she wanted to be a slave, to truly serve her master, the more difficult the test the more she could prove herself. The psychology might be twisted, but that did not mean it wasn't accurate.

But it wasn't only that. Highfield's cock was hard and large. And, almost despite herself, Andrea found the penetration welcome. Her cunt had been neglected since she'd been at the house. After last night, after the softness and subtlety of a woman's mouth, the unsubtle hammering of Highfield's cock was exactly what she needed. 'Oh God,' she mumbled.

'Christ, I wish I could have done this to you over my desk in the office,' Highfield said between gritted teeth. 'Why didn't you tell me you were into all this, you little bitch? I'd have tied you up and whipped you every fucking day!'

Suddenly he stopped. He pulled out of her. 'I have a better idea,' he said, breathing heavily. 'Kneel down.'

He spun her round and forced her to her knees, his large cock bobbing in front of her face. Andrea looked up at him. His body showed little sign of muscle; in particular his legs and arms were soft and unexercised. He cupped her chin and the back of her head, told her to open her mouth, and fed his erection between her lips. She instantly tasted her own juices on his pulsing flesh as it stretched her jaw.

'Come on, girl, suck on it,' he ordered crudely.

She did exactly that. She sucked hard and Highfield moaned. She pulled back and pushed forward so his cock would saw in and out of her mouth, but with her hands still strapped to her sides it was difficult to maintain her balance.

'Faster,' he urged, seizing her head tighter and guiding it back and forth until she achieved the rhythm he required. She felt his erection pulse ever more urgently. As he forced her head forward his cock was driven right down to the back of her throat. Her forehead nudged the underhang of his well-fed belly. It was difficult with her lips stretched and her mouth full, but she used her tongue as best she could to lick the ridge at the base of his glans. Her nostrils flared as she breathed deeply to quell the impulse to gag.

'You little bitch,' he hissed, 'you're fucking good at this… Now drink!'

She sucked hard again as he pulled her back, then ran her tongue over the top of his glans. His cock jerked violently and he rammed it back into her mouth, just as his spunk began shooting thick pearly liquid down her throat. He clamped her head in both hands, his fingers as unforgiving as steel, and exhaled long and slow.

Andrea swallowed obediently. His copious offering tasted salty.

'Your turn,' he said, grinning between heavy pants as he pulled away.

'W-what do you mean?'

He sniggered in a way that unsettled her immensely. 'You'll see,' was all he said.

He went to the corner of the room. What Andrea had thought to be part of the wall was in fact a flush-fitting cupboard door, also covered in black carpet. Highfield pulled the door open, then dragged a strange-looking frame into the middle of the room. It looked like a barstool but, instead of a flat surface, the sturdy legs of the stool supported what looked like a leather saddle, complete with stirrups. The saddle had an American-style pommel at the centre in the front.

'Climb up here,' Highfield ordered.

'What are you going to do to me?' After four days of training herself not to respond spontaneously, it felt strange to be able to talk freely again.

Highfield leered. 'You'll see. Or rather, you won't. Now do as you're told and sit up here, on the saddle.'

With her arms bound it proved difficult to climb onto the top of the stool. Highfield had to help her put one foot in a stirrup then lift her leg over the saddle, just as she would do had she been mounting a horse. As she did so, she noticed there were a series of holes in the centre of the saddle.

The stirrups were adjustable, and Highfield pulled them higher so Andrea's legs were bent up with her heels immediately under her buttocks. Straps had been provided to make sure the occupant of the stool remained in this position, and Highfield buckled them tightly round her ankles.

'That's better,' he said, standing back to admire his

103

handiwork.

He went to the cupboard on the other wall. Andrea heard the door open. When he came back he was carrying a long strip of black silk. Without a word, he placed it over her eyes, then bound it tightly around her head.

'Lovely hair,' he said. She felt his hands stroking it.

The blindfold intensified her trepidation and excitement. Deprived of one sense, all the others seemed to over-compensate. She was able to listen to all the little grace-notes of arousal that were playing within her.

She heard Highfield moving again. The cupboard door creaked. Then she thought he was kneeling in front of the stool. She felt a hand touch her leg, then something was pushing up through one of the holes in the saddle. It butted into the top of her labia, pushed forward, then was retracted again. A second later it re-emerged through another of the holes, this one immediately under the opening of her vagina.

'That's the one,' Highfield grunted.

The object thrust upwards, and Andrea gasped. It was a phallus, hard and cold and very large. It filled her completely.

'Like that, do you?' his voice taunted.

Andrea had to admit that she did. Her sex reacted violently, contracting around the dildo. It was so large it splayed her labia apart and exposed and stretched her clitoris, which began to throb. This was, after all, what she loved. She was bound and helpless. A slave. An object to be used in whatever way her master saw fit. Giving her to Highfield was part of Hawksworth's largesse. In the darkness she could see herself mounted on the horse, clad in tight black leather, her arms tied to her sides, the black silk banding her eyes, her legs tucked up beneath her. The image excited her immensely. She found herself pushing down on the phallus, grinding her hips from side to side so her clitoris rubbed against the pommel of the saddle.

'Let's warm you up a bit.'

She knew what that meant. Another surge of excitement

swept over her. He was going to whip her. She could hear him crossing the room again. She held her breath…

Thwack! A thin whip landed viciously against her leather-covered arse. She bucked up on the saddle as much as the bonds on her ankles would allow, pulling up off the phallus, then sinking back down again. God, that felt good!

Thwack! She rocked forward and rose again. The pain from the whip transmuted to pleasure. She dropped down onto the dildo for a second time, using her weight to force it deep. It wasn't going to take long to come like this.

'I – I have to have permission,' she panted urgently.

'I told you, this is your turn. I want to see you come.'

That was all she needed. He cut two more blows down onto her vulnerable buttocks, and the stinging pain speared straight to her sex as she rode the unforgiving dildo buried so deep inside her. Like a wave crashing on the beach, her orgasm gathered all its strength, mounting higher and higher before finally breaking on the shore. She squirmed and writhed, spreading her legs as far apart as she could to get the dildo deeper still. A stream of juice coated the phallus and the saddle, as a long low guttural moan of ecstasy slowly died in her throat and head lolled forward.

Andrea was taken to the bathroom to shower. Her hair was pinned up in a tight chignon and her make-up retouched, then she was permitted to eat.

Ten minutes later, Laurie arrived. As usual, she dropped clothes onto the bed. 'Put these on, quickly,' she ordered, before leaving again, closing and locking the door as usual.

Andrea wasn't sure what time it was, but she had the feeling it was early evening. That was heartening, she thought. Until now the master had always called for her in the middle of the night. If he wanted her now it was possible he wanted to spend more time with her.

Highfield had left Andrea tied to the saddle in the punishment room, with the blindfold still covering her eyes and the dildo firmly lodged in place. Laurie had removed it and unstrapped her before returning her to what Andrea thought of as her cell in the stable block.

She had plenty of time to think about what had happened. That afternoon had been one of the most humiliating experiences of her life. Previously she had been able to pretend that Hawksworth and the almost hypnotic effect he had on her caused her extraordinary responses. But that afternoon he had not been present. She had been used. Totally used. And yet she had still responded with a degree of arousal that had astonished her. It appeared that as long as she was bound and helpless, and was required to be completely submissive, her body responded with unquestioning arousal. She had no idea why. There was undeniably something deep in her psyche that yearned for such treatment. And she was terribly grateful that Charles Darrington Hawksworth was there to provide it in spades.

She picked up the clothes Laurie had left: a red strapless tube dress, a white strapless bra, a pair of flesh-coloured shiny hold-up stockings, and red shoes with gold heels and a gold motif on the toe. As usual, there were no panties.

Andrea pulled on the outfit. The dress was tight, clinging to the curves of her body, the material smooth and glossy, its bodice displaying a great deal of cleavage. The skirt was just long enough to conceal the tops of the stockings.

The door opened again.

'Good,' Laurie said, with a glint in her eye of undisguised approval. The brunette floated close to Andrea, their faces only inches apart. 'Kiss me,' she breathed, her breath crisp and fresh.

Andrea was puzzled; Laurie had never made any attempt to use her without Hawksworth being present. But she didn't think she had any choice. She leaned forward a little and lightly brushed Laurie's heavily rouged and slightly parted lips with her own. The voluptuous brunette immediately wrapped her arms around Andrea and plunged her tongue

106

into her mouth. Andrea was sure she could feel the little gold rings that pierced her nipples, hard and cold, as they pressed into her own breasts.

'One day…' Laurie whispered huskily as she pulled away from the sexy embrace. Andrea could see the lust in her eyes. Her own body was tingling, all the memories of what Laurie had previously done to her instantly revived.

The brunette used a manicured finger to remove a smudge of lipstick that had smeared onto Andrea's chin. 'Hands behind your back now, and turn around,' she ordered quietly but firmly.

Andrea obeyed. The cold metal of a pair of handcuffs clicked around her wrists.

Once again they walked from the stable block and into the main house. As on her first night they went into the sitting room, then through to the smaller scarlet dining room. Charles Hawksworth was sitting at the table on his own. A maid stood by the kitchen door.

'Good evening, my dear,' he welcomed, with a warm smile.

Andrea wasn't sure whether she should respond, so she remained quiet.

'You look stunning,' he went on, and then nodded at Laurie, who was standing quietly beside her charge. 'You may leave us.'

A faint smile flickered in the brunette's eyes, and then she left the room.

'Please sit down.' Hawksworth was wearing slacks and a white shirt. He indicated the chair next to him, but made no effort to pull it out from under the table. Rather awkwardly, Andrea managed to reach around and grip the back of the chair, and then drag it out. She sat down.

The master leant forward. Those piercing blue eyes burned into her as he studied her for long unsettling minutes.

'Highfield was very pleased with you,' he eventually said. 'He reported that you were most responsive. He was surprised and annoyed that he'd never before realised your full potential.'

Andrea squirmed slightly. She could still feel the shadow of that monstrous dildo deep in her sex.

'I was right about you, wasn't I?' Hawksworth's dulcet tones continued. 'You are a natural, aren't you?'

'Yes, master,' she answered with sincerity. 'I think I am.'

He gestured to the maid at the door. Andrea had seen her on her first night in the house. She was tall with red hair. 'Another brandy, Philippa.'

The maid disappeared into the kitchen. Hawksworth leaned forward, and possessively cupped Andrea's breasts. Her whole body tingled. It was the tenderest gesture he had ever made toward her.

'I'm going to take you into the punishment room, Andrea,' he said. 'I have something very special in mind.'

'Yes, master.' Andrea felt her heart leap. The idea of being alone with Hawksworth was thrilling no matter where he was taking her. She could see real desire deep in his eyes.

Hawksworth rose gracefully as Philippa reappeared with the brandy. 'Come with us,' he said to her, whilst guiding Andrea to her feet.

Andrea felt instant disappointment. It looked as if they were not going to be alone, after all. Did he plan to use the redhead as he'd used Julia on Andrea's first night there?

They walked through the big house. Hawksworth opened the door of the punishment room and ushered both women inside ahead of him.

The room had clearly been prepared for this visit. The saddle stool had been put away, and in its place, suspended from two chains in the middle of the room, was a long tubular metal bar. Six thick leather straps were bolted to the metal.

'Stand against the bar, Andrea,' Hawksworth said, closing the door.

'Yes, master.' Andrea did as she was told. The bar was at shoulder height and she felt the cold metal against her bare shoulder-blades. Hawksworth took the brandy balloon from

Philippa and savoured the amber liquid. Then he took a key from his pocket and gave it to Philippa, who walked over to Andrea and used it to unlock the handcuffs.

'Extend your arms along the bar,' Hawksworth instructed.

Andrea stretched her arms out so they were at right angles to her body.

'You know what to do,' he said to the maid.

Philippa nodded. She moved behind Andrea and began wrapping the leather straps around her arms. She started on the left, buckling the first strap around her wrist, the second just above the elbow and the third at the top of the arm. As she repeated the process on the right, Andrea felt a new surge of excitement.

'Spread your legs apart,' Hawksworth ordered.

Andrea tried to do as she was told, but the skirt was too tight and she could barely get them more than a foot apart.

Hawksworth saw the problem. He moved in front of her, took hold of the hem and wriggled it up over her thighs until it was banded across her flat stomach.

Andrea felt Philippa's hand gripping her left ankle. She pulled it over to a metal ring set in the floor and used a length of white nylon rope to bind it to the ring. She bound Andrea's right ankle to another ring, splaying her legs wide apart.

'That's better. Bondage excites you, doesn't it?' Hawksworth touched his glass to her erect nipple, its shape protruding through the red dress.

'Yes, master, it does,' Andrea admitted softly.

'And whipping, does that excite you too?'

'No master,' Andrea said quickly. She didn't know if that was true. Being spanked or whipped brought her pain, but it was always accompanied by pleasure too. Could she have one without the other?

He smiled indulgently. 'No? That surprises me. Shall we put it to the test?'

'Anything you want, master.' That was definitely true.

She didn't care what he did to her as long as he was here with her, his full attention riveted on her. It was that which she craved.

He went to the rack of whips and selected one. It had a braided handle with six or seven long thin lashes, each one knotted at the end.

'Hold this for me,' he said, pressing the handle to Andrea's mouth. She took it between her teeth. 'Don't drop it,' he warned, and then, to her immense surprise and disappointment, he turned and left the room, closing the door behind him.

The handle of the whip was so thick it was difficult to get a good grip, so Andrea bit down hard and tensed her jaw.

Philippa was still lurking behind her. 'Looks like you're his favourite,' she said quietly, her breath ruffling the soft blonde hair at Andrea's temple. Andrea felt the girl's hands snaking around her body, her fingers digging into her breasts. She pinched both her nipples simultaneously through the sleek dress and ground her lithe body into Andrea's back. It felt firm and muscular. 'Have you had the nipple clips yet?' she breathed, twisting the bound girl's nipples as if they were the dials on a radio. Andrea whimpered and squeezed her eyes tightly shut, trying desperately not to lose her grip on the whip.

One persistent hand stroked her side, running over her buttocks, now exposed by the raised dress, and down between her legs. There was nothing Andrea could do to stop it worming its way to her sex. The fingers pinched Andrea's labia, and again she almost lost the whip as she gasped in tormented surprise. Philippa thrust two fingers up into her victim's vagina and ground her warm groin against Andrea's rounded buttocks. Andrea shuddered within the intimate embrace. Her sex was wet, very wet, and she responded to the sudden intrusion with a sharp intake of breath and a quivering sigh.

'I hope he lets me whip you,' Philippa purred, her lips

fluttering seductively against Andrea's ear like a delicate butterfly. 'I just *love* to whip a gorgeous girl like you.'

The door started to open. Philippa immediately pulled away from Andrea, the intrusive fingers withdrawing from the moist haven of her sex.

Hawksworth reappeared. He was wearing the same scarlet velvet robe he had worn before.

The muscles of Andrea's jaw were beginning to ache intolerably, and she was breathing deeply from the stimulation so recently snatched away from her. If he didn't remove the whip from her mouth soon she would inevitably drop it. Perspiration dampened her forehead and her blonde fringe as she tried desperately to suck the handle back into her mouth. She tried to hold it with her lips, but it was just too awkward. She desperately didn't want to fail at the one task he'd set her.

Hawksworth spoke to Philippa, 'And what have you been doing?'

The redhead did not reply.

'Well? Answer me when I ask you a question.'

'Nothing, master,' she said guiltily.

He looked from her telltale glistening fingers to Andrea. 'Did she touch you?' he asked.

Andrea did not dare move. If she nodded her head the whip would definitely fall out of her mouth. He appeared to accept this as a no. To her enormous relief, he reached up and plucked the whip from between her lips. Her saliva had darkened the braided leather.

'You may go, Philippa,' he said.

'Thank you, master,' Philippa replied, her voice betraying her relief, before scurrying from the room.

'Now, where were we?' Hawksworth continued, once she was gone and the door firmly closed once again. He looked into Andrea's eyes. He raised his hands and cupped her breasts, just as he had done in the dining room. Andrea felt a wave of emotion. She had been totally entranced from the moment she had set eyes on him. He had affected her more deeply than any man ever had before, and now, at last, they were alone together.

'Master,' she murmured, needing to say the word and hoping he would not object to her speaking out of turn.

'So needy,' he said. He raised one hand to the top of the tight tube dress and peeled it down, exposing her delicious breasts. He stared at them, the flesh quivering, the nipples as tight as knots. Three or four red stripes criss-crossed the soft flesh.

'Highfield whipped them, didn't he?'

'Yes, master.'

Hawksworth flicked the end of the whip against her left nipple, then ran it down over the bunched material of the dress. He trailed the lashes against her inner thigh, above the tight elasticated welt of the hold-ups.

'It's neat, isn't it?' he said, his eyes feasting on her vulnerable beauty. 'I have a need to dominate, and you have a need to be dominated. A perfect match.'

He pushed the handle of the whip between her legs. It nestled between her labia, and she gasped as it crushed against her swollen clitoris.

'Sex is not just a physical thing.' His low tone was hypnotic, and Andrea swooned in her bonds. 'It's dependent on emotional need. This is your emotional need, isn't it Andrea?'

'Oh yes, master.' She tried to squirm closer to him, urging her breasts forward, the metal bar swaying with her slight movement. Her clitoris was throbbing violently against the braided leather.

He walked around her. His hand caressed her buttocks with such tenderness she felt a whole new wave of emotion sweeping over her. He wanted her. He cared for her. That thought was totally intoxicating. For a fleeting second she felt his fingers run down between her labia.

'Have you ever been buggered?' he asked.

112

She groaned at the unexpected bluntness of the question. 'No… master…' Her sex lips trembled as she felt his fingers slid between them.

'You haven't? How interesting.'

He pulled his fingers away. She heard the heavy velvet rustle as he raised an arm.

Swish! The whip cut across her exposed buttocks. Instead of one single line of searing pain the lashes created six or seven simultaneously, each one biting like a thousand needle pricks. Andrea gasped, and the leather bonds creaked as she rocked forward from the impact of the cruel blow.

'Thank you, master,' he said, obviously meaning her to repeat the same. 'Please may I have another?'

It was what she'd heard Julia say. 'Thank you, master,' she managed. 'Please may I have another?'

'You may.'

The next volley strokes came in such quick succession she had no time to repeat the litany he had taught her. She thought she counted four, each making her buttocks explode with pain. But she knew the pain wouldn't last. In seconds her body had twisted it into a furnace of sensual excitement. The fact that it was her master's own hand that was applying the punishment made it much more pleasurable.

'Thank you, master,' she panted the moment the assault had stopped. 'Please may I have another?'

Three more strokes came in quick succession. One cut higher, rendered ineffective by the material bunched around her waist. The other two were much lower, stroking against her thighs, the lashes seeming to curl inward and brush her sex.

'Thank you, master—' she began, but before she could finish the whip was falling again. This time he seemed to be angling the blows so that the knotted lashes did indeed hit her sex directly. A new pain lanced through her body. She found herself struggling against her bonds, trying to pull her legs together and free her hands. The chains that held the metal bar clanked noisily. The fact that she could not move a muscle dramatically increased her arousal.

'No!' she screamed, as yet another stroke lashed against her inner thigh.

'Don't say no unless you mean it. The word no, in this house, carries very unpleasant consequences.' He moulded his body against her back and whispered in her ear. 'Now, shall I continue?'

'Oh yes, master… please master.' She knew what he meant, of course; if she refused to co-operate she would be sent away. And she just couldn't bear the thought of that – especially as every sinew in her body was now tingling with the pleasure of the whip and screaming out for more.

'Very well. Three more. Count them.'

Thwack! The whip coiled up between her legs. But this time the pain was muted, the multiple lashes that cut into the tender flesh only seeming to increase the strength of the pleasure that was coursing through her.

'One…' Andrea sobbed.

Thwack! The second was the hardest yet, the lash curling right up to her anus. She felt her sphincter contract reflexively.

'T-two…' Her breasts swelled invitingly as she filled her lungs in readiness for the final onslaught.

Thwack! The whip whistled as it lashed up between her legs. One of the knots seemed to catch her right on the clit, causing a momentary explosion of pain that turned instantly to the hottest, most penetrating ecstasy. Her whole body felt the impact.

'Thu-three…' she just managed to gasp. The last stroke had set her nerves on edge. She could feel all the familiar sensations gathering in her body. Her head lolled forward and she looked down at herself through lowered lashes; her breasts thrusting out of the tube dress so lewdly, her legs bound and spread – and the sight only amplified her arousal. She was helpless, completely vulnerable. Why was that so exciting? It was the tightest bondage she had yet experienced, and it was adding fuel to the fire that was consuming her senses.

Desperately she tried to relax, but neither mind nor body would let her. Her mind was telling her that Hawksworth must really care for her to want to be alone with her and administer the punishment personally. And her body was alive with sensation, the tails of the whip having created a hundred new areas of sensitivity, each throbbing quite as madly as her clit.

Hawksworth had made it quite clear she was not allowed to come without permission. Tonight the master had given her special treatment. If she repaid him with disobedience who knew what his response would be? It might be days before she was allowed to see him again. He might even lose patience and send her away for good. She tried to hang on to that thought as a way of cooling her ardour, but it was only partially successful.

Hawksworth dropped the whip to the floor. Andrea heard a rustle of the robe and suddenly felt his hands wrapping around her body. They cupped both of her breasts, squashing them flat against her chest as he pulled her back towards him. Her superheated bottom butted against his comparatively cool belly, his fully erect cock pressing into the cleft of her buttocks. He bucked his hips and she felt his phallus push inward. She could feel it sliding between her labia, their wetness making it instantly slippery. His cock was hot and she could feel it pulsing.

This new development gave a new twist to her spiral of excitement. She was so close to orgasm now that she knew if he pushed into her cunt she would instantly come – she wouldn't be able to help herself.

He tongued her ear, setting her nerves on fire. At the same time he bucked his hips and suddenly his lubricated glans was nestling against her tiny puckered rear entrance.

He was going to bugger her, she knew. Almost before she'd

115

absorbed the notion, she felt him pressing forward. Her sphincter resisted, then yielded, and a stretching discomfort racked her body. But the pain did not last long. In seconds it was replaced by a sensation of the most ecstatic pleasure. He had not penetrated far, but she felt her anus clenching around his glans, as if trying to suck him in deeper. But there was no time.

Hawksworth threw his head back and came, his cock jerking violently in the tight confines of her bottom, his sperm seeping into her virginal rear passage. Andrea could feel every jet as the liquid fire of his essence created beautiful sensations in a place where no man had ever been before. She had started to orgasm the moment he ejaculated, each new spurt of semen creating a new torrent of delight. It seemed to go on forever, her bondage somehow trapping the orgasm inside her, like a thunderstorm in a canyon.

Only the sudden feeling of his softening cock being squeezed out of her anus by an involuntary contraction brought Andrea back to reality, and the consequences of what she had done.

'I'm sorry, master,' she muttered, knowing that even saying this was wrong. 'I'm so sorry.'

'Shhh…' he soothed. He moved away and stood in front of her, wrapping the robe around his body. 'It doesn't matter,' he said. He stooped slightly and kissed her on one flushed cheek, so tenderly that Andrea thought she was going to cry.

'You're very special, Andrea. A lot of the girls have rebelled at the raffle. But you were perfect. It must have been hard for you to submit to Highfield.'

'Yes, master,' she said honestly, still swooning in the afterglow of her shattering orgasm.

'I have to go away for a few days,' he continued. 'You must obey Laurie as you would obey me. You understand that, don't you?'

'Yes, master, I do.'

'When I come back it will be time to take you to the next stage. I think you're ready. Don't do anything to change my mind.'

'No, master.'

Andrea wanted to ask how long he would be away, but dare not. She did not want to spoil the mood that had been created between them. Instead she wanted to wallow in it.

At the door Hawksworth paused and took one last look back at Andrea, then he was gone.

Chapter Six

Laurie pulled Andrea forward by the chain leash attached to the steel collar.

It felt strange for Andrea to be naked. On every other occasion when she'd been taken from the stables she'd been dressed in some outré outfit or other. This afternoon she was naked, apart from a pair of black high heels that clacked noisily on the stone flags.

Laurie, on the other hand, was fully dressed in a smart black suit over a white blouse and grey nylons.

It had been three days since Andrea's night with Hawksworth. She had heard the helicopter arrive the next morning and imagined him being driven to meet it by Laurie in the Range Rover. An hour later, Laurie had come into the stable block and explained to her that she would be given light household tasks for the next few days until Hawksworth returned. She had been given a set of cotton overalls and set to work cleaning and helping in the kitchen, though not without some form of bondage. On the first day it had merely been metal handcuffs securing her wrists together in front of her body. On the second, a leather belt had been strapped around her waist, with a chain linking her wrists running through a ring on the front. This meant that Andrea couldn't extend one hand without the other following. The device made even the simplest of chores difficult and exhausting.

Andrea had been grateful for the distraction. The thought of spending days alone in her cell, wondering how long it would be before Hawksworth returned, was not appealing.

On the third day, after lunch, Laurie took her back to the stable block without explanation. After being ordered to shower, Andrea had been made up and her long hair brushed out over her shoulders. It occurred to her that Hawksworth might have come back. But when Laurie returned to collect her with no clothes for her to wear any hope began to fade. Hawksworth had always given instructions for her dress. Without a word the brunette secured Andrea's hands behind her back in padded leather cuffs, and clipped the chain leash into the collar.

Any vestige of hope that she was being taken to see the master was quickly dashed as Laurie led her through the house; they mounted the stairs but walked past Hawksworth's bedroom and down the landing.

'In here,' Laurie finally said, opening a door and ushering her charge inside.

Andrea suspected that they were in Laurie's bedroom. It contained a chest of drawers, a wardrobe, a dressing table, a large double bed and two bedside chests. The décor was plain, with beige-coloured walls and a sandy carpet. The bed had square wooden posts at each corner that stuck up about three or four feet above the mattress. Two metal rings, similar to the ones in the punishment room, hung menacingly from chains that were set into the top of each of these posts.

'Stand by the foot of the bed,' the beautiful seductress ordered brusquely, clearly enjoying her role without her boss resident in the house.

Andrea obeyed. The bed was covered with a pretty patchwork quilt. The sun had been shining all day, and the room was comfortably warm and still.

Laurie drew the heavy curtains, plunging the room into semi-darkness.

'Do you know why you're here?' she asked, turning to face her vulnerable plaything.

'No, Ms Angelis.'

'You're here to learn.' Laurie smiled that enigmatic smile. 'Mr Hawksworth wants you schooled in the art of lesbian love. As I am the expert in that field…' The sentence trailed off. Laurie slowly unbuttoned her jacket, took it off and hung

119

it in the wardrobe. She unzipped her skirt and stepped out of it with breathtaking movements of fluid elegance. She hung that up in the wardrobe too. She unbuttoned her blouse and allowed the diaphanous material to fall open as she walked over to the bed. 'You were very responsive the last time we were close.' She ran cool fingers down Andrea's spine. 'Do you remember?'

'Y-yes, Ms Angelis,' Andrea replied hesitantly. She wasn't sure whether she felt excitement or apprehension at the prospect of what lay ahead. She had convinced herself that her reason for being so aroused by Laurie was because of Hawksworth and that it would please him. Without his presence, it might be different.

Laurie slipped the blouse from her unblemished shoulders. She was wearing a translucent black bra that pushed her breasts into a deep cleavage, the flesh spilling out of the low-cut cups, and matching bikini style panties. Her grey nylons were supported by a wide suspender belt of the same black material.

The stunning brunette drifted to her dressing table, where she sat and began brushing out her lustrous hair. She took a small bottle of perfume with an atomiser and sprayed her breasts and the top of her thighs. The scent was heady, a mixture of musk and flowers.

'Let's get started then, shall we?' she said huskily to the reflection of Andrea behind her.

She rose and moved back to Andrea, where she unclipped the chain from the silver collar and placed it on one of the bedside chests.

'You understand that you must obey me totally, don't you, my dear?' she said. 'As if I was Mr Hawksworth?'

Andrea felt herself blushing as the breathless tension in the room increased. 'Yes, Ms Angelis.'

'Excellent.' The woman smiled, her ringed nipples pushing slightly through the shimmering black bra. 'I think this is going to be a lot of fun.'

She opened the bottom drawer of the chest and extracted a snake's nest of belts, straps and leather harnesses. She placed them reverently on the bed. Then she reached behind her back and unclipped the bra, and her large breasts thrust free. Her nipples, pierced by the gold rings, stood out prominently.

She bent over the bed and picked up a thin gold chain with a tiny snap-lock at each end. She opened the locks and clipped them onto her nipple rings.

'Some masters insist all their slaves are pierced,' she said. 'Mr Hawksworth is not one of them.'

The chain looped between her breasts. She grasped the middle of it with finger and thumb and pulled it up until her already firm breasts were lifted too. Andrea saw a flash of self-indulgent pain in her eyes, but it was soon replaced by very obvious pleasure.

'Lovely…' Laurie muttered, almost to herself.

She dropped the chain and bent over the bed again, sorting through the leather harnesses. She found two thin straps. Moving silently behind Andrea, she unhooked the central link that held the two padded cuffs together.

'Now turn around and move forward a little, to the foot of the bed.' She guided Andrea until her knees were touching the mattress. 'Good. Now, raise your left arm.'

Laurie threaded the thin strap through the D-ring on the cuff, then stretched it over to the metal ring dangling from the top of the bedpost. She threaded it through that too, then buckled the strap tight so that Andrea's arm was stretched out tautly to the side. She then repeated this procedure with her right arm.

'Mmm… very nice…' Laurie again ran her hand down Andrea's back, and across her buttocks. She stroked up the side of her body, then cupped her right breast. 'I can appreciate exactly what Mr Hawksworth sees in you.'

With a wistful smile she moved away again and rooted through the pile of belts. She quickly found a more complicated harness. It consisted of a thick belt, which she secured tightly around Andrea's trim waist. Hanging from the belt were two narrow bands that joined into a single strap. Laurie pulled it between Andrea's thighs and up into the cleft of her buttocks, buckling the harness into the waistband at the back, the leather cutting deeply into Andrea's sex.

Two more padded leather cuffs followed. She knelt and wrapped them round Andrea's ankles, then clipped them to metal rings which were attached to the foot of the bedposts by chains, spreading her legs wide apart.

After a short pause to admire her handiwork, Laurie hooked her thumbs into the waistband of her panties and pulled them down her long legs. She swept the coil of belts and straps off the counterpane onto the floor, and lay back on the bed. She opened her legs and bent her knees, allowing Andrea a clear view of her hairless sex. Her labia pouted and Andrea could see the scarlet flesh within, glistening with juice. Laurie's hands ran up and down the soft inner surface of her thighs.

'I think stockings are *so* sexy, don't you?' she said, her hands moving over the welts of the stockings, stretched into peaks by the taut suspenders. Her thighs were firm, with deep hollows just below her sex. 'I asked you a question,' she suddenly snapped, when Andrea didn't reply.

'Yes, Ms Angelis,' Andrea hastened to respond.

Laurie's fingernails were painted bright red. She stroked her hand over her mons, then pushed her fingers between her labia and splayed them apart, allowing her middle finger free access to her clit. Andrea could see her tapping it aggressively. Laurie's other hand slipped down to her vagina. She drove two fingers deep inside, then pushed a third finger into the puckered hole of her anus. She screwed her fingers inward until they were buried up to the knuckle. Her eyes were closed. She stopped tapping her clit and rubbed instead, pressing it hard.

'So *good*...' she muttered.

Laurie's body trembled. She tossed her head violently to the right and moaned, pulling her fingers quickly from her body as if that pleasure had suddenly become too much to bear.

After a moment she sat up. The chain that looped between her nipples clinked, her breasts quivering.

There was a knock on the door.

'Come in,' Laurie called. 'I asked Julia to join us,' she then said to Andrea as the door opened.

Andrea twisted her head around as Julia walked into the room. She was wearing a tight body made from sheer black nylon, so her breasts and the bush of her pubic hair were clearly visible. Her legs were bare, but she wore black high heels.

'Julie, just in time.' Laurie smiled warmly. She leaned across the bed and opened the top drawer of the bedside chest. 'Come over here, my darling.'

As Julia crossed the room she glanced at Andrea, her eyes flickering over her naked and trussed body.

'Put this on our dear Andrea,' Laurie said, taking out a large flesh-coloured dildo from the drawer. It was not like any other Andrea had seen. While one end was shaped crudely to resemble a male phallus with a glans and a distinct ridge separating it from the rest of the shaft, the other end was flared. Laurie also held a triangle of black leather, in the centre of which a large hole had been cut. She handed both items to Julia.

The newcomer stood behind Andrea, fitting the flared dildo through the hole in the black leather. She then reached around Andrea's body and pushed the dildo down into the straps that extended from the harness. There were three small studs on the straps which snapped into corresponding fasteners on the leather harness. Julia secured them all one by one, so the black leather triangle and the dildo were held firmly in place.

Andrea looked down at her body. She had sprouted a cock.

'Now this,' Laurie said. She was holding up a smaller dildo, not much bigger than a little finger. Attached to it was a long thin flex, at the end of which was a rectangular box.

Julia took the device from Laurie. Quickly she unbuckled the belt of the harness that ran up between Andrea's legs from the thicker belt at her waist. Dropping silently to her knees, she prodded the little dildo up between Andrea's labia until she found the mouth of her vagina and pushed the instrument home. Immediately she pulled the belt up tightly and buckled it to the waist belt again, much more tightly than before. The flex hung down between Andrea's legs, the rectangular box resting on the floor.

'You know what to do now,' Laurie said to Julia.

This was obviously something they had done before. How many of Hawksworth's slaves had been tied to this bed and used in this way? Was it all part of the usual training?

Andrea felt her sex twitch. The leather strap cut up into her sex so tightly now that it was pressing directly against her clitoris. It didn't take much imagination to guess what Laurie had in mind, and Andrea was aroused by the prospect. Strangely, the dildo that stuck out obscenely from her belly seemed to be alive, as though it had become a part of her.

Julia had taken a jar of cold cream from the bedside chest and was slathering the greasy unguent all over Laurie's sex, working between her legs and over her anus.

Then she turned to Andrea. Scooping some of the cream into her palm, she coated it over the bulbous head of the dildo. Again, Andrea had the strange feeling that the dildo was producing little thrills in her lower belly.

'Would you like her gagged?' Julia asked.

'Yes,' Laurie confirmed, with a wicked smile, 'I would like that very much.'

Julia disappeared behind Andrea's back. A moment later a large wedge of black rubber attached to a leather strap was being pressed against her lips. Andrea had little option but to open her mouth and allow Julia to push the rubber in, securing it with the strap buckled tightly around her head. The rubber reached right to the back of her throat, the wider end forcing her lips apart.

Laurie knelt on all fours and positioned herself so her buttocks were only inches away from the tip of the phallus.

Andrea looked down at her, the suspender belt banding her narrow waist, the suspenders so taut they cut into her thigh flesh. Her buttocks were oval and fleshy, and between them her sex pouted eagerly. Guilt gnawed at Andrea's insides as she realised the kneeling vision was both intoxicating and irresistible.

Julia took the base of the dildo in her hand and, as Laurie pushed back, guided it into her waiting cunt. Andrea watched it slowly disappear. It was almost as if she could feel the warmth and wetness that enveloped it.

'Oh yessss…' Laurie hissed, squirming her buttocks from side to side and dipping her back. 'You know what to do now.'

Julia stooped and fiddled with the box on the floor. Immediately a strong vibration coursed through the little dildo in Andrea's cunt. The vibrations spread outward into the leather strap that held the dildo in place, making that vibrate against her clitoris.

Once more Julia disappeared from Andrea's line of sight. Then she felt the girl's hands looping around her body and fingers sinking into her breasts, pinching the nipples viciously. Andrea moaned quietly with pleasure at the feel of Julia's body pressing into her back, and then with disappointment as Julia stepped away. As Laurie pushed back, driving the big dildo deep into her cunt, Andrea heard a familiar swish and twisted her head around in time to see the whip in Julia's hand. Before she could prepare herself for the impact it cut into her buttocks.

Thwack! A stripe of pain exploded across her bottom. At

the same time the blow had the effect of making her jerk her hips forward, further impaling Laurie's sex. Laurie gasped.

Thwack! Another stripe of searing pain. Another reflexive forward thrust. Another gasp of pleasure.

But pain was not all that Andrea was feeling. Each cut of the whip not only sent the dildo slithering deeper into Laurie's buttery vagina, but pushed Andrea's clitoris against the leather strap. As usual, the pain from the whip routed itself down to her sex, mixing and amplifying the extraordinary pleasure the vibrations were creating.

Thwack! Thwack! Two blows in quick succession, one landing directly on top of the other, causing a huge wave of pain that made Andrea whimper into the gag. But by the time the next blow fell the discomfort had become indistinguishable from the throbbing pleasure that invaded her. She looked down at Laurie. The brunette was balancing on one hand and using the other to manipulate her clitoris while she wriggled back on the dildo, the flesh of her buttocks quivering. She tossed her head back and cried out as her sex clenched around the dildo and she came, her whole body rigid and glistening with a sheen of perspiration.

Julia threw the whip aside. She wrapped her arms around Andrea and rubbed her nylon-covered belly against her abused buttocks. At the same time the girl pulled on Andrea's nipples and feverishly kissed Andrea's shoulders. Andrea was fighting the myriad of provocations that assailed her; the vibrations in her sex, the sight of Laurie coming as if she had fucked her, the blows of the whip, each producing that peculiar mixture of pain and pleasure. But it was the touch of Julia's lips, the softness and tenderness of them, that she found totally irresistible. Pulling against her bonds, she came, her body filled with delicious sensations. The vibrations from her sex seemed to have extended right down to the phallus strapped to her belly, and she had the odd feeling that her orgasm was focused at its tip, deep inside Laurie's hot wet cunt.

It was days before Andrea could sit down without discomfort. Charles Darrington Hawksworth had been away for at least a week, and Andrea was beginning to wonder if he was ever coming back. He probably had other houses all over the world, and each was probably stocked with willing women dying, just as she was, for his attention. Perhaps some new slave had taken his eye and Andrea's star had waned. He had told her she was special and, what's more, he had shown she was by using her so intimately – but that didn't mean she couldn't be replaced in his affections by another.

Since the lesbian seduction in Laurie's room, Andrea had hardly seen her either. She had been given light household duties, which she shared with Julia and the other two girls who appeared to be in residence, but Laurie had barely said a word to her.

In her better moods she hoped the neglect was deliberate, part of her training and therefore something that Hawksworth had ordered. As long as Hawksworth was behind it, as long as this was all part of his plan for her, it was easier to bear. He had already taught her that being deprived of her master was a punishment, and therefore that being in his presence was a reward for good behaviour. She had behaved well with Edward Highfield and received her reward. She was sure that this absence was another lesson, a way of showing her that she was now totally and absolutely dependent on Charles Hawksworth. As he had once said, a slave is not complete without a master, and the emptiness she'd felt in the last week was a clear demonstration to her that she was a true slave, physically and mentally. If she had ever doubted that this was what she wanted, it had long gone. Even without Hawksworth, even in the middle of the night when she feared he had forgotten her, she knew that she had no regrets.

The sex she'd experienced at the manor had far exceeded her wildest dreams. Though she was aware that other women had similar fantasies and yearned as much as she did for

127

complete domination, she imagined that most found it hard to turn their desires into reality. She'd had no idea that there were places where this had become institutionalised. Hawksworth had created a whole world where such needs had become the norm. Andrea remembered the couple on her first night talking about The System, which implied that Hawksworth was not the only man who operated a similar establishment. They had made it sound like a sort of club, though no doubt the membership was confined to those wealthy enough to afford the large house and the necessary accoutrements to keep their operations strictly private.

After yet another morning when the woman in the black dress had taken Andrea to the bathroom and then given her breakfast, she had expected to spend the day working much like all the others. But when she returned to her cell, Laurie was waiting for her.

'Good morning, Andrea,' she said. The brunette was smartly dressed in a tailored red suit.

'Good morning, Ms Angelis.'

'Make her up would you, Betty?' she said to the woman in the black dress. 'And put her hair up. She's required, and she's to wear these clothes.' On the cot lay a white designer suit, a cream silk blouse and a set of white silk lingerie. 'I'll be back in thirty minutes.'

Andrea felt her heart begin to pound. Was it possible that the master had returned?

Betty collected her large make-up bag and proceeded to attend to Andrea's face and do her hair. Though this had occurred several times, Andrea had not got used to the experience. It was a symbol of how much she had given up to her master, and as such it never failed to excite her.

The woman pinned Andrea's hair on top of her head, leaving her shapely neck bare, then left without a word. Andrea examined the clothes – a white bra with lacy three-quarter cups, a thin suspender belt, a teddy with a delicate lace bodice, and sheer silk stockings.

Quickly Andrea clipped the bra on, settling her breasts into the cups. It pushed them up and together into an attractive cleavage. She wrapped the suspender belt around her waist and then sat on the bed to pull on the sleek stockings, adjusting the suspenders to hold them tight. Getting to her feet again, she pulled the teddy over her shoulders. The gusset was undone and she leant forward to fasten the three poppers that held it in place. This, she realised, was the first time she had worn any sort of panties since she'd arrived at the manor. Her labia were moist with anticipation already.

The blouse was cut low at the front, allowing a good view of Andrea's spectacular cleavage. The A-line skirt of the suit was just long enough to hide the stocking tops. It clung to her buttocks and thighs. Andrea pulled on the jacket – a perfect fit.

The door opened and Laurie entered, carrying a pair of white high heels. 'Put them on,' she said, placing them on the floor. 'And these.' She dropped a pair of white leather gloves on the cot.

Andrea obeyed, and then followed the lovely woman out of the cell as ordered.

Once in the house, instead of going into one of the rooms as usual, Laurie led the way to the front door and out to where the big black Mercedes was parked on the gravel drive, the chauffeur standing by the open passenger door.

'Get in,' Laurie said.

Andrea settled herself on the back seat. She wasn't sure whether she should be excited or disappointed. She tried to work out the implications of this development. Was she being taken to see Hawksworth? Or had he ordered something else for her? She would have loved to ask Laurie, but knew she must not.

Laurie sat beside her. The morning was sunny and warm, but the interior of the luxury car was air-conditioned and comfortably cool. The car smelt strongly of leather. Andrea couldn't help remembering what had happened the last time she'd been inside it.

The driver slipped behind the wheel, and the car pulled off down the drive with a reassuringly expensive crunching of gravel.

Laurie took a small bottle of perfume from her handbag and dabbed the stopper behind Andrea's ears. She dipped it into the bottle again, then applied it to Andrea's cleavage. The scent was heady and rich.

Laurie put the bottle back into her bag and took out a pair of handcuffs. 'Arms behind your back,' she said easily.

Andrea twisted around awkwardly on the seat, presenting her back and her wrists to Laurie. The handcuffs were snapped in place.

'That's better,' she said, matter-of-factly. 'Now stay as you are.'

Andrea felt a thin strap being wound around the top of her elbows, cinching them together. When she was satisfied they were tightly bound, Laurie pushed her back onto the seat.

Sitting back was uncomfortable. With her arms pinned so tightly behind her, Andrea found that leaning her weight on them only increased the pressure and made it necessary to sit leaning forward a little, making it difficult to keep her balance every time the car took a corner.

In fact, as they turned sharply to take the main road, Andrea was thrown right across Laurie's lap.

Laurie appeared to find this funny. 'Since you insist,' she said. 'You'd better get on your knees.' She pushed Andrea to the richly carpeted floor of the car, then tugged up her tight red skirt. Raising one foot, she planted it over Andrea's shoulder, then lounged back in the seat and sprawled her legs apart. She was wearing sheer black tights and black panties, but the tights had an open crotch. With languid movements she peeled the gusset of the panties to one side. 'And make it good,' she said with menace.

Andrea wriggled forward, dipping her face between Laurie's silky warm thighs. The musky female scent drew her ever closer. As recently as two weeks ago the idea of doing this to another woman would have revolted her, but now she felt nothing but excitement. Laurie's hand wrapped around the back of her head and pulled her forward. Andrea kissed the other woman's sex as if it were a mouth, pressing her lips against it. She pushed her tongue between the brunette's velvety labia, searching until she could feel the tiny nut of her clit. She heard Laurie gasp as her tongue pressed the button of flesh against the pubic bone, then dragged it from side to side. She could taste Laurie's juices. They were sweet. If Andrea had had the use of her hands she would have eased her fingers into the other woman's sopping vagina and anus, just as she'd seen Laurie do to herself three days before. But now she had to be content with using her tongue. She pressed the tip against the lozenge-shaped protuberance, then circled it slowly. Laurie moaned huskily.

Andrea wondered if the driver was watching in his rear-view mirror, as he had the day he'd driven them to the manor.

Laurie slid forward, tilting her sex to meet Andrea's mouth. Andrea thrust her tongue into the sticky maw, trying to get in as deep as possible, then licked the outer rim, drinking the juice of the brunette's increasing excitement.

'Back on my clit,' Laurie breathed.

Andrea shifted her attentions to the top of the gaping slit as she felt Laurie lift her buttocks. Then Laurie's hand slipped beneath her raised thigh and Andrea saw brightly varnished fingers plunge inward, two at first, and then three, deep into her open sex. As Andrea concentrated on stroking Laurie's clit with a regular rhythm, the brunette adopted the same tempo to slide her fingers in and out of her cunt. A sticky squelching sound echoed in the confines of the car.

'Oh *yes*…' Laurie gasped, her toned thighs instinctively squeezing Andrea's head. She arched up off the seat and

131

mumbled a long, breathless groan. For a moment the two women were frozen together, locked in a rictus of passion.

As her orgasm faded, Laurie raised her foot and gave Andrea a contemptuous shove. With no arms to help her balance Andrea sprawled back on the floor of the car.

Laurie took a handkerchief from her handbag, wiped her sex with it, then leaned forward and dabbed Andrea's mouth and chin as though cleaning a child that had eaten too much chocolate.

'You can spend the rest of the trip on the floor,' she said dismissively, her skirt rustling expensively as she straightened it down over her thighs.

It was another twenty minutes before the big car slowed and Andrea heard the crunch of more gravel under the tyres.

Laurie helped Andrea back up onto the seat, quickly taking a lipstick from her bag and retouching Andrea's slightly smudged appearance. As she sat pouting and allowing the woman to make her presentable once again, Andrea could see they were driving up to an impressive Georgian country house. A big pink sign read: THE GRANGE RESTAURANT. The car drew to a smooth halt by the front entrance and a doorman in a smart black uniform appeared from nowhere to open the passenger door.

He clearly noticed that Andrea was tightly bound, but training and professionalism overcame all, and his poise was unfaltering.

'Give us a minute, would you?' Laurie said calmly.

'Certainly, madam.' The car door closed again with a sturdy thud.

Laurie unbuckled the strap around Andrea's elbows, then unlocked the handcuffs. Andrea whimpered as she brought her arms around to the front and blood flowed freely again.

Laurie nodded and the door opened again. The doorman held it for them and stared respectfully into the distance as the two women climbed out of the car.

Four stone steps led up to the glass-panelled entrance.

Another doorman touched the rim of his top hat and dipped his head very slightly as they went inside.

They were greeted by a frock-coated *maitre d'* standing by a lectern with a fat reservations book.

'Mr Hawksworth,' was all Laurie said to her.

Andrea's pulse rate leapt as she heard Hawksworth's name. She was being taken to him after all.

'This way, please.' The *maitre d'* led them across the large and elegant restaurant. The tables were covered with crisp pink tablecloths and laid with sparkling silver and crystal, and each had its own small vase of roses. On the plain cream walls, old-looking oils depicted scenes from country life and stern portraits of lords and ladies in all their finery. In the large fireplace, burning logs had been replaced by a huge bowl of dried flowers, no doubt due to the good spring weather.

As they walked Andrea caught sight of her reflection in a large gilt mirror. She hardly recognised herself. Betty had put mascara on her eyelashes and a much heavier eyeshadow than Andrea normally used. The colour tones on her face contained a pink tinge, rather than the subtle blues that she preferred.

Andrea spotted Hawksworth at a corner table, between two windows with a view out onto the carefully manicured garden and the parkland beyond. He stood as they approached.

'How nice to see you, my dear.' He took Andrea's hand and kissed the white leather glove. 'Thank you, Laurie, that will be all for now,' he said, and the brunette turned with her usual style and poise and left them.

'Please sit down, my dear,' he said to Andrea. 'What can I get you to drink?'

A waiter drew a chair out from the table and Andrea sat down. The *maitre d'* hovered. Andrea was so surprised by this treatment that she wasn't quite sure what to say.

'A glass of champagne, perhaps,' Hawksworth suggested.

'Yes, thank you, ma—' She was just about to say 'master' but stopped herself. Surely he wouldn't want her to use that form of address in a public place?

'Champagne for my guest, please, Ernesto.'

'Certainly, sir.' The *maitre d'* dipped his head curtly and was gone.

'You look radiant,' Hawksworth said.

'Thank you…' she glanced round; there was no one within earshot, '…master.'

'How discreet.' He smiled, as though enchanted by a cute child. 'But you can drop the formalities here.'

'Thank you.' Andrea blushed a little, feeling reprimanded for being so silly.

'In fact, I would prefer it if we spoke normally. Do you understand?'

'I think so.'

'Good.'

A waiter brought a glass of champagne on a silver tray and set it down before her.

'Laurie is a very beautiful woman, isn't she?' He raised his glass of what looked like malt whisky, and touched it against her own.

'Yes, she is,' Andrea agreed, unsure of where this line of conversation was leading.

'Tell me,' he continued smoothly, having taken a sip of his drink, 'what did she do with you?'

Andrea hesitated and lowered her eyes.

'It's all right, she had my permission to do whatever she thought fit. Laurie was a slave once. I told you that, didn't I? She thought that was what she wanted. She knew she was missing something sexually but she didn't know what it was. She thought being a slave would be the answer for her. Interestingly enough, it was quite the opposite of what she needed. Of course, she hadn't discovered she was more attracted to women than men at that point. When she did she was very… grateful. Now she can be quite uncompromising towards others, which is ideal in most circumstances.'

Another waiter arrived with two large menus bound in leather. He opened one and handed it to Andrea.

'What did she do to you?' the question came again, demanding an answer.

The waiter had moved away, but not far, and Andrea was sure he could still hear their conversation. She lowered her voice. 'She took me to her room and made me…' Her eyes flitted anxiously in the direction of the waiter.

'Go on,' Hawksworth encouraged. 'I'm interested in all the intimate details, Andrea. Were you naked?'

She thought it was the first time he'd used her name. It sounded wonderful on his lips.

'Yes. She has a bed with posts at the corners.'

'I know.'

'She tied me to it.'

'And then?' The tone of Hawksworth's voice remained level and controlled, but she noticed he had a hand in his lap under the table and his arm was moving, almost imperceptibly.

The waiter seemed to edge closer, his face turned away but his ear directed towards them. Andrea looked at the waiter, trying to indicate to Hawksworth that he was there. But her master took no notice. He sipped his drink and stared at her intently.

'She had a… a dildo. With a harness. Julia came in and strapped it on me.'

'Sounds interesting. I wish I'd been there. Go on… was Laurie naked too?' Clearly all the details were exciting Hawksworth. Andrea was encouraged to see his eyes were sparkling keenly.

'Yes. Well, she had on a suspender belt and stockings.'

'Mmmm… I bet she looked a picture. And then?'

'And then Laurie knelt on the bed.'

'Good… Good…'

135

'Julia got hold of the dildo and put it in Laurie's…'

'Pussy?' he prompted. The word sounded strange in his cultured tones.

'Yes, in her pussy. Then Julia began to whip me, while I fucked Laurie.'

Suddenly Hawksworth leant right back in his chair, staring up at the ceiling. His eyes glazed, as if he were playing the scene through in his mind. 'And you came?' he asked.

'Yes, master.' The 'master' had slipped out, but he appeared not to notice or be perturbed. She realised that might not be a wise confession; Laurie hadn't given her permission to come.

'Mmmm…' His eyes closed and his body stiffened.

After a moment he sat forward again. 'Let's order,' he said, raising his hand. The *maitre d'* appeared in seconds.

Hawksworth ordered smoked salmon and grilled Dover sole for them both, then summoned the wine waiter to bring them a bottle of Chablis.

He leant forward and put his hand on her knee, beneath the table. His touch made her melt.

'Open your legs,' he said, exactly as a waiter arrived to offer them bread. Andrea obeyed, declining the freshly baked rolls, and from his attitude she sensed the man knew what was happening beneath the table.

Hawksworth's fingers inched their way up her trembling thigh. The skirt was too tight to allow her to do more than spread her legs a few inches apart, but he managed to work his way right up to the top of her stocking.

'So deliciously smooth,' he said, the tips of his fingers caressing the top of her thigh.

A bevy of waiters appeared with the first course, placing the salmon down in front of them and serving buttered brown bread, but Hawksworth's hand remained where it was.

The waiters dispersed. The hand crept higher. Andrea could feel it against the silk gusset of the teddy. The material had folded itself into her labia. She knew the gusset was wet. After what Laurie had made her do in the car it was not surprising.

'Lovely,' Hawksworth said softly, his fingertips following the line of the material right up to her clit.

'Your wine, sir,' the *sommelier* said, pouring half an inch of the Chablis into a crystal glass. Hawksworth sipped it.

'Excellent,' he said.

The *sommelier*, too, was looking at Andrea. She wasn't sure whether his expression was one of disgust or excitement. He walked away.

Hawksworth hooked his finger under the gusset of the teddy and pulled it outward. Then his index finger pressed down between her labia and brushed against her clit. Andrea was so surprised she gasped involuntarily.

The couple at the next table turned to see what had caused this exclamation. Fortunately, from their angle, they could not see Hawksworth's hand.

'Oh master,' she whispered. He had never touched her so intimately before. After the last week, her need for him had built up to such a level that she thought she might come by this caress alone. She felt her whole body throbbing, her clitoris on fire.

Slowly he moved his finger from side to side. She whimpered, holding on to the edge of the table, her fingernails making impressions in the thick linen cloth. He was leaning forward with his other elbow on the table, his face only inches from hers now. He stared straight into her eyes, hungry for her reaction. She gazed back, her sex convulsing every time he moved his finger. She was near to coming, though she knew that was not allowed.

She tried to distract herself. She picked up her wine, but her hand was shaking so much she had to put the glass down again.

'I give you permission,' he said.

'Oh, master...'

His finger pressed her clitoris hard, trapping the throbbing

137

nerves. She looked straight into his eyes, feeding off the predatory excitement she saw there. This was humiliating, being made to come in the middle of a restaurant while people bustled around her, but it was incredibly exciting too. She couldn't keep her eyes open any longer and screwed them tight as the wave of her orgasm flowed through her body. She felt herself rocking back in the chair.

'Oh *God*,' she sighed, much too loudly.

Hawksworth withdrew his finger, then settled the gusset of the teddy back where it had been. This produced another wave of feeling as the wet silk rubbed against her clit. Andrea moaned again.

'Is everything all right, Mr Hawksworth?' The *maitre d'* had hurried over.

'Everything's fine, Ernesto. Could you bring me another napkin?'

'Certainly, sir.'

Hawksworth wiped his hand on the pink napkin in his lap. A waiter took it and replaced it with a freshly laundered one.

'Are you all right?' he asked Andrea solicitously.

'I'm not sure. My body's still floating.'

'Eat something,' he said, spearing a piece of salmon with his fork.

'Yes, I will.' But for the moment Andrea could do nothing. It had all been so sudden and totally unexpected.

'Charles, how delightful.' A short but elegant woman had walked over to their table. She was about forty with an attractive face, her cheekbones high and her nose straight. She had piercing green eyes, a small mouth with thin straight lips and short auburn hair. Her jersey dress was yellow and clinging, with a V-neck and a knee-length skirt.

Hawksworth got to his feet and kissed her hand. 'Georgina, how are you?' he greeted her.

'I'm as randy as hell if you really want the truth,' the woman said bluntly, but with a manner that couldn't offend.

Her eyes were devouring Andrea as she spoke.

The couple at the next table stopped eating their *hors-d'oeuvre* for a moment and glanced around to see who had made such a remark.

'Nothing changes then,' Hawksworth chuckled. 'And what about Miles?'

'Oh, you know Miles, he needs a lot of encouragement,' the woman said with a dismissive wave of her hand, her alert eyes never leaving Andrea. 'She's pretty,' she said.

'She's not yet fully trained.' He changed the subject. 'Why don't you come over to the manor some time? I'm sure we could arrange something to suit Miles's tastes.'

'She would *definitely* suit his tastes,' the woman said suggestively, nodding towards Andrea, who sat quietly under the lurid scrutiny, her eyes respectfully downcast.

'As I say, she's not yet fully trained,' Hawksworth repeated.

The woman smiled theatrically. 'Oh, that doesn't matter, surely? We'd obey the rules. You know we would.' The woman pouted her heavily rouged lips and simpered, 'Charles, couldn't we just borrow her for a teensy-weensy while? We'd have her back to you before you know it.'

Andrea could hardly believe the way they were haggling over her... and in public! From first impressions she didn't like the woman, and she didn't want to go anywhere with her. But she knew she had little choice if her master agreed to it. She nibbled her lip anxiously and gripped the pink napkin tightly in her lap.

Hawksworth was pensive for a long while. Andrea held her breath, and then her heart sank as he said, 'Okay, but as long as you *do* obey the rules. I'll be extremely annoyed if I hear you haven't; and you know what I'm like when annoyed.'

The woman clapped her hands gleefully.

'And I want her back tonight,' Hawksworth finalised the brief details and sealed the deal. 'By ten o'clock at the latest.'

'I promise!' the woman enthused. 'Ten o'clock at the latest.

Come along, sweetie, you're coming with me for a ride.'

'She hasn't eaten yet,' Hawksworth said.

'Don't worry about such minor details,' the woman mocked, with a lewd grin.

Hawksworth glanced at Andrea. 'Obey her,' he said, as casually as if he were ordering another bottle of wine.

Chapter Seven

Georgina's fingers bit into Andrea's upper arm like talons, guiding her through the busy restaurant. The *maitre d'* stood aside as they reached the exit, his eyes watching Andrea's every step, his expression clearly puzzled.

Outside the main entrance, a pack of uniformed drivers stood by six or seven large limousines parked at the front of the car park. Georgina gestured to one of them, who immediately marched to a claret-coloured Rolls Royce. Moments later, the big car drew to a stately halt in front of the stone steps and the chauffeur got out and opened the passenger door for the two females with military-like precision.

'Sorry, madam,' he said. 'I thought you were staying for lunch.'

'A change of plan, Dobson,' Georgina replied, pushing Andrea into the car.

Andrea's emotions were reeling. After a moment of real intimacy with her master, when he had touched her physically and emotionally in a way he had never done before, he had apparently abandoned her without the slightest qualm. She'd looked back at him as she'd been hurried out of the restaurant. He'd been busy eating his lunch, apparently not giving the matter a second thought.

Andrea knew she mustn't dwell on this. She was his slave after all. For all she knew, this was another carefully rehearsed test and Georgina's arrival was not as coincidental as it appeared. Whether that was the case or not, Andrea was determined not to fail him. She'd been ordered to obey and that's what she would do, no matter how hard it seemed. She wanted this Georgina woman to report tonight that she had done everything she'd been asked to do, no matter what it was.

The interior of the Rolls, like the interior of the Mercedes, smelt strongly of leather. The long back seat was deeply padded, the floor covered with a thick wool carpet. Unlike the Mercedes, however, the windows were clear glass. Nor was there a divider between the driver and the passengers.

As the car drove off, Georgina turned towards Andrea.

'And how long have you been with Charles, sweetie?'

Andrea thought for a moment. It was difficult to keep track of time. It felt like she had been at the manor for a lifetime. 'Two or three weeks, I suppose.'

'You address me as mistress,' she snapped, her eyes cold and hard.

'Yes, mistress... I'm sorry.'

'Take your jacket off, let's see what we've got,' Georgina order without warning. And kneel on the floor, here.'

Andrea knelt on the soft carpet of the Rolls and slipped off her jacket.

Georgina leant forward and examined her breasts closely. 'Now the blouse,' she said.

Andrea pulled the blouse out from her skirt and took it off.

'What's that, a slip or a teddy?'

'A teddy, mistress.'

'Push it off your shoulders and remove your bra. I want to see your lovely breasts.'

Andrea extracted her arms from the satin shoulder straps of the teddy and pulled it down to her waist. Reaching behind her back, she unclipped the bra. She was glad they were travelling through the countryside and there was no one to look into the car as she bared her bosom.

'Mmmm, very impressive,' Georgina said, lifting her left breast by the nipple and pulling it this way and that. 'Turn a little, so Dobson can see.'

Again Andrea obeyed. She saw the chauffeur's eyes

142

examining her in the rear-view mirror. He was young, with large blue eyes and a square solid face. It looked as though his nose had been broken and badly re-set; it had a distinct ridge about halfway down.

'What do you think?' Georgina asked of him.

'Nice,' was all he said.

'Dobson's not really into big tits.' Georgina pulled Andrea closer. 'But my husband most definitely is.' Georgina moistened her rouged lips with the tip of a fat tongue and pinched her long fingernails into Andrea's right nipple. 'Are they sensitive?'

'Yes, mistress,' Andrea gasped, wanting desperately to squirm away from the cruel molesting, but not daring to. When the woman released her, Andrea saw the nails had left livid crescent shapes in her poor flesh.

'Good, I like my girls to be sensitive. Now take your skirt off.'

Andrea unzipped the tight garment, then sat up on her haunches to pull it down to her thighs. If she'd been uncertain of her feelings when she got into the car, she felt no such dilemma now. As long as she was debased and made to feel totally subservient, it seemed her body responded with unadulterated excitement.

She wondered if that was why the master had agreed to let her go – to teach her a lesson. No matter who was in charge of her, the feelings and emotions her submission generated were the same. What she felt for Hawksworth, the effect he'd had on her from the moment she'd first seen him, had allowed her to be honest about her sexual needs. He had recognised something in her and had the means to satisfy it. But now she was beginning to realise that her needs were not specific to him. She had taken an instant dislike to Georgina, but even that did not change the way she responded to her commands.

Andrea rocked back onto her bottom and wriggled the skirt further down her legs.

'And the teddy,' Georgina said.

The white silk teddy was banded around her waist. Andrea pulled it off, leaving her naked but for the gloves, white suspender belt, stockings and high heels.

'Hold your hands out in front of you,' the instructions continued, 'thumbs up. You can keep the gloves on.'

From her bright yellow handbag, Georgina extracted a pair of what looked like miniature metal handcuffs. She opened the metal loops and snapped them over Andrea's leather-covered thumbs, effectively binding her hands together.

The car turned off the main road and headed down a country lane into a small village. It slowed to a halt at a roundabout by the village green, just as two cars swung by from the left. Andrea found herself staring straight into the eyes of a young cyclist who had pulled up alongside. He was young and fresh-faced, and blushed nearly as deeply as Andrea as he drank in her voluptuous and exposed body.

The Rolls pulled away. A few minutes later it slowed again and pulled into the tarmac driveway of an impressive Georgian house, a beech hedge surrounding the whole property. The driveway was short and the big car rolled up to the front door.

'Take her around to the back, Dobson,' Georgina instructed. 'I'll go and tell Miles about our lovely little plaything.'

'Yes, madam,' Dobson said.

Georgina got out of the car, which immediately pulled away. It followed the drive around to the back of the house and stopped by a garage block.

The chauffeur got out and opened the passenger door.

'Out,' he said brusquely.

Andrea did as she was told, and Dobson took her by the arm and led her inside the open door of the garage. They walked past a red Ferrari to a door at the back, which Dobson unlocked with a key.

144

'In here,' he said.

The narrow room beyond was clean but bare, with white walls and a stripped wooden floor. There were no windows and it was lit by a single bulb hanging from the ceiling. A wooden frame about the size of a double bed was positioned in the centre of the floor. A large pine chest of drawers was the only item of furniture.

Dobson closed the door. 'Are you really into all this?' he asked.

'Yes,' Andrea said simply, because it was true.

'You must be bleedin' mad,' he said, a Cockney accent suddenly evident. 'Well, come here then.' He walked over to the far side of the room where a single metal ring was set in the wall at a height of about seven feet. He pulled Andrea's hands above her head and tied them to a rope hanging from the ring. She was stretched almost on tiptoe, her naked breasts pressing against the cool plaster of the wall.

'Nice arse,' Dobson said thoughtfully. He caressed her buttocks roughly. He was still wearing his driving gloves. 'Have fun.'

He started to move back to the door just as Georgina entered. 'Surely you're not leaving us, Dobson?' she cooed.

'With respect, madam, you know I'm not into all this stuff.'

'Such a straight fellow, aren't you? It's a pity.' Georgina gripped his upper arm tightly, blowing an elaborate kiss into his face.

The chauffeur smiled patiently. 'Each to his own,' he said, and then left, closing the door behind him.

Georgina drifted to where Andrea was trussed against the wall. Her hands traced her buttocks, then her fingers ran down the crevice between them. They probed Andrea's vagina.

'Juicy,' she said. Which was true. What had happened in the car had seen to that. Andrea's nipples were so erect.

Georgina opened the bottom drawer of the chest of drawers. Straining to peer over her shoulder, Andrea saw the woman taking out a long leather tawse, its tongue split into three. Georgina slapped it against her own palm.

'Unfortunately we can't afford slaves of our own,' she said conversationally. 'Much too expensive for poor little us. But dear Charles can sometimes be very generous.'

The door opened. A gaunt man in a white cotton robe walked into the room. He had tousled brown hair and a long face with a lantern jaw.

'She's a pretty one,' he said, his protuberant eyes staring at Andrea's naked body. 'How long do we have her for?'

'Miles, darling...' Georgina welcomed him flightily, 'I'm afraid Charles wants her back tonight. He was very insistent.'

Andrea realised that was true. She hadn't thought of that. Did it mean Hawksworth had something in mind for her?

'Nice tight arse,' Miles said, rubbing his prominent jaw.

'I was just going to warm it up a bit.'

'Good idea. Give me one of those. We'll take it in turns.'

Georgina took another tawse from the drawer and handed it to her husband.

'Shall we tie her legs?' he asked.

'No, let's watch her wriggle. It all adds to the fun.'

Georgina put her tawse down on the top of the chest of drawers, then pulled the jersey dress over her head. She was wearing beige-coloured French knickers, inset with lace, and a pair of flesh-coloured ultra-sheer hold-up stockings, but no bra. Her breasts were the size of inverted saucers with bulbous dark brown nipples. Her body was evenly tanned. She picked the tawse up again and advanced towards her prey.

'She hasn't been fully trained,' she told her husband.

'Really? Does she know how to respond properly?' He raised the tawse and slashed it down across Andrea's left buttock, as if to test his own question.

'Thank you, sir,' she gasped, hoping that was the response he expected. The pain from the tawse was quite different from the whip; less intense but covering a broader area.

'Apparently she does,' Georgina drooled. She slashed her tawse down across Andrea's right buttock.

Andrea flinched and tugged on the rope that bound her wrists. 'Thank you, mistress,' she whispered.

The man raised his tawse again and cut it down powerfully. Andrea instinctively tried to squirm out of the way but, as she moved to the right, Georgina caught her full across the bottom with another vicious stroke.

'Keep still!' Georgina ordered.

The blows fell thick and fast, one after the other, the flesh of Andrea's buttocks trembling, the skin soon a livid red. Despite Georgina's injunction, Andrea found it impossible not to squirm against the wall, her breasts rubbing against the plaster and her poor bottom on fire.

She lost count of the number of strokes they gave her, but she was sure there wasn't a single part of her bottom they had not thrashed. Several strokes fell on her upper thighs too, the tip of the tawse coiling inward to lash the delicate flesh of her labia. But any pain she felt had long turned to breathless excitement.

'That's enough,' Miles suddenly announced.

'Nice and red.' Georgina caressed the blotchy flesh. Her hand felt deliciously cool and Andrea moaned loudly as it soothed her blazing arse.

'Turn her round,' Miles said, his voice still expressionless.

Georgina gripped Andrea's hips and manoeuvred her until she faced her two tormentors.

Miles stripped off his robe. His body was unattractively thin and hairless, but a large cock sprouted from his loins. He raised the tawse again and smacked it against each of Andrea's breasts in turn, watching them as they quivered under the impact. 'Nice tits,' he murmured.

'I thought you'd like them,' purred his wife, clearly pleased with herself for acquiring such a tasty morsel.

'Spread your legs apart, girl,' he ordered, without acknowledging his wife's smugness.

147

Andrea tried to obey but her wrists were tied above her head and she was almost at full stretch. Parting her legs put more pressure on her already tortured arms.

Miles ran his hand up her thigh until his fingers were touching her labia. 'It's running down her legs,' he sneered crudely. Andrea decided she liked him even less than she liked his phoney wife.

'They're all like that, darling.' The woman was prattling on. 'This is what turns them on, you know that. Especially Hawksworth's girls. He seems to find the ones that need it the most.'

Miles's bony fingers nudged against Andrea's clitoris, and she couldn't suppress a moan.

'Her clit's swollen too.'

'Come on darling, I'm so randy…' Georgina whined like a spoilt teenager, pushing herself into her husband's arms and kissing him wetly.

Miles broke away from the slobbering embrace. He took a small key from the chest of drawers and reached up to insert it into the thumb cuffs, his erection prodding obscenely into Andrea's diaphragm, and then he untied the rope around her wrists.

As Andrea gratefully lowered her hands she felt a wave of pain, the cramped muscles in her shoulders and arms registering a sharp protest.

'Bring her over here,' Georgina said, indicating the wooden frame.

'If she's not been fully trained she might not have been with a woman before,' Miles pointed out.

'Have you?' Georgina asked her, as though it was the most normal thing to ask.

'Yes, mistress.' Andrea blushed. 'I have.'

'Kiss me then,' Georgina ordered. She hooked a hand around Andrea's neck and engulfed her with her full lips, her tongue thrusting into Andrea's mouth, exploring it aggressively. Despite her revulsion towards this couple,

Andrea felt a surge of lust knot her stomach. She didn't think she would ever get over the shock of kissing another woman. But it was a shock that aroused her. It felt so different from a man; the lips more pliant and knowledgeable and, of course, the butter-soft breasts and belly and thighs moulding against her own. As Georgina pushed her thigh between Andrea's legs she could feel the juices from her sex leaking over the other woman. For a moment Andrea was completely transported, lost in a world of sensuous pleasure, her eyes closed and her body throbbing with delights.

'Come on, I'm randy too,' Miles interrupted irritably.

Georgina pulled away, jolting Andrea back to reality. 'Lie down on the frame,' the woman instructed, 'right in the middle.'

Andrea did as she was told. The surface was made from wooden slats that were uncomfortable against her back.

Georgina took hold of her left wrist and pulled it back above her head. The cramped muscles and nerves responded with a new stab of pain. Georgina buckled Andrea's wrist to a leather cuff attached to the top corner of the frame. Then she secured Andrea's right wrist to the opposite corner.

'Now for your legs,' she said. 'Stretch them apart.'

She strapped Andrea's ankles into cuffs at the foot of the frame until Andrea's body was stretched out taut. Though it was impossible for Andrea to do anything other than wriggle her torso helplessly, Georgina took four strands of rope and, looping them beneath the wooden slats, tied them to Andrea's arms, just above the elbow, and to her legs, just above the knee.

As Georgina stood back to admire her handiwork with her husband, Andrea felt the familiar effects of such complete bondage. The more her body was constricted, the more her sex seemed to palpitate. She could feel her clitoris pulsing and was sure her labia were throbbing visibly. Of course, tied like this, with her sex open and completely exposed to the gaze of the lecherous man and woman, the effect was even stronger. They were both staring at her, their eyes focused between her legs, and that provoked Andrea quite as much as if they had been touching her. She longed to run her finger over her clit and hold her labia firmly against her palm, but the fact that she couldn't only increased her arousal. She could actually feel a little trail of juices running out of her vagina and down over her anus. She struggled for a moment, not trying to escape, but to feel exactly how powerless she was.

Georgina turned to her husband. Though he was fully erect, his foreskin still partially covered his glans. She pulled it back sharply, then took his cock in her fist and squeezed it.

'Are you ready?' she asked unnecessarily.

He nodded, taking hold of the waistband of her French knickers and pulling them down to her thighs. She shook her legs until the flimsy knickers fell to the floor, then stepped out of them.

Georgina knelt on the frame at Andrea's side. She swung one thigh over Andrea's body so she was straddling it, and moved back until her sex was poised above Andrea's face. Andrea gazed up at her, the flesh above the stocking tops soft, with deep hollows just under her sex. The cunt itself was covered with auburn hair. Over her labia it was matted with juice, and Andrea could see the scarlet flesh of her pouting vagina.

Miles knelt on the frame as well, between Andrea's outstretched arms. He shuffled forward on his knees until his cock was waving above Andrea's face, his glans no more than an inch from his wife's sex. A tear of fluid was running down his gnarled shaft.

'Lick it,' Georgina instructed.

For a moment Andrea hesitated, then Miles lowered his throbbing cock onto her face, pressing his glans against her lips. Andrea shuddered with excitement, licking the rock-hard flesh as if it were an ice cream cone. She managed to get the bulbous head into her mouth, wrapping her lips around it and sucking it in. Again the bondage aroused her. The fact that she could hardly move any other part of her body seemed to concentrate her senses on her mouth. She sucked him avidly, trying to raise her head off the frame to get him deeper.

Miles pulled away, his cock covered with Andrea's saliva. Almost immediately, Georgina thrust herself down and her hairy sex planted itself firmly on Andrea's mouth.

'My turn,' she said huskily.

Andrea kissed her sex greedily, crushing her lips against her labia. The cunt lips were thick and very wet. She tried to plunge her tongue into Georgina's satiny vagina, but could not get it very far.

'My arse,' Georgina said, her voice strained with passion. 'Do my arse.'

Andrea pulled back slightly, her tongue working its way to Georgina's puckered anus. She had never done this to either a man or a woman, but was much too aroused to give it a second thought. She pushed her tongue forward and felt the little circle of muscle resist. She persisted, flicking her tongue from side to side, and suddenly the muscles relaxed and her tongue was enveloped in a tight tube of flesh.

Georgina moaned and shuddered.

Andrea's own anus seemed to be reacting too, clenching convulsively as she explored Georgina's rear. Her legs were stretched so far apart that her clitoris appeared to be stretched too, like the string of a harp, its reverberations playing throughout her excited body.

'Now,' Miles said.

Georgina raised herself out of reach of Andrea's probing tongue, then backed her splayed cunt towards her husband's bursting cock. Three inches above her face, Andrea saw Miles's big penis slipping into Georgina's vagina. She watched with total fascination as the labia stretched around the broad shaft and the whole phallus was buried deep inside Georgina. She saw the woman wriggle her hips from side to side, savouring the complete penetration of her cunt.

'Take his balls in your mouth,' Georgina ordered.

Miles's scrotum was bobbing just above her chin. Ignoring the searing cramp it created in her shoulder muscles, Andrea raised her head and opened her mouth. She took his balls between her lips and heard Miles moan loudly.

He made no attempt to drive his cock in and out of his wife. Instead, he ground the base of his shaft against her labia ever so subtly, hardly appearing to move at all, while Andrea sucked on his balls.

'Yes, like that,' he said, as she jiggled them in her mouth.

The intimate sight of the couple's coupling had provoked new waves of excitement in Andrea's body. She could feel pulses of sensation right at the neck of her womb and knew she had produced another wave of juices, the sap flowing from her cunt and inundating the wooden plank beneath her arse.

But these feelings were overtaken as Georgina suddenly lowered her head between Andrea's thighs and pressed her lips to the girl's wide-open labia. Georgina's tongue darted out, first exploring the tender lips of her cunt, then moving up to her clitoris, exposed and vulnerable and already pulsing wildly.

Andrea's feelings and sensations coalesced. It felt as if Georgina's tongue had somehow worked its way inside her clitoris, its writhing tempo producing such soaring pleasure. There seemed to be a direct connection between her hot wet sex and her mouth, wrapped around Miles's balls. Like an arc of electricity, sensations leapt from one to the other, bringing her closer and closer to an inevitable orgasm. She didn't know whether the master's prohibition against coming still applied but, even if it did, there was simply nothing she could do to stop herself – especially as she knew Georgina was coming too, her sex clenching rhythmically around her husband's cock. The woman was gasping, trying to maintain contact with Andrea's clit, her breathing hot and heavy.

'Oh my God!' she screamed, the words muffled against Andrea's sex, the movement of her lips creating a plethora of new delights.

Andrea watched Georgina's labia throb and the muscles of her thighs spasm as she climaxed. Then it was Andrea's turn, this last provocation irresistible. Every part of her body seemed to shudder with excitement, from the bonds that held her to the frame, from her sex melting beneath Georgina's kiss, to the images in her mind as she pictured herself being so obscenely used. Exactly as her orgasm exploded, Miles pulled his cock out of his wife's vagina and came too, the hot liquid of his semen spattering over Andrea's face. He thrust his phallus down into her mouth and she felt more spunk jetting out of him, over her lips and tongue and down her throat, giving her orgasm another dimension. It was almost as though she had come again.

It was a long time before they moved. Georgina used her French knickers to wipe her husband's thick deposits from Andrea's face.

'You're really into this, aren't you?' she said quietly.

'Yes, mistress,' Andrea replied. It was true. Somewhere in the back of her mind she knew this was a turning point for her. Even alone with Laurie her submission had had a direct connection to her master, she'd been in his house with his overseer, obeying his instructions. But these people were complete strangers to her with little or no apparent connection to her master. She couldn't kid herself that it had been his hypnotic presence that created her soaring responses to what they had done to her. In the beginning Hawksworth had told her that no slave is complete without a master. But it appeared it did not matter who that master was.

'Take her back to the manor,' Georgina instructed her chauffeur. 'You know where it is, don't you?'

'Yes, madam.'

Andrea had been led into the house, given some food, and allowed to use the bathroom. She dressed herself and tried to re-pin her hair in the style Betty had created that morning. She had no cosmetics, however, so she could not repair the damage to her make-up.

Georgina and Miles had waited for her by the front door, the Rolls waiting in the drive.

'She can't go back like that,' Miles said.

'Why not?' Georgina asked.

'Hawksworth wouldn't like it.' He walked back into the house. A few minutes later he came back with a thin white cord. 'Put your hands up in front of you,' he ordered.

Andrea obeyed. He looped the cord several times around her wrists, binding them together, then threaded it into the ring on the steel collar she'd worn around her neck since her first day as a slave. She had been tied in the same way on that first day too.

'That's better,' Miles said.

'You're right, it is,' Georgina agreed. 'Now get in the car.'

With her hands tied in front of her throat, Andrea climbed awkwardly onto the back seat.

'I hope we'll see you again, Andrea,' Georgina said. She took her husband's hand and Andrea watched them walk back into the house as the car pulled away.

Once they were away from the house and gliding through country lanes the driver looked at her in the rear-view mirror. 'Did you have a good time?' he asked.

'I'm not supposed to talk,' she said.

'Who's going to hear you? I'm not going to tell. Come on, what did they do to you?'

Andrea said nothing. The cord bit deeply into her flesh and she tried to ease it by wriggling her wrists into a more comfortable position, flattening her palms together.

'So it turns you on, does it, being submissive?'

Andrea remained silent, and tried to ignore him by

enjoying the passing fields and trees.

'Come on, we've got an hour's drive,' he encouraged. 'We might as well talk to each other.'

'I'm not supposed to,.' she insisted.

'Yeah, so you say. Come on, darling, I'm curious. Those two are always trying to get me involved in their games, but I'm not interested. I've always been real straight about sex. Do you like straight sex too?'

Andrea looked at him in the mirror. His eyes were staring at her. Her skirt had ridden up over her thighs to reveal the tops of her stockings but, with her hands tied to her collar, she couldn't do anything about it.

'You're really something, you know that?' he persisted. 'Look at those legs.'

He drove for another ten minutes without saying another word, but he kept glancing at her in the mirror, clearly savouring the view. She saw signs saying that the motorway was three miles away.

'Hey, I've got a good idea,' he said suddenly. He slowed the car.

A gap in the hedge to the left led to a small copse of trees at the corner of a ploughed field. He pulled into it. The sun was setting, but there was still enough light to see by.

'What are you doing?' she said sharply.

'I thought you weren't allowed to speak,' he sneered. He got out of the car and opened the rear door. 'Out,' he said bluntly.

'No. Take me back to the manor, please.'

'We're having a comfort break,' he said. He walked over to the large horse chestnut tree under which they were parked, opened his flies and started to pee.

'That's better,' he said, walking back to the car. His cock was still hanging out of his fly. 'Come on, the fresh air will do you good.'

'No, I'm not allowed to,' Andrea insisted.

He laughed, and said sarcastically, 'So you're allowed to

fuck those two sad bastards but you aren't allowed to get out of the car?'

'Please,' she said, 'can't we just—'

'Just do it!' he suddenly snapped. 'You get your kicks by being a slave, right? Well, I'm your master now.' He reached into the car and caught hold of her arm. 'Come on, don't mess me about.' He hauled her out into the slightly chilly evening air. 'Now let's see what makes you so special.' He pushed her to her knees on the dewy grass and took her head in his hands. His circumcised cock had already started to swell. He entwined his fists in her hair and pulled her towards it. 'Take it in your mouth,' he grunted. 'And that's an order!'

Andrea's emotions were mixed. Even though she hadn't cared for Georgina and Miles very much, what had happened with them had been undeniably exciting; so exciting that her body still tingled with arousal. Her orgasm had been exquisite, but it had left her with a deep-seated need for penetration. The thought of a pulsing cock thrusting into her was overwhelming. Dobson was an attractive man but she doubted he was supposed to be behaving in this way without the presence of his master and mistress and, therefore, co-operating with him would be wrong. If it came out that he'd stopped the car and taken advantage of her Hawksworth might believe that she'd encouraged him. On the other hand, it was extremely unlikely that anyone would ever find out. Hawksworth had demanded her return to his house by ten o'clock, and it was nowhere near that hour yet. No one would ever know what had happened. And she could tell herself she was not breaking her private oath of obedience to her master. Dobson was strong enough to force her to do whatever he had in mind, especially with her hands tied securely to the steel collar.

Of course it could all be a test; that this had all been organised with Georgina ahead of time. But she dismissed the thought. The meeting with Georgina had been spontaneous; there had been no time to set up such a charade.

Resignedly she opened her mouth and sucked in his spearing erection, feeling it engorge rapidly.

'That's better,' he sighed, throatily.

She ran her tongue over the ridge at the base of his glans, then sucked the whole shaft as hard as she could. It stiffened further, pushing to the back of her throat. Her own sex throbbed, clenching involuntarily, as she imagined how it would feel to have this large erection pounding into her. Bound as she was, the tips of her fingers were within reach of his balls, so she cradled and massaged them.

'Shall I untie you?' he panted.

'No, please,' she said with real alarm. If he untied her she would not be able to convince herself that none of this was her fault.

'Well, if that's what you want...' He pulled out of her mouth and raised her to her feet. He dragged her around to the back of the car and opened the boot. Andrea saw it contained a big box of tools and other equipment. Dobson opened the box and removed a nylon tow-rope, then dragged her to the horse chestnut. One of its lower branches had broken off and lay on the grass under the tree. Part of the twisted and gnarled limb was at about waist height.

Dobson tied the towrope to the cord that bound her wrists, then climbed over to the other side of the bough and pulled the rope down, so that Andrea was forced to bend forward from the waist. He stretched under the branch and looped the other end of the rope around her left ankle, making it impossible for her to straighten up again.

'Is that what you want?' he sneered.

'I... yes, master,' she intoned, the bondage creating its usual wave of excitement. She was bent so far over the branch she could only look backwards between her legs.

'Master,' he chuckled derisively. 'Is that what you call your men? I like it. Say it again.'

'Master,' she repeated.

Dobson stood behind her. He took hold of the hem of her skirt and wriggled it up over her hips. 'Well, look at that...' he breathed.

The gusset of the teddy had worked its way up between the cheeks of her bottom, concealing nothing. Her buttocks were red and tender from the whipping they'd received. They tingled in the cool air.

'Gave you a whipping, did they? Are you into that, too?'

'Y-yes, master,' she admitted quietly.

He ran his hands slowly down her tensed thighs, following the line of the tight white suspenders to the top of her stockings. 'Shall I tell you what I'm into?' he asked.

'Yes please, master.'

'I'm into fucking… simple as that.'

The coarse phrase excited Andrea. It was exactly what she wanted. She was not supposed to speak unless she was spoken to, but under such circumstances it was academic. 'Fuck me then, please master.'

'You've changed your tune,' he snorted. 'I could have fucked you in the car. Do you only get off if you're tied down?'

'Yes, master.'

He undid his belt and pulled his trousers and briefs down to his knees. He then reached for the gusset of the teddy and pulled it out of the cleft of her buttocks, and stared hungrily at her moist labia. 'Very smooth,' he said, a little emotion betrayed by his tone. 'Do they have you shaved?'

'No, master, that's how I am naturally.'

His fingers ran down into her sex. He found the opening of her vagina and slipped a straightened finger into it. 'Christ, you're wet.'

'Yes, master.'

He pushed another finger inside, while his other hand worked its way down from her neck to her breasts, kneading and squeezing her luxurious flesh. Finally he pulled his fingers out of her cunt and took hold of her hips, pushing his cock between her legs. Andrea gasped. He was hot and hard.

'Ask me again!' he panted.

'Fuck me, master, please…' she pleaded. She really meant it. The proximity of his cock to her cunt was making her whole body tremble in anticipation. Having been neglected all afternoon, her vagina was eager for penetration. Her back ached, her belly was pressed against the rough bark of the bough, and her neck and arms ached from being bound so tightly together, but these irritations only aroused her. The more the discomfort, the more her level of excitement rose.

'Again!' he insisted.

'Fuck me,' she begged again. 'For Christ's sake, fuck me!'

She felt his grip on her hips tighten. His cock was throbbing against her labia but, instead of directing it up into her vagina, he pushed forward so his glans parted her labia then butted against her clit. Andrea gasped as he made little prodding movements, his cock pressing against her sex again and again, each movement producing a wild pulse of sensation that coursed through her whole body.

'Please,' she begged. She knew he was teasing her, deliberately holding back the moment of penetration, and that excited her too. Even in this secret tryst she was still a slave, unable to assert her own needs.

Then he pulled his cock back and angled it up towards the mouth of her vagina. As it settled between her lips, the satiny flesh responded with a huge jolt of feeling. Andrea felt it clench, her labia desperately trying to draw him in. But he did not move. Instead she felt a hand snaking down over her bunched skirt to her mons. His fingers slid onto her clit, rubbing over the top of it. The sensation was electric. She shouted out loud.

'Please, please, please,' she begged.

'Please what?' he taunted.

'Please, master!'

Almost before she had finished the last word, Dobson

pulled back, and then rammed his cock into her. She was so wet the penetration was effortless, the long hard phallus filling her until she felt his glans at the neck of her womb and his pubic hair grazing the cheeks of her bottom. With both hands on her hips he began pounding into her, pulling her back against her bonds as he lunged forward.

The feeling took Andrea's breath away. Though she'd had countless orgasms in the last two weeks, it had been a long time since she'd been so comprehensively fucked. She had been penetrated with fingers and dildos front and back, been licked and sucked and wanked but, apart from the time the master had used her anus, she had not had a throbbing hot poker of flesh hammering into her like this. Dobson was hard – and big. His cock stretched the silky walls of her vagina, filling her completely.

There in the copse, with darkness falling, she knew there was nothing to stop her from savouring an explosive orgasm. Hawksworth would never find out. Of course, it would be an act of disobedience, but for once there would be no consequences; she would have only her conscience to deal with. Which was just as well because, even if she wanted to there was no resisting the feelings Dobson's cock was generating. Now she was coming for the third time that day, coming with renewed intensity, every nerve in her body screaming with pleasure.

Her cunt gripped the sword of flesh that stabbed into her and her clit pulsed. Deep inside her vagina her sex seemed to open, like the blossoming of a flower, allowing him in deeper. As he plunged into this new territory she came again, her eyes screwed shut, her whole world narrowed to the compass of her sex.

Dobson must have felt her orgasm erupting, but he did not pause for a second. If anything, he increased his tempo, hammering into her faster and deeper, each stroke pushing her into the rough bark of the tree. Andrea raised her head as far as her bonds would allow and opened her mouth to beg him to stop for a moment but, before she could get the words out, another orgasm seized her. In a split second, she was coming again, her body trembling from head to toe, her cunt convulsing violently and her mind wiped clean of everything but the uncontrollable ecstasy of fucking.

As her senses began to return, she became aware that his rhythm had slowed. Suddenly he pulled out of her altogether, producing a paroxysm in Andrea's cunt that made her whimper. Before she could protest, the bulb of his glans was nudging into the little crater of her anus. He pushed forward, not at all gently, and encountered no resistance. Andrea was so turned on her sphincter was already relaxed. She felt his glans piercing her rear, the flesh so wet with her juices it slid home effortlessly.

Then Andrea felt a wave of fierce pain. Unlike her master, Dobson did not hold back. He thrust forward again, his large cock penetrating deeper until it was completely buried inside her arse. The pain she felt was as intense as her former pleasure. She shuddered and heard herself scream, though the noise sounded as if it was coming from a long way away, as though it wasn't really her at all.

Dobson was in no mood for subtleties. He began ploughing her anus as hard as he had fucked her cunt. Each forward stroke produced a tremor of pain and, after the third or fourth, Andrea could bear it no longer. She closed her legs and tried to twist her hips to one side to pull away. But as his hands gripped her more tightly, forcing her buttocks back towards him, something inside her changed. A flood of acute pleasure washed over her, inundating her with sensations so strong they made every nerve in her body convulse. Inevitably, this huge reaction kicked in yet another orgasm, this one so sudden it took her completely by surprise. One moment she was writhing in agony, the next she was trembling in helpless ecstasy.

And that was not all. As she struggled to keep control she felt his cock jerk convulsively inside her. Dobson pulled her hips back towards him one last time and buried his cock up to the hilt in her arse. As he came hot semen erupted into the tight confines of her rear. She could feel each throbbing jet, and each one drove her higher and deeper into her orgasm. With her eyes shut tightly she pulled on the rope that bound her to the branch, and allowed the sensations to overwhelm her.

When she opened her eyes it was dark. There were no lights on the road that ran alongside the copse, and no houses nearby.

She felt Dobson's spent cock slip from her body. He knelt at her feet and untied the rope. As she straightened up and stretched her back she felt the strange sensation of a creamy liquid oozing between the cheeks of her bottom. It was a feeling that made her tremble, renewing in miniature everything she had felt before.

He untied the rope from her hands. 'We'd better be going,' he said, looking at his watch. The fluorescent dial shone out in the gloom. 'Are you all right?'

'Yes, master,' she said, managing a weak smile.

Chapter Eight

The white skirt was marked with moss from the tree and badly creased. The blouse and jacket showed signs of dirt too. Her left stocking was laddered and the white shoes muddy and stained with grass. The frantic activity as she'd been bent over the branch with her head down had dislodged most of the pins from her hair and it looked ragged and unkempt.

It was only as she climbed back into the car and caught a glimpse of herself in walnut framed mirrors that were set into the sides of the car above the back seat that she realised how unkempt she looked. What's more, there was nothing she could do about it. Even if Dobson released her hands she wouldn't be able to make any impression on the stains or change her stockings, and she doubted she would be able to do much with her hair without a brush and more hairpins.

She would have to hope that Hawksworth would blame Georgina. Perhaps he would think they had taken her out into the woods. But as they got closer to the manor she became apprehensive. What made it worse was that the master had told Georgina she was needed back at the house by ten. Maybe he had something special in mind for her. If she was taken straight to him, would he question her closely about what had happened and, if so, would she be able to lie? Lying was, after all, the ultimate disobedience.

She became increasingly gloomy and depressed. It was true that there had been nothing she could do to stop Dobson but she knew that, in the end, she had actively encouraged him. She felt guilty; a guilt compounded by the fact that the orgasms she'd enjoyed were still giving her little tremors of pleasure. Her bottom was still tingling from its rude violation.

Ironically, if she hadn't enjoyed it, if she hadn't orgasmed so profusely, she wouldn't feel she'd betrayed her master's trust.

Dobson did not say a word as they drove through the gates of the manor and up to the front door.

As soon as the car appeared, Laurie emerged wearing another of her skin-tight catsuits, this one of dark violet, the material woven with a glittering metallic thread. Her suede ankle boots were black and her long hair was brushed out over her shoulders. She strode to the passenger door and opened it as the car came to a halt.

'Out,' she said.

Andrea held her breath as she clambered awkwardly out of the back seat.

'Thank you,' Laurie said to Dobson.

'My pleasure, madam,' Dobson said, grinning broadly. He glanced at Andrea, who rapidly looked away. 'My pleasure,' he repeated. Laurie closed the door and the car pulled away.

Laurie examined Andrea critically, but she didn't comment on her disarray. She took Andrea's arm firmly. 'Come with me,' she said.

When it was obvious they were going straight to the stables, Andrea breathed a sigh of relief, though she also had to confess to feeling disappointed. Even at the risk of him asking her difficult questions, her desire to see Hawksworth again was overwhelming.

Inside her cell Laurie untied the cord that bound her wrists. 'Take off all your clothes,' she said.

Andrea obeyed, handing Laurie each item until she was naked. The gusset of the white silk teddy was still wet and had creased into a long thin strip. But, though Laurie must have noticed, she made no comment. After all, it could have been explained by what Georgina and Miles had done to her.

'Betty will take you for a shower,' was all she said. 'I'll be back in thirty minutes.'

Andrea's heart leapt. Maybe the master was waiting for her, after all.

Betty arrived moments later and took her to the bathroom. Andrea used the toilet then showered, avidly washing away all evidence of Dobson. Then she sat on a bathroom stool while Betty made her up again.

Andrea felt better now. The suit and the lingerie would be sent for cleaning. The evidence of her misbehaviour had been destroyed. Admittedly, her bum was still red and raw, but if Hawksworth asked her about that she wouldn't have to lie.

Back in her cell, Andrea found a scant collection of clothes lying on the bed: a waspie corset of black satin, boned to cinch tightly at the waist, with four long ruched satin suspenders; a pair of sheer black stockings; and black patent leather ankle boots with a narrow four-inch heel.

As she wrapped the corset around her waist, breathing deeply to enable her to fasten it, her excitement mounted. Everything that had happened that afternoon had distracted her from what the master had said and done over lunch. It had been a rare moment of intimacy between them. Twice now he'd been alone with her and each time she'd felt they had shared something very special. A unique bond existed between a master and his slave. It was not love or even friendship, but an emotion like no other. She hoped she would experience it again that night.

As she finished dressing, squeezing her feet into the boots, Laurie unlocked the door.

'Are you ready?'

'Yes, Ms Angelis,' Andrea confirmed.

'Hands behind your back.'

Andrea turned and pressed her hands together over her bottom. She felt the familiar weight of metal handcuffs being clipped into place. A tremor of excitement and trepidation ran through her body. Bondage had become a precursor of sexual pleasure.

Laurie clipped the chain leash into the metal collar and pulled her out of the room. To Andrea's surprise they did not head down the corridor to the house, but walked in the other direction. At the end of the block, by the bathroom, there was another door. Laurie opened it with a key.

The room beyond was large, with a high sloping ceiling. The floor was polished wood block and the walls were covered in dark blue velvet. Spotlights had been trained on a circular dais in the centre of the room.

Andrea was astonished to see three other girls on the dais, all wearing an identical outfit to her own. The only difference was the colour. Julia's corset was in white satin, while the other two girls, whose names Andrea did not know, wore bright red and navy blue. The stockings and ankle boots were of matching shades.

The girls were standing with their hands raised above their heads, their wrists secured in leather cuffs attached to a metal bar hanging from a chain that disappeared up into the ceiling. The shorter of the three had smallish breasts that reminded Andrea of Georgina's. Several thin red lines criss-crossed them, indicating they had been whipped recently.

The third girl was the redhead Andrea had seen previously. As tall as Andrea, her legs were just as slender and shapely.

'I don't think you've met Donna.' Laurie pointed to the shorter girl. 'And this is Cherry,' she indicated the redhead.

Then it took Laurie a few minutes to hitch Andrea to the metal bar so that she, too, stood with her arms secured above her head. Then, without a word, she left the room and locked the door behind her.

'Bitch!' Donna spat.

'Shut up,' said Julia.

'Are we going to just stand here and keep quiet then?'

'That's exactly what we're going to do.'

'Huh…' Donna huffed but did not say another word.

This was not what Andrea had expected at all. The bondage

brought back all the aches and pains she had experienced during the afternoon when she'd been tied to the wall in the room behind the garage.

As time dragged by the girls began to whimper. Andrea noticed that Julia had inched closer to Cherry and was moving her body against her, as though trying to comfort her. The girl responded in the same way, rubbing her calf against Julia's, the nylon stockings rasping together.

That stopped the moment they heard the key in the lock. The two girls moved apart as the door opened and Charles Hawksworth strode in. A tall rangy boy, probably no more than twenty years old, followed the master into the room. Both wore dinner suits and black bow ties, though the boy's jacket was white.

'Here we are,' said Hawksworth. 'Now you can see for yourself.'

The boy stopped dead in his tracks as he set eyes on the lovely collection of trussed girls. His eyes widened and his mouth dropped open as he stared at their semi-naked bodies.

'My God!' he drooled.

'Introduce yourselves, girls,' Hawksworth commanded.

'Good evening, sir,' Julia immediately simpered.

The other three followed suit.

The boy walked right up to the dais, still staring, his eyes level with their crotches.

'Who... who are they?' he asked incredulously. 'Where do you find them? Where do they come from?'

Hawksworth smiled. 'So many questions. However, none of that really matters. As I said to you over dinner, it may be hard for you to understand at your age, but there are women who have, shall we say, a penchant for being submissive. Some take years to discover it, others are more open. Of course, wanting and getting are two different things. Many women go through life desiring to be a slave and yet never finding a man who is prepared to give them what they crave. In that respect, these four are privileged.'

'How long have they been standing like that?'

'Half an hour… an hour perhaps.'

'Doesn't it hurt them?'

Hawksworth laughed. 'Of course it hurts them. That's the whole point, Martin. Pain, the sort of pain they are experiencing now, is entirely relative. It's a function of the mind. I'll get you a whip. Use it on them. See the effect it has.'

'A whip?!' The youngster's expression was a confused cocktail of disbelief and undiluted excitement.

'Yes, a whip,' Hawksworth said, as though it was the most natural thing in the world. He strode across the room. He pulled aside the velvet curtains to reveal a rack of whips like the one in the punishment room in the house. He selected a short riding-crop with a large leather loop at the end of the lash. 'Here,' he said, handing it to the youngster.

'Is this some kind of wind up?'

'Martin,' said Hawksworth, with a patient smile, 'I promised your father before he died that, when you were old enough, I'd see to this aspect of your education.'

'My father knew about this?'

'Yes. He was one of the founder members of The System. Now that you're twenty-one and have inherited his estate, you're entitled to join.'

'He had a collection of gorgeous females like this?' He looked like a child locked in a sweet shop.

Hawksworth nodded. 'Yes, indeed he did.'

A grin slowly lit up Martin's face. 'Well, well, I never knew father had it in him, the old bugger!'

'And your mother. There are also women who enjoy the other side of the coin. Like Laurie Angelis, for example.'

'Mother too? No! Really?' Martin was clearly having trouble taking all this in.

'Oh yes,' Hawksworth chuckled, 'you mother too.'

'So, what do I do?' Martin asked. It was plain that any unease he felt was rapidly disappearing. His bright blue eyes were sparkling with expectation.

'You were asking me about pain, remember? Use the whip and you'll see how easily they can convert pain into pleasure.'

'On their bums?'

'Wherever.'

'Christ!'

Andrea saw Martin swallow hard. He stepped forward and raised the whip, taking aim at Julia's full buttocks. 'Like this?'

'Yes, Martin,' urged Hawksworth. 'Just like that.'

The lad swept the whip down a little gingerly. *Thwack!* The noise of leather on flesh echoed throughout the room. Andrea watched Julia's eyes close. She knew exactly what she was experiencing.

'What do you say, Julia?' prompted Hawksworth.

'Thank you, sir, may I have another?'

'Again?' Martin asked.

Hawksworth nodded. 'If you wish.'

The whip lifted again. This time the blow was lower, the whip cutting across the top of Julia's thighs. She yelped and bucked in her bonds.

'That hurt her,' Martin said, reprovingly.

'Of course it hurt her,' agreed Hawksworth. 'But feel the effect it had. Go on, Julia, you know what to say.'

'Please, sir,' she whispered, choking back a little sob, 'please feel my cunt, sir.'

Martin looked like a man in a trance. He stepped up onto the dais and put his arm round Julia's waist. Andrea saw his hand slipping over her buttocks. 'Christ, she's so hot,' he said.

'Yes, she will be,' said Hawksworth.

The hand delved lower. Tentatively, it slotted into the cleft of her buttocks, then slid deeper. 'Christ,' he said, drawing his hand away as though it had been stung by a bee.

'You see?'

'I – I don't believe it,' gasped Martin. 'They're all like

that?'

'All of them,' Hawksworth confirmed with unerring confidence. 'What I suggest now is that you pick just one of them and take her back to the house. Spend some time alone with her. Allow yourself to get comfortable with the idea that she will do anything you want. Enjoy yourself. Then tomorrow, perhaps, you can indulge yourself with two of them together.'

'Two of them? Together? Bloody hell!'

'Of course.' Hawksworth smiled. 'I'm going up to bed now. Take your time, Martin. The girls will show you where everything is. They will obey. We'll talk again over breakfast. Good night.'

'Good night, uncle,' he replied dreamily, his eyes devouring the four available beauties before him. The door shut quietly and he was alone with them.

Martin stepped off the dais and began to circle it. 'What's your name again?' he said to Julia, his hand caressing the two weals he had raised on her buttocks.

'Julia, sir,' she said.

'Well, open your legs, Julia,' he instructed, his confidence growing visibly.

Julia moved her legs apart and Andrea saw the boy stoop slightly to look at her sex. She was sure it would be glistening with her juices.

'And you?' he said to the petit girl.

'Donna, sir.'

'Open your legs too, Donna. In fact, all of you open your legs.'

They all obeyed. He continued circling the dais. He extended his hand and stroked Cherry's leg, running it over one of the suspenders that held her stockings taut. 'Nice legs,' he said.

The door opened and Laurie entered. 'Mr Hawksworth asked me to see if you needed any help, Mr Phillips,' she said politely. 'Have you made your choice for tonight?'

'Not yet.' He looked at Laurie, who was still wearing the tight catsuit. 'This all came as quite a surprise.'

'I can imagine.'

'So, how long have you worked for my uncle?'

'Five years.'

'And how long has this been going on?'

'A lot longer than that.'

He turned back to the four girls. 'They're all so lovely…' he said pensively, rubbing his chin. 'I'll choose her,' he suddenly blurted, making his mind up and pointing to Andrea.

Laurie made no comment. She climbed onto the dais and unhooked Andrea's cuffs from the metal bar.

Gingerly, Andrea lowered her arms. She gasped as her muscles and sinews reacted to their new freedom.

'And where shall I take her, Mr Phillips?' Laurie asked, her apparent humility almost bordering on disrespectful.

'My bedroom, I suppose.'

'Certainly.'

Laurie took the metal leash that hung between Andrea's breasts and led her to the door.

'I'm going to get a drink first,' Martin said. 'I think I need one.'

Laurie led Andrea to Martin's room at the back of the house, overlooking the stable block. It was luxurious, with a dark green carpet and trellis-work-patterned wallpaper. A walnut wardrobe and an armchair upholstered in matching trellis-work stood by the foot of the bed. The counterpane of the large bed had been turned down to reveal white linen sheets.

Laurie unclipped the chain from Andrea's collar.

'Tell him we've provided some equipment for his use,' she said, pointing to a chest by the door. 'All the usual toys. And if he wants to take you to the punishment room you know the way, don't you?'

'Yes, Ms Angelis.'

171

Laurie took a single strap from the chest and undid one of the handcuffs. 'Hands behind your back,' she ordered.

Andrea obeyed. She felt the cuff being re-buckled behind her, then Laurie wrapped the strap around her arms just above her elbows and drew it tight, pulling her shoulders back and thrusting her breasts forward.

'Don't let us down, Andrea. This is very important to Mr Hawksworth.'

'I'll do my best,' Andrea whispered sincerely.

Laurie left, closing but not locking the bedroom door behind her. The house was silent. Andrea listened. She was sure this room backed onto the master's bedroom. She yearned to be with him, but she supposed this was the next best thing. If she could impress Martin, he was bound to mention it to his uncle and that would be a point in her favour. Then, perhaps tomorrow night, he would reward her by spending some time alone with her.

Her shoulders and arms began to ache. It was a familiar sensation. In all her fantasies about submission she had never been able to imagine what the pain would be like. Tying herself to her bed had only been a pale imitation of the real thing. The pain was a hundred times worse and, by the same token, a hundred times better.

Ten minutes later the bedroom door opened and Martin came in, carrying a large brandy balloon.

'It's Andrea, right?' he said.

'Yes, sir.' She wasn't sure whether she should call him master, but since Julia had called him sir, she thought she'd better do the same.

'You can sit down,' he went on. 'Sit on the edge of the bed. I'm going to take a shower.'

Martin's excitement seemed to have evaporated. Now he looked dazed and very young, his unblemished complexion creased with worry. He stepped into the bathroom, but did not close the door. Andrea heard him peeing, then the noise of the shower.

It was a long time before he came back into the room. He was wearing a short white towelling robe, and his black hair was wet.

He moved over and sat on the bed beside her. 'Look, this is really quite a shock. I'm not sure I want to do anything.' He was staring at her jutting breasts. 'Doesn't it hurt you to be tied like that?'

'Yes, sir,' she said, 'it does.'

'Please drop the sir. I don't like it. I could untie you, if you like.' But he didn't. Instead he continued to stare at her, his eyes roaming over her body, examining the sheer black stockings and the way the waspie bit into her waist. 'Unbelievable,' he said to himself. 'Quite unbelievable.'

Very tentatively, he extended his hand and touched the top of her breast. 'You've got really great tits,' he said.

'Thank you.' Andrea felt sorry for the boy. He'd been plunged into the deep end. He clearly had no inkling of the world his uncle had created and, from his obvious shock and surprise, she doubted he had ever shown the slightest inclination towards his uncle's more outlandish appetites.

'You'll do anything I say, right?'

'Yes, anything,' Andrea confirmed, wishing he'd at least get on with something.

'Lie back on the bed then… can you do that?'

Andrea wriggled back and lay down. With her arms bound so tightly behind her it was not easy.

Martin knelt up on the bed beside her. With one hand on her knee, he pulled her legs apart and stared at her sex. She knew it would be wet; the bondage had seen to that.

His hand slid up her thigh, over the opaque black stocking top, and on to her thigh. As she was lying on her arms her buttocks were raised and her sex was angled upwards. Gently he pushed a finger into it.

'You're turned on, aren't you?' he breathed.

'Yes, I am.' She desperately wanted to add the word master. His finger moved up and down. 'Christ,' he whispered, shaking his head as if he could not believe what he was doing.

'Ms Angelis told me to tell you there's equipment in the chest over there,' Andrea said softly, her own pleasure slowly building.

'Equipment?'

'Harnesses and whips and toys,' she added. 'Things like that.'

'Oh.' He looked alarmed. 'I wouldn't know what to do with them.'

'I could show you, if that's what you'd like.'

'To tell the truth, Andrea, I'm not sure what I want. This is all a big surprise. I've never really had much to do with my uncle before. Then suddenly he invites me down here a day after my twenty-first birthday and presents me with all this. Apparently, my father had a house like this too. I never imagined such things existed. I mean, I'm not a virgin, but I've always been pretty straight.'

His finger probed the mouth of her vagina.

'Does that feel good?' he asked.

'Yes, it feels very good,' Andrea replied honestly.

'Why are you here?' he asked. 'Why do you let him do this to you?'

'Because it's what I've always wanted,' Andrea said with total conviction.

He shook his head in disbelief. Andrea noticed there was a large bulge tenting the front of the robe.

'You're very beautiful.' He pushed another finger in alongside the first and drove them both in, right up to the knuckle. Then he pulled them both out again. 'I shouldn't be doing this,' he said decisively. He jumped up off the bed and started to head towards the bathroom. But after two steps he stopped and turned around, looking down at Andrea again.

Suddenly, he tore the towelling robe off and jumped back on the bed. He rolled on top of Andrea and she felt his erection poking up between her legs. Martin kissed her fiercely, crushing his lips against hers and forcing his tongue into her mouth as he bucked his hips and slid his cock into the wet tube of her sex.

She gasped, the sound muffled by his mouth.

Still kissing her, squirming his mouth down on hers, he pumped his cock into her two or three times. Then he stopped as suddenly as he'd begun.

'No,' he whispered. He tore his mouth away from hers and buried his face in her throat, his body as rigid as a board. He remained completely still for long silent seconds, obviously battling with himself, and then Andrea felt his cock twitch inside her violently. She felt his juice erupting into her body.

'Oh *Christ*,' he groaned, rolling off her immediately. 'I'm sorry. I'm really sorry. It's always happening to me.'

He stood up, his expression full of anguish. His cock was softening rapidly.

'Look, I'm *really* sorry,' he bumbled, wringing his hands and avoiding her eyes. 'This was all a terrible idea. I've always had this problem with women. I think I want you out of here now.'

'It's all right,' Andrea tried to reassure him. She supposed she should have kept silent, but if she didn't say something, if he called Laurie now and had her returned to the stables, she imagined Hawksworth would not be pleased. If she was going to impress her master she had to help his nephew. She struggled to sit up, her breasts swaying with the effort. 'Please, don't send me back yet.'

'It's no good, Andrea. I thought…'

'Won't you at least let me try to help you?' she urged.

'Help me?' At last he looked at her, his expression hopeful but cautious. 'What can you do to help me?'

Andrea wasn't at all sure. But she wanted to try. If she could get him aroused again she thought there was a chance his ejaculation would not be so premature next time.

'Untie me.' It sounded strange for her to be saying those words, but she couldn't do what she had in mind with her hands tied behind her back. She twisted around and presented her arms to him.

With obvious uncertainty Martin unstrapped her elbows, then unbuckled one of the cuffs. 'Look,' he said, 'wouldn't it just be better if we called it a day?'

'Let me know if you think that in ten minutes.' She rubbed the circulation back into her arms. 'Come with me,' she said, taking his hand.

She led him into the bathroom. It was tiled in grey marble with a free-standing tub and a separate shower cubicle.

'But I've just had a shower,' he complained.

'I know, but we're going to have a bath – together.' She bent over the big white tub and turned on the taps. She poured bath oil into the steaming water. It was the first time she'd acted independently in weeks, and it felt very strange. 'Undo my stockings, would you?' she directed, rather than asked.

She put her feet up on the edge of the bath in turn and he unclipped the four suspenders, his hands trembling slightly. She made him unzip the ankle boots and pull those off too. 'Now the corset,' she said.

Turning her back on him again, she felt his fingers fumbling with the hooks and eyes of the waspie. The tight garment had left creases in her flesh that ran all the way around her body, above and below her waist.

'Come on.' She turned off the taps, stepped in, and carefully sank into the luxuriously hot water. He followed, and sat opposite her.

'What now?' he asked sheepishly.

'Give me your foot.'

He raised one foot out of the water. She took hold of it and pushed it back down, between her legs. 'Use your toes,' she encouraged.

'My toes?' He looked puzzled, then caught on. Without looking very enthusiastic, he pushed his toe between her labia. The water had washed away all her natural lubrication and the opening of her vagina was tight.

'Push,' she said, wriggling down on his big toe.

He pushed forward and the seal was broken. Inside, her cunt was hot and wet.

'Christ,' he said.

'Feels good, doesn't it,' she sighed, squirming down on him.

'It feels so hot.'

'Mmm…' She snaked her foot over his thigh and pushed it up into his crotch. His cock was floating in the water. It was beginning to engorge again. 'Put your other foot on my tits,' she said.

This time there was no reluctance as he lifted his foot and pressed it against her left breast. The feel of that pliant flesh under the sensitive sole of his foot clearly excited him, and Andrea felt his cock twitch.

'Now the other one,' she said.

He transferred his foot to her right breast. This time he flicked at her nipple with his big toe before he squashed it against her ribcage.

She took his foot in her hand and pulled it up to her mouth, sucking on his toes. This too produced a sharp twitch in his cock. She pressed it against his belly with the sole of her foot, rubbing it up and down.

'That feels good,' he murmured dreamily.

'You're getting hard again,' she purred.

'I know. That doesn't usually happen.'

'Perhaps you've never given yourself a chance before.'

She sucked on his big toe. This made his cock jerk against her foot. It was fully erect now.

'Come on,' she said, 'this is only the beginning.'

'What do we do now?'

'You'll see.'

She stood up, his toe making a distinct plop beneath the fragrant water as it was pulled from her vagina.

177

She grabbed a large white towel from the heated rail next to the bath and wrapped it around his body as he stepped out too. She rubbed him aggressively until she got to his cock, which she dried with the gentlest of touches.

'Now you can dry me,' she said.

He did. He rubbed the towel over her body as vigorously as she had done, then knelt and dried her legs, his erection standing up proudly. She turned around so he could gently dab her buttocks. He pushed the towel down between her thighs.

Andrea took his hand and led him back into the bedroom.

'Lie down,' she said.

He lay on the bed.

'Open your legs.'

Again he did as he was told. She knelt up on the bed between his thighs and took his cock in her hands.

'Don't,' he protested, leaning up on his elbows. 'I'll only come too quickly again.'

'When you've been with other girls, Martin, what did you do?'

'What do you mean?'

'After you'd come the first time?'

He blushed sheepishly, 'I usually took them home,' he admitted.

Andrea smiled comfortingly. 'You see, I used to have a boyfriend who had the same problem. He was young like you. The younger you are, the quicker your recovery rate. You can see that for yourself.' She eyed his spearing erection, and wet her lips. 'You're as hard as you were before. Instead of running away, you must persist. You won't come half as quickly this time, I promise. Now you're nice and relaxed from all that hot water, just lie back and trust me.'

Martin gave her an uncertain look, then lay back on the bed again.

Andrea wrapped her hands around his cock and began to wank him very gently. His cock was hard and smooth. She pulled his foreskin back and bent forward to slip his glans between her lips.

'No…' he gasped.

As she sucked him into her mouth, his cock began throbbing violently. She saw the muscles of his thighs go rigid and, for a moment, she thought she was going to be proved wrong. His hands clawed at the linen sheet and he was panting for breath. But the crisis passed. The throbbing stopped and his breathing became more regular. She saw and felt the tension leave his muscles.

Tentatively, Andrea swallowed his whole erection, sucking it back into her throat. Very slowly, she began sliding her mouth up and down on him.

'Yessss…' he hissed this time, very quietly.

She increased her pace, mouthing his shaft a little harder.

'Yessss…' he repeated, but much more firmly this time.

She pulled away, holding his cock in her hand.

'It's working,' he said. Although obviously still anxious, he tried to smile. 'I… I think you're right.'

'Do you want to try the big test?'

The smile disappeared. He looked into her eyes. 'I suppose I've got this far…'

She nodded reassuringly at him, and then straddled his hips so that her sex was poised above his standing erection. She took hold of it and guided it between her labia.

Martin moaned. She felt his cock twitch. 'I don't know if I…' he groaned, his voice trailing off.

'Just try,' she coaxed.

She lowered herself onto him. As he slid into the silky wetness of her cunt, she felt his cock throbbing as violently as it had done before. Again his muscles locked. His hands grabbed at her thighs, his fingers digging in like steel claws.

Andrea remained motionless. If he came again, she doubted he would give her a second chance. Slowly she felt the urgent throbbing subside and his hands relax. Almost imperceptibly, he began pumping into her. Gradually each stroke got stronger, his hips bucking up off the bed.

'Slowly,' she chided, as he began thrusting into her.

'You were right,' he panted, his voice strained. A tentative smile returned to his face, and as he powered his cock into her and grew in confidence, it broadened into a triumphant grin. 'This is fantastic,' he enthused. 'I never knew how good it felt.'

'You're very hard,' she cooed, her own body beginning to respond now that she wasn't so worried about him.

'This is so *good*,' he said. 'Let me get on top.' Before Andrea could do anything, he pulled her down on top of him and rolled over. As soon as she was on her back, he began pounding into her again, with even more enthusiasm than before. His body was fit and strong, his muscles toned, and he concentrated every one of them on driving up into her.

'Oh yes...' Andrea encouraged.

He went on and on, his cock ploughing into her. She raised her legs, pulling her knees back to allow him even deeper access.

'It's fantastic,' he breathed.

His cock began to throb again. She knew he was going to come but it didn't matter this time. He was in control of his ejaculation now.

'I'm going to come,' he confirmed, his voice strangled in his throat.

'Yes, let me feel it.'

His cock jerked violently and she felt him spurting into her body, as copiously as he had the first time.

Instead of pulling away the moment his ejaculation had subsided, he remained where he was, panting for breath, his cock still buried inside her.

'Bloody marvellous,' he beamed, with evident pride in his achievement. 'That was bloody marvellous.'

He kissed her, sucking on her lips, then plunging his tongue into her mouth. She responded, but her excitement was muted. She'd helped Martin for her own reasons but, if she needed confirmation of her desires, her own arousal had not reached the heights she had achieved when bound and helpless.

Martin was pressing his body against hers as he kissed, his chest crushing her breasts.

'You feel so good,' he whispered, without moving his mouth away.

To Andrea's amazement, she felt his cock begin to stiffen again. At first she thought it might be her imagination but, as he continued to kiss her, his cock was definitely growing hard.

He pulled away and looked down at her, mischief twinkling in his eyes. 'Like you said, a rapid recovery rate.'

He started gently, easing in and out of her again, while he supported himself on his elbows and looked down into her face.

After a few moments he stopped and rolled off her. He took his cock in his hand and squeezed. 'Now it's your turn,' he said. He got up. His whole attitude had changed. He was no longer diffident and hesitant.

'It's all right,' she said. 'You don't have to do that.'

Martin smiled. 'I know I don't have to,' he said. 'What do you call my uncle?'

'Master,' Andrea said. The word gave her a pang of arousal.

'Master.' He pondered for a moment. 'And you're his slave?'

'Yes, I'm his slave.'

'And you submit to his will,' he persisted, 'is that it?'

'Yes.'

'Well, you'd better start calling me master.' Martin's voice was suddenly stern.

'Yes, master, anything you say.' His new-found confidence and attitude evoked another thrill, deep in her tummy.

'That's better. Now get on your knees, beside the bed. Start behaving like a slave or I'll get one of the other girls up here instead.' It was as though he was trying out a new role for himself, seeing whether he was comfortable with it. It appeared that he was. She had given him back his masculinity and now he was going to give her back her subservience.

Andrea meekly dropped to the floor immediately, while Martin rummaged in the chest.

'This looks interesting,' he eventually decided, 'put it on.' He threw a leather harness to the floor in front of her. She picked it up. The mass of thin leather straps consisted of a bra-shaped top, which fitted around her breasts but not over them. Extending down from each breast, two more straps formed a long V that looped into a metal ring over her mons. From the bottom of this ring, two thinner straps ran down between her legs and up into the cleft of her buttocks to connect with another ring in the small of her back. A thick strap then ran up her spine, where it divided in two and met the shoulder straps of the bra. All the straps could be adjusted to fit tightly.

Andrea struggled into the garment while Martin watched.

'That's much better,' he said, when she had finally buckled all the straps tightly. 'You can stand up now.'

She obeyed immediately. The tight leather was not overly restrictive, but it suggested bondage, and the smell of it provoked an instant reaction deep inside her sex.

Martin produced a length of white nylon rope from the chest. 'This is what you want, isn't it?' he demanded.

'Yes, master.' It was *exactly* what she wanted.

'Come here, then. You don't think I'm going to come to you, do you?' Martin was beginning to enjoy his role. His cock jutted arrogantly from his belly.

Andrea walked over to him.

'Hands out in front of you.' He looped the rope around her wrists, and then between them, leaving a long length of it trailing. He pulled her forward. 'Stand behind the chair,' he ordered.

Andrea was on familiar territory once again. Martin's growing confidence was matched by her excitement.

'That's better,' he continued. 'Now I'm going to gag you.'

'Yes, master.'

She felt another sharp stab of anticipation. She loved being gagged, having her mouth stretched open and invaded. She could suck on a gag and pretend it was her master's cock.

Martin produced a rubber ball-gag from the chest and secured it in her mouth with a leather strap, tying it tight around her head. She felt his erection nudging against her buttocks as he did so. Suddenly, something descended over her eyes. It was a thick band of black rubber. It was wide enough to cover the tops of her flushed cheeks, and was shaped in the centre to accommodate her nose.

'Oh no...' she breathed, almost to herself.

'Oh yes.'

She sensed him kneeling at her feet. 'Legs apart.'

As she shuffled her feet, his hands grasped her ankle and he wrapped a leather cuff around it. The cuff must have been attached to a bar between her legs because, when he'd finished with both ankles, she could not close them.

'I could get to like this,' he said. She heard him moving around in front of her, then stop. She was sure he was admiring his handiwork. A few minutes before she had been naked, now she was trussed up in black leather and rope, a fetish icon made flesh.

She felt a tug on the rope, pulling her forward. She toppled face down over the back of the chair until her head was a few inches from the seat and her hands were practically touching the floor. She could feel him pulling the end of the rope beneath the chair and tying it to the bar between her feet.

'Isn't this how you should be treated?' he teased.

Andrea nodded. The bondage had induced a level of arousal that was making her feel quite elated. She was completely helpless and vulnerable, her sex exposed and available, her limbs rendered useless. She could feel the leather harness biting into her flesh, particular the two thin straps on either side of her labia and the tight rope that encircled her wrists. The darkness seemed to concentrate her feelings and magnify them.

'Let's see you try and get out of that then,' her new tormentor challenged. 'Come on, I want to make sure I've done a good job.'

Andrea pulled with her hands and tried to kick her legs free of the leather cuffs but, though she could wriggle from side to side, moving her head and shaking her bottom and breasts enticingly, she could not escape.

'That's very sexy,' he said slowly. 'I like watching you do that.'

Andrea felt his hands on her buttocks. In this position, the purse of her sex was spread wide open. His fingers slipped into her briefly, and she moaned as they nudged against her clit.

'Downstairs, when I whipped that girl, I felt something, you know?' He was almost talking to himself. 'Perhaps I inherited the urge from my father. Do you think that's possible?'

Andrea wasn't sure whether she should respond or not, so she held her breath and didn't move.

'I'm going to whip you now, Andrea,' he continued. 'It doesn't seem fair, but I'm going to do it because I know that's what you want. It is what you want, isn't it?'

She nodded. She'd been whipped many times now and it always brought pain. But there was also pleasure too.

She heard him walk away. A few seconds later she heard a tap running. He'd gone into the bathroom. Why had he done that?

He returned and a hand touched the small of her back. It was wet. She sensed him raise his other hand. Drops of water landed on her back. She heard a whistle of air and then a searing line of pain exploded right across the rump of her buttocks with a whooping noise. The pain was like no other she'd experienced. It made her whole lower body vibrate.

'We used to do this at school,' he said. 'It's a wet towel, in case you're wondering.'

Whoop! The towel landed again. Andrea screamed into the gag but very little sound came out. She felt her buttocks quivering. The towel was being stroked down so strongly it flattened her buttocks and actually hit her labia, stinging them too.

Whoop! The third blow was the strongest of them all, but already the pain was turning to that sticky hot pleasure she'd felt so often since she'd been at the manor. This time, the sound she tried to push past the gag was much more to do with a moan of utter delight than a whimper of pain. She felt her clitoris pulse and realised her body was undulating as she pushed her belly against the back of the chair.

She heard Martin throw the towel aside. He grabbed her hips and unceremoniously rammed his cock into the depths of her cunt. She was hot and incredibly wet, his two ejaculations adding to her own juices. As he ploughed into her for the third time, she strained against the bonds that held her. This time, as they fucked, she was a slave again, unable to do anything for herself. But if she were a slave, she was not allowed to come without permission.

He held himself deep inside her and reached down to her breasts, pinching both nipples in turn. In response she clenched her sex tightly around his shaft.

He straightened up and pulled his cock back slowly, then jammed it in again, grinding his hips from side to side.

Andrea simply could not suppress the oncoming orgasm.

'Come on, I want to feel you come!' he hissed through gritted teeth, right on cue.

And that was all the permission she needed. Instantly her sex seemed to melt over him. Previously that day her orgasms had been intense, sharp, almost painful, and centred on her clit. This was different. This was a warm feeling that was not centred at all and which seemed to start from every part of her body simultaneously, then turn inwards to her sex; an implosion, not an explosion. Every muscle in her body seemed to soften and her body turned to liquid.

Martin pulled out of her. He was still vibrantly erect.

'And now,' he crowed proudly, as he bent to loosen the rope around her wrists, 'I think it's time I properly met one of those other gorgeous girls.'

Chapter Nine

Andrea had to be helped up the narrow steps into the helicopter. It would have been impossible for her to do it by herself. For one thing, her heels were too high and, for another, her hands were bound to her sides so she could not use her arms.

Laurie pushed her forward into the cabin, then settled her in one of the chairs and fastened the seatbelt for her.

Andrea was wearing a black suit and a white silk blouse. The skirt of the suit was a rather unusual design with two small slits on each side that, to a casual glance, looked like pockets. But they were not pockets. They were holes that allowed Andrea's wrists to be chained to her thighs, making it impossible for her to move her hands from the top of her legs. Another clever piece of tailoring allowed the cuffs of the jacket to hide the chains on her wrists.

The helicopter engine and rotor arm began to increase in pitch and tempo.

A steward arrived, the same man who had attended Andrea on her first helicopter ride – it seemed like a lifetime ago. The steward fitted a set of headphones over Andrea's ears, then handed another pair to Laurie.

'Can I get you anything, Ms Angelis?' He didn't even glance at Andrea.

'No.'

'Off to town?' he said cheerily.

'Yes.'

He disappeared as Laurie put on the headphones, clearly not wanting to engage in small-talk with him.

That morning Laurie had marched into Andrea's cell and ordered her to dress. The austere brunette had buckled leather bands around Andrea's thighs, above her flesh-coloured hold-up stockings, then made her put on the blouse and the suit without underwear, not even a bra. Wrist cuffs had followed and been clipped through the skirt to the thigh bands. Then, as usual, Betty had arrived to do her make-up. As the older woman was brushing out her hair Andrea heard the helicopter arrive.

Fifteen minutes later they were in the air.

She had not seen Martin since the previous night, nor her master. She hoped she was being taken to him now.

The helicopter banked and rose over the house. She glimpsed the carefully cultivated gardens beyond the wall, then they were heading east, tracking alongside a major motorway towards London.

Andrea's wrists began to ache, the thigh bands pulling them down at an unnatural angle. The thigh bands too were tight and chaffed the tops of her legs. But Andrea didn't care. She was confident that Martin had given a favourable report of her to his uncle and that, for the second day running, she was being taken to him.

The helicopter reached the city in less than fifteen minutes, then turned north. After another ten minutes it banked and headed for a twenty-storey tower whose black glass windows reflected the bright morning sun.

As they descended Andrea saw a large white H within a circle painted on the flat roof of the building. The helicopter landed with a gentle bump, the engine noise dropped to a loud hum. Andrea felt a thrill of anticipation. It seemed Darrington International had its headquarters in a large office block on the south bank of the river.

Laurie took off her headphones and undid her seatbelt. She leant forward and did the same for Andrea. 'Up,' she ordered.

Andrea got to her feet. The high heels meant she had to stoop as she tottered out of the cabin. Laurie went down the steps first then held Andrea securely as she climbed out.

The draught from the rotor blades sent both women's hair flying in all directions and the noise of the engines was deafening. Laurie took Andrea by the arm and pulled her over to a metal staircase that led down into the main building.

Inside, the noise dropped to a gentle hum. They were standing in a small hallway in front of a single door made from lime wood and elaborately carved with an art deco design. Laurie took a key from her small clutch bag and unlocked the door.

'Follow me,' she said.

The room beyond contained two banks of lifts. The floor was of polished ash and a huge abstract tapestry dominated the space, its primary colours so bright they seemed to vibrate.

Opposite the lifts were two large double doors, also of lime wood and carved with the same design. Laurie led Andrea through them into a large rectangular room. One entire wall, from floor to ceiling, was glass, and it presented a spectacular view over London. To the right she could see the National Westminster Building and St Paul's and, to the left, the Houses of Parliament and the gardens of Buckingham Palace.

The room was full of desks, at least eight of them, all manned by secretaries working at computer terminals. Laurie led Andrea to another lime carved door. If any of the secretaries noticed anything strange about her, none of them gave the slightest indication of it.

Laurie opened the door.

Charles Hawksworth was sitting behind a large curved rosewood desk. He was talking on the phone, but put down the receiver when he saw them.

'Come in, my dear. I'm sorry to bring you all this way, but business must take precedence over pleasure – on some occasions.'

The room was large, with another floor-to-ceiling window, and very little in the way of furniture. Apart from the desk there were two chairs, a sofa and a cocktail cabinet, all in classic art deco.

'Thank you, Laurie, that will be all,' he said.

Laurie closed the door, leaving them alone.

'Come over here,' he said.

Andrea tottered forward. It was not only that the heels of the shoes were precipitously high, but that the cut of the knee-length pencil skirt only allowed her to take tiny steps.

'Sit down, won't you?'

He indicated one of the chairs in front of his desk, then returned to his telephone call.

Andrea managed to sit down, the cuffs round her thighs pinching hard.

She watched Hawksworth as he talked, his deep blue eyes flashing, his long fingers making small gestures in the air as he made his point. He had an innate air of authority, whether sitting in his office, at the very centre of his global empire, or in bed, commanding her to obey his slightest whim. She trembled as she remembered how he'd touched her only the day before.

The telephone call ended.

'Well, my dear,' he said, getting to his feet and moving around the desk. 'I hope you had a pleasant flight?'

'Yes, master,' she answered politely. 'Thank you.'

'Good.' He stood behind her and put his hands on her shoulders. The touch made her start. 'I'm very pleased with you, Andrea. Very pleased indeed. Martin has given me a glowing account of your behaviour last night. He seemed to think you were very special. So I have decided to embark on the final part of your training straight away.'

'Thank you, master.'

His hands slid down under her jacket to her breasts, cupping them and lifting them slightly.

'But first there is some urgent business I have to attend to. Once that is over...' He squeezed her breasts sharply then let them go, returning to his desk with the flicker of a smile on his lips.

On his desk were a telephone console, a computer terminal and a small bronze nude of a slender woman with over-large breasts. Despite her heavy chest, she stood proudly with her head up and her legs apart.

As Hawksworth sat down the telephone rang.

'Yes.' He listened, then began to talk in rapid French.

The door opened and one of the secretaries from the outer office walked in, carrying a file of papers. She had blonde hair and wore a short black skirt and a tight sleeveless blue blouse. Her legs were spectacular, her thighs slender and contoured, the firmness of her calves and buttocks emphasised by her high spiky heels.

She ignored Andrea and stood at the side of Hawksworth's desk, waiting for him to finish his call.

'Yes, Diana?' he said as he put the receiver down.

'The French contract you wanted, sir,' she said, handing him the file. 'Thank you. Has Lloyd arrived yet?'

'Yes, sir. And Mr Highfield.'

'Tell them I'll be with them in a few minutes. Take Andrea in, will you?'

'Yes, sir.'

'Go with her Andrea,' he said.

Andrea got to her feet and felt herself blushing. It was possible the girl might have thought she was sitting in an awkward position but, as Andrea struggled to her feet, it was obvious that her wrists were bound to her sides.

But Diana was clearly not in the least bit shocked. She took Andrea's arm and guided her across the room, and led her through a door opposite Hawksworth's desk.

The room beyond was as spacious as Hawksworth's office, with the same huge window and decorated in the same art deco style. At least twenty chairs surrounded a large oval table, but the room was dominated by a large oil painting depicting a riverside picnic. It was no ordinary picnic, however. With one exception, all the participants were women in various stages of undress, some wearing simply skirts or blouses, others naked but for stockings held up with frilly garters, while others wore tightly laced corsets. Their attention was centred on the single male, who sat at a picnic table being served an array of food. He wore a dark scarlet robe, and a large wolfhound sat at his feet.

'Over here,' Diana said abruptly.

Next to a small table laid with coffee and other soft drinks, stood an odd-looking metal device which Andrea at first took to be a piece of modern sculpture. A flat black spine of metal, about six foot high, was attached to the wall. Near the top and in the middle were two metal hoops, and the metal crossbar at the bottom had two further hoops at each end.

As they approached this odd contraption, Andrea could see that each of the metal circles was hinged, with a lock at the front. Diana opened all four rings.

'Stand here,' she said.

Before Andrea could obey she snatched her arm again and pulled her round so her back was against the vertical metal bar.

'Chin up,' she said.

Diana swung the first of the metal loops around Andrea's neck and locked it underneath her chin. The metal bit into Andrea's throat, forcing her head up so she could not see the girl snapping the larger ring around her waist or securing her ankles to the hoops on the crossbar. This was difficult to accomplish, as Andrea's tight skirt constricted her legs and Diana had to pull it up to her thighs.

Now Andrea was completely helpless. With her hands still secured to her thighs, and her throat, waist and ankles encompassed by steel, she could not move.

Diana looked at her critically for a moment. She unbuttoned Andrea's jacket and folded it back. The material of the blouse was thin and Andrea's breasts were clearly visible beneath it.

'Rather you than me,' she said, in an expression that could

be best interpreted as a sneer.

Diana's heels clacked on the polished wooden floor as she walked away, her pert round bottom swaying from side to side. As Andrea watched her retreating rear, she felt a pang of desire. She was shocked to realise it was the first time she had felt like that about another woman.

Andrea had no time to dwell on this discovery, however. Almost before the echo of the girl's steps had died away, a tall man with a bushy black beard and a briefcase entered the room. He was followed by white-haired man who walked with a limp. They closed the door and walked to the conference table, glancing at Andrea briefly, as if she were an interesting piece of furniture. They were talking in a language Andrea thought might be Swedish. The bearded man took a sheaf of papers out of his briefcase, and both men began to read.

The door opened again. This time Andrea recognised the newcomer: Edward Highfield. He smiled at her briefly then turned his attention to the other two men, greeting them effusively. Behind Edward, two much younger men had edged into the room, both in grey suits. They shook hands with the others and sat down at the table. Only then, apparently, did they notice Andrea. They stared at her with their mouths open, their faces white, but obviously neither dared comment. Diana returned to place four or five files on the table just as Charles Hawksworth entered the room.

He sat at the head of the table. Diana sat to his left, taking out a notebook and pen.

'There's coffee over there,' he said, pointing to the table beside Andrea. 'Please help yourselves. We have lunch for you later in our executive dining room. I think you will find our chef to be excellent. Now, to business.'

They began discussing a deal for the acquisition of a patent in an electronic circuit which the bearded man appeared to own. Weeks ago, when she was working for Silverton, Andrea might have found the details fascinating. Now all she could think of was what her master had said to her. The 'final stage' of her training. What could that mean? She yearned to be alone with him again to find out.

The metal frame was extremely uncomfortable, particularly the collar around her throat, which was too high and dug into her chin. Her legs were hurting too. Diana had only pulled the skirt up far enough to allow her to lock Andrea's ankles into the metal rings. The hem of the skirt was still incredibly tight and bit into her thighs, just as the metal dug painfully into her ankles.

One of the younger men got to his feet and walked over to the coffee table. He stole furtive glances at her as he approached. As he poured himself a coffee, he allowed himself a longer look, his eyes dwelling on her breasts and her legs, the skirt pulled up enough to reveal a hint of the leather that banded her thighs.

Unfortunately for him, while Highfield and the bearded man discussed some aspect of the contract in detail, Hawksworth looked his way.

'Beautiful, isn't she?' he said, getting to his feet. He came over and put his arm around the young man's shoulder.

'Very,' the young man agreed.

'You haven't been here before, have you?'

'No, Mr Hawksworth.'

'Artists spend a great deal of time trying to create objects of beauty, often not achieving it in a whole lifetime. But, in my opinion, real women are far more beautiful than anything they can ever create. Other people have sculptures in their homes and offices, but I prefer the real thing.' He looked at the young man seriously. 'And, like all good sculptures, she deserves to be touched, don't you think?'

'T-touched?' The man looked agitated and fiddled with the knot of his silk tie.

'Of course,' Hawksworth smiled confidently. 'Go ahead. Stroke her. Feel her. She's in no position to refuse you.'

The young man's hands were trembling so much he had

to put his cup of coffee down. He was clearly intimidated by Hawksworth and, even if he had wanted to refuse the invitation, saw no way of doing so without incurring Hawksworth's wrath.

He moved over to stand directly in front of Andrea. She held her breath and watched a hand moving slowly towards her. His fingers trailed down over her breasts. He blushed a beetroot red and exhaled audibly.

'Gary!' the bearded man called.

The young man snatched his hand away as though he'd been scalded, and hastily beat a retreat back to the table, clearly relieved to get away. Hawksworth winked at Andrea, and then followed him.

They were all soon engaged in conversation again.

The discomfort in Andrea's body increased. She wished she could edge the skirt up her thighs an inch or two to relieve the pressure on her legs. She tried to use her fingertips to tug on it, but made very little difference. She found that if she ground her bottom in a circle she could transfer the worst of the cramp from one leg to the other, but she had to be careful that no one noticed what she was doing.

'Well, gentleman,' Hawksworth eventually sat back in his chair and announced, 'I think it's time for lunch.'

The chairs scraped against the floor as the five men and one woman got up from the table. Still chatting together, they headed for the door. The bearded man led the way, followed by the other three, leaving Highfield and Hawksworth alone for a moment.

'I think it's going well,' Highfield said. 'Two million less than we'd budgeted for.'

'That is impressive,' Hawksworth agreed, with a pensive nod of his head. 'Come on, let's eat.'

'Do you mind if I have a word with Andrea first?' Highfield asked, glancing back to where she stood locked in the metal contraption.

'Of course I don't. If it hadn't been for you, I'd never have found her. She's perfect. I have high hopes for her.'

'Are you going to put her into The System?'

'That's her decision. She has to complete her training first. You know what Marie-Claire's like.' Hawksworth patted Highfield on the arm, then walked out of the room, closing the door after him.

'I'm sorry I couldn't say hello earlier,' Highfield said as he walked over to her. 'You're looking suitably uncomfortable.' He stood directly in front of her and took her left nipple between his thumb and forefinger, pinching it hard. 'Are you excited?'

'Yes, master,' Andrea admitted. 'I am.'

'I bet you are.' He took hold of her skirt and tugged it up her thighs. The relief was enormous. His hand snaked between her thighs and onto her labia. A finger pressed against her clit and she gasped.

'If Hawksworth puts you into The System, I'm going to bid for you, Andrea. You're the most exciting woman I've ever met.'

She could see a bulge tenting the front of his trousers. He wrapped his free arm around her body and embraced her, his erection pushing into her belly.

'I haven't been able to keep my eyes off you all morning,' he breathed into her ear, his lips brushing her cheek. He was undulating his hips so his cock slid up and down against her soft flesh. 'I haven't stopped thinking about being with you since the last time. None of the other girls...'

Suddenly he threw back his head and gave a little gasp. Even through the layers of material that separated them she could feel his cock pulsing heavily. He pressed harder, then pulled away. There was a damp stain spreading rapidly across his navy-blue trousers.

'See what you do to me,' he croaked, his face flushed.

He took some paper napkins from the table and tried to wipe the damp stain away. Then he left the room without another word.

So far Andrea hadn't given much thought to what the master had said about The System. But now it was puzzling her. Hawksworth had spoken of her having to make a choice at the end of her training, but he hadn't explained what that choice would be. From what he'd said to Highfield, it seemed she would be offered a chance to enter The System. But what that meant she could only guess. Highfield said he would bid for her, but she didn't know what that meant either – though the thought of being with him again was not one she cared to contemplate too much.

The door of the conference room opened and Gary slipped into the room. He closed the door quietly and examined it for a moment, as though trying to see if it could be locked from within, but apparently it couldn't.

'Don't worry,' he said softly. 'I'm not going to hurt you.'

He brought a chair over and sat down next to her. With her head fixed as it was, it was impossible for Andrea to see much more than the top of his mousy-coloured hair. Gary appeared to realise this and got up, examining the metal collar around her throat. He touched the lock on the front of the ring and it sprung open, Andrea's head falling forward so suddenly she gasped with relief. She stretched her neck back and forward, easing the cramped muscles.

Gary sat down again. He stared at her thighs and began rubbing the front of his trousers. 'Why don't you say anything?' he asked.

'I'm only supposed to talk when I am spoken to, sir,' she answered.

'Hawksworth said I could touch you. Can I?'

'Yes, sir, you can.'

'Hawksworth also says you're often whipped,' he delved. 'On the bum and the tits. Is that true?'

'Yes, sir, that's true.'

Gary looked nervous and uncertain, though Andrea could see a distinct bulge lifting the front of his trousers. It seemed he was wrestling with his conscience. He looked from her thighs, up to her breasts, then back down to her thighs.

He suddenly sprang to his feet and unzipped his trousers. His cock sprang out from beneath the tails of his shirt. He took it in his fist and began to wank aggressively. With his other hand he cupped a breast, then ran it down her body, over her flat belly and up under her skirt. She felt a finger insinuate between her labia, thrusting into the hot hole of her vagina.

'You're so wet,' he grunted, his jaw clenched tight.

Hawksworth had clearly given these men licence to do what they liked to her, Andrea thought. And, as with Martin the previous night, serving them was a way of serving her master. She wanted to make sure Gary was impressed with her.

'I'm very excited,' she whispered.

'You are?' Gary's eyes were glued to the soft breasts in his hand as he spoke. His expression was one of total disbelief.

'I am, because I want to take you in my mouth. I want to suck all the spunk out of your cock and empty your balls,' she said, with intentional crudity. She felt her sex clench around his finger and watched her sultry words make his bulbous end engorge even further and turn a deeper shade of purple.

'Really?' he croaked. 'You really want to do that to me?'

'Mmmm...' she licked her lips hungrily. 'But do you want to whip me instead? Would you like that? Would you like to see the marks on my poor bottom?' she pouted theatrically. Strictly speaking she should have been silent, but she thought the ends justified the means. This was what her master would have wanted, she was sure.

'Yes...' His reply was barely audible as his fist pumped up and down his cock like a piston.

'Whip my tits instead,' she urged. 'Then put that cock inside me. Fuck me. Would you like that, Gary?'

Suddenly he went rigid and his eyes bulged. He just managed to twist to one side so the arc of spunk missed her skirt and blouse and spattered on the wooden floor. He shuddered and let out a long low mewling sound.

'Oh God,' he said eventually. He looked at his watch, then at Andrea. Quickly he pulled his finger from her body and snapped the metal collar shut again, forcing her head up. He examined her clothes to make sure none of his juice had landed on her, then grabbed paper napkins from the table to clean up the floor.

Just as the door of the conference room started to open he hastily dumped the soiled napkins in a waste bin under the table.

'Your zip,' Andrea whispered.

His cock was still hanging from his trousers. He pushed it back in and tugged his fly up – just in time.

'Well, gentleman, shall we get on?' said Hawksworth, as the door opened fully and he and the others filed back into the room.

The meeting lasted a further hour or more. Andrea saw Gary glance at her surreptitiously from time to time but, other than that, the group ignored her. Hawksworth brought the meeting to a close, declaring himself satisfied with the deal that had been struck, and shook hands with the bearded man.

All five men then left the room, talking animatedly of future successes, leaving Diana to clear up. The blonde didn't speak to her either. She stacked all the files and papers and carried them out of the room.

Andrea's body ached from standing still for so long. The effort of keeping her head up so her chin would not chafe against the metal collar was giving her cramp in the neck; she also had a burning desire to go to the loo. But her overriding feeling was still one of anticipation. She had no idea what was going to happen next.

The silence continued. The pressure in her bladder became worse. She tried to think about Hawksworth and what he had said, but the desire to pee was making it hard to think of anything else. As Hawksworth was such an expert in devising humiliations for his slaves she wondered if this was another one; that she would be discovered standing in a pool of her own pee. But that would surely be a punishment and, after what he'd said about Martin, it did not make sense that he should want to punish her.

She wriggled and squirmed, trying to find a position that would put less pressure on her belly. It would have helped if she could close her legs together. In her mind, she kept imagining the pee sprinkling out of her, thinking of the relief it would bring. It was only a matter of time before she lost control.

The door opened, and Diana entered.

'Did you think we'd forgotten about you?' she said in a mocking tone.

'I need to go to the loo, please,' Andrea implored.

'I thought you weren't supposed to speak unless you were spoken to.'

'It's urgent,' Andrea groaned. 'I'm getting desperate.'

'I bet you are.' Diana was clearly enjoying tormenting her victim. In no particular hurry she unclipped the metal collar at Andrea's throat. She placed a hand over Andrea's belly. 'Bad, is it?' she taunted.

Andrea closed her eyes and nodded.

The metal band around her waist was opened, then those at her ankles. Andrea pressed her legs together. The relief was only momentary; she still needed to pee.

'Come on then,' Diana said, walking across the room.

Andrea tottered after her, each step jolting her bladder and making the need worse. A small door to the right of the boardroom led into a long corridor. Halfway down were two doors marked with symbolic men and women. Diana held the appropriate one open and allowed Andrea to go through first.

Andrea rushed into one of the cubicles. But even though her skirt was partially hitched up around her hips, she still needed to pull it up further; a feat she could not perform with her hands bound to her thighs. She tried to inch her skirt up by clawing at it with her fingers, but the process was altogether hopeless.

'I need help,' Andrea said. The fact that she could see the water in the toilet bowl was making her need a hundred times worse.

'From me?' Diana asked, sardonically. She wandered over to the cubicle and held the door open.

'Please,' Andrea said, straining her hands against the leather cuffs so Diana would see the problem.

'It must be terribly difficult like that,' the blonde mocked.

'*Please*... help me,' Andrea pleaded.

Diana took one step forward. The links that joined the leather cuffs to Andrea's thighs had a small snap-lock, which she opened, allowing the skirt to be hoisted up over her buttocks.

Andrea sank down onto the loo, and a stream of pee immediately burst forth. Diana stood watching, her eyes locked to Andrea's sex, the cubicle door still open.

'It must be bad,' she said pensively. 'I've always wondered what it would be like. To be so helpless, I mean. To be totally dependent on others. You can't even pee if Hawksworth doesn't allow it.' Diana shuddered dreamily. 'Is it exciting to be dominated like that?'

Eventually the powerful stream slowed to a tinkle, and then stopped altogether. Andrea wiped herself with the available tissue paper. 'Yes, it is exciting,' she said.

'Well then, aren't you going to thank me?' Diana said.

'Well... yes, thank you,' Andrea replied.

'No, not like that,' Diana said. She closed the cubicle door. 'I think I deserve something a little more intimate. I saw the way you were looking at me this morning. I've never tried it with a woman before, but, looking at you, I think it's time for a little experiment. You wouldn't mention it to Hawksworth, would you?'

'I don't know, what do you want me to do?' Andrea said.
'Kiss me.'

Diana caught Andrea by the shoulders and pushed her back against the cubicle wall. Tentatively, she kissed Andrea on the lips, not using her tongue, just brushing their lips together. But slowly she increased the pressure, her tongue slipping into Andrea's mouth. Then she crushed her body against Andrea's, her belly grinding from side to side, their breasts squashing together.

Andrea felt a jolt of excitement. She knew she shouldn't be doing this, but she didn't see that she had much choice.

'That's nice,' Diana said. 'I've always wondered what it would feel like.' She hitched her short skirt right up over her hips. She was wearing tights, but no panties. She braced herself against the opposite wall of the cubicle with her legs apart. 'Come on then.'

'What do you want?' Andrea asked.

Diana grabbed her hand and pushed it into the top of her pantyhose. 'Hawksworth makes you take women, doesn't he? That's what I heard. You must know what to do.' She thrust Andrea's hand down until it was on her mons.

The girl's sex was covered with a thick bush of hair. Andrea prodded her finger into the slit of her labia. It wasn't particularly wet. It was awkward with her forearm tangling in the tights, but she managed to angle her finger inward and find Diana's clit.

The girl gasped as Andrea rubbed the little nut of nerves.
'Oh yes…' she sighed.

Andrea pushed her finger inside the girl's vagina. This too was dry, but, as she nosed her finger into the soft flesh, she felt the juice beginning to flow.

'Can you feel that?' Diana asked. 'I'm so turned on.'

'Uh huh,' Andrea replied. She moved her finger back to Diana's clit, leaving a trail of wetness along her labia, then pressed the nub of flesh back against the pubic bone. This caused the girl's whole body to shudder. Andrea jiggled her

202

finger from side to side.

'Like that, yes, like that,' Diana urged. She raised her left hand and wrapped it around Andrea's neck, her fingers digging into her flesh.

Andrea frotted Diana's clit more rapidly. The girl moaned loudly and threw her head back against the wall. 'Don't stop, don't...'

But she couldn't say the last word. It turned into a long cry of pleasure. She banged her head back against the thin cubicle wall once again, a noise that echoed through the tiled room. She pulled Andrea's head onto her shoulder and came, her clitoris pulsing under Andrea's fingertip.

As the orgasm faded she pushed Andrea's head away, and looked her in the eye. 'I've never come so quickly before,' she panted. 'I always knew it would be good with another woman.'

Andrea removed her hand from the girl's tights.

'I'd better get you back.' Diana pulled her skirt down and took a few deep breaths to compose herself.

Andrea's own sex was throbbing. Feeling Diana come had aroused her own needs. She would have liked to kiss her again and pull those tights right down. She would have liked to press her mouth against her damp sex and make her return the compliment. But she knew she could not do any such thing.

Diana caught hold of the hem of Andrea's skirt and tugged it down her legs. She quickly found the slits on either side and clipped the leather cuffs back to the thigh bands.

'Don't say a word about this to anyone,' she warned, as she pulled Andrea out of the cubicle and led her to the washroom door.

'I won't,' Andrea said. Diana had used her. She supposed she should have refused to co-operate but, like Laurie, Diana was acting on behalf of her master. By obeying her, Andrea was obeying her master too. At least, that was how she convinced herself that what she had done had not compromised her role of perfect slave. Which didn't mean it was wise to tell Hawksworth what had happened. 'I won't,' she repeated quietly.

Chapter Ten

The black Mercedes cruised along the motorway. Charles Hawksworth sat in the back with Andrea at his side.

'Is that bondage uncomfortable?' he asked, as he sipped the malt whisky he'd poured himself from the cocktail cabinet.

'Yes, master, it is,' she replied. Sitting down, with her wrists still secured to her thighs, the leather cuffs bit into her flesh.

'I saw you looking at Diana earlier,' he said. 'She's a lovely woman, isn't she?'

She felt a jolt of alarm. What did he know?

'Yes, master.'

'Do you think she would be suitable?'

'I don't understand, master.'

Hawksworth smiled. 'She wants to come to the manor. But I'm not sure she has what it takes. She's not a submissive. She has a dominant personality.'

'Yes, master.'

Had there been a video camera in the toilets? Had Diana been yet another test? If so, it was one she had patently failed. Andrea felt her heart beating faster.

'Perhaps I need to set her a little test,' he said, almost to himself.

Andrea remained silent. As Hawksworth showed no signs of being angry with her, she relaxed slightly.

The car slowed, then pulled through the tall wire gates of a private airfield. It drove straight up to a small white jet parked on the runway. The driver got out and opened the passenger door.

'Come on, my dear,' Hawksworth said, helping Andrea

out of the car.

A uniformed stewardess stood by the steps that led up to the plane. She had short dark brown hair and a curvaceous figure. 'Good evening, Mr Hawksworth,' she said, with a gorgeous smile.

'Good evening, Isabel. Take Andrea in would you, and get her settled.'

'Certainly, sir.'

Isabel took Andrea's arms and helped her up the steps. The main cabin of the plane was luxurious, with large comfortable armchairs, a sofa, and a dining table surrounded by four chairs. In one corner stood a bar and a large television screen.

Isabel pushed Andrea down into one of the armchairs and fastened her seatbelt. With her arms secured to her thighs, she was once again completely helpless.

Hawksworth sat in the other armchair, facing Andrea. 'I'll have another malt, Isabel, please.'

Isabel poured the drink and set it down on the small table next to his chair.

'Now leave us,' he said.

'Take off in five minutes, sir.' Isabel walked to the door at the front of the cabin and closed it behind her.

Andrea had never been in a private plane before, but she was not in the mood to take notice of her surroundings. It was obvious that wherever they were going Hawksworth was escorting her personally, and she was intoxicated with delight. What's more, his whole attention was focused on her now, his eyes examining her secured body. In all the long hours at the manor, she had done nothing but think about what it would be like to have him all to herself. Now it seemed that wish had come true.

The plane's engines roared into life and it taxied forward. After the briefest of waits at the end of the runway, they took off, climbing rapidly. Andrea wanted to ask where they were going, but she dare not. As long as she was with her master, she told herself, she did not care.

As the plane levelled out there was a knock on the cabin door.

'Yes,' Hawksworth said.

Isabel entered. 'Is there anything you would like, sir?' she asked, still smiling cheerily.

'Get Andrea a drink, please,' he said. 'What would you like, my dear?'

That took Andrea by surprise. Having spent so long without making a single decision it was difficult to make a choice.

'Fetch her a glass of champagne,' Hawksworth decided for her.

Isabel opened a bottle and poured a glass. She held it to Andrea's lips so casually that Andrea was sure she had performed this service before. Some of the champagne spilled over her lips and down her chin, dripping onto the white blouse.

'Undo her seatbelt.'

Isabel flipped it open.

'Stand up.'

Hawksworth's attitude had changed. His voice was authoritative and the relaxed manner he'd adopted in the car had disappeared. Andrea got to her feet.

'I want her stripped, Isabel,' he continued.

'Yes, sir.'

Again, Isabel seemed to know exactly what to do. She unclipped the leather cuffs from the thigh bands and pulled off Andrea's skirt. She took her jacket off, then pulled the white blouse over her head. Andrea's breasts quivered as she raised her arms.

'Take the thigh bands off,' he said. 'Bind her hands behind her back.'

Isabel immediately drew Andrea's arms behind her back and used the snap-lock on the D-rings to secure the cuffs together. The thigh bands were held in place by Velcro, which made a tearing sound as she pulled them off.

The leather had wrinkled the tops of the stockings. Isabel pulled them up until they were tight and smooth again, her hands pressing against Andrea's naked sex rather more than Andrea thought was necessary.

'Leave us,' Hawksworth ordered.

As she left, Isabel took a lingering look at Andrea's exposed body.

'Kneel,' Hawksworth commanded, once they were alone again.

Andrea obeyed with difficulty, sinking to her knees on the thickly carpeted floor.

Hawksworth levelled his deep blue eyes straight into hers. She was riveted to the spot. Then he got to his feet and poured himself another malt from the crystal decanter. He sipped the golden liquid for a moment.

'Would you like some more champagne?' he asked.

'Yes please, master.'

He tilted her head up by touching her chin and put the glass to her lips. It was a tender gesture and one that made her heart leap. The look in his eye was caring too. The wine was cold. It dripped down her chin and splashed onto her breasts. Her nipples stiffened.

Hawksworth took off his jacket. He unzipped the fly of his trousers and extracted his cock. It was flaccid.

'Here,' he said. 'Suck on this for me, Andrea.'

She felt her pulse racing. He had been intimate with her before, but never like this. She thrust her head forward eagerly. For once she wished she was not in bondage so she could hold his cock in her hands and cup his balls while she took him in her mouth. But she would just have to make do with her lips and her tongue. She opened her mouth and sucked him in, then used her tongue to rub against his glans and the ridge below of it.

'Good girl,' he said.

His cock began to swell rapidly. She pushed forward until

it was buried in the back of her throat, then sucked hard on the whole length. Pulling right back, she dipped her head lower to run her lips down the underside of the shaft, sucking and nibbling. When she reached his balls, she sucked on them one after another. His cock, resting against her cheek, throbbed strongly.

The master stepped away.

He tugged off his tie, undid his shirt, then kicked off his shoes.

The phone built into the side of the plane rang once. He leant forward and unhooked it, cradling it to his ear with his shoulder while he sat on the chair and pulled off his socks.

'Yes.' He listened for a moment. 'I'll call you back,' he said. Getting to his feet again, he undid the belt of his trousers and stepped out of them. His black briefs followed.

'I don't really have the time for this,' he said, taking a step towards the beautiful kneeling Andrea, the pulsing tip of his erection an inch from her lips. But as much as she wanted to suck it into her mouth, she knew better than to do anything without being told.

'Now, where were we?' Hawksworth said. 'Oh yes, you were just about to take me into your mouth again. Make it good, my dear.'

Andrea dipped her head, licking the length of the gnarled shaft. She used her tongue to jiggle his balls, then sucked avidly on his cock, working all the way up to his glans. Then she used her teeth, nipping the rigid column lightly, until her lips were firmly against the base of his shaft and she could taste his wiry pubic hair.

Slowly she moved back up, nibbling her way along his phallus, delaying the moment she plunged her mouth down and swallowed him again. Her own sex was running with her juices, the wetness leaking out onto her thighs. She remembered how she'd felt as she watched Julia do exactly this to Hawksworth, and how she'd wished it had been her.

Now her wish had come true. She hadn't understood what the 'training' he'd spoken of meant, but now she knew. It was not a question of obedience or discipline, though that was obviously important. What her time at the manor had done was to narrow her world down until it was entirely focused on Charles Darrington Hawksworth. She cared about no one else. No one else mattered.

She still cursed herself for being so stupid on her first day at the manor, but she had begun to wonder if placing her in that room with the rope pulled up between her legs and many other similar provocations had been deliberate. Hawksworth had wanted to punish her with his neglect to show her right from the beginning exactly how much she needed his attention, and how little he needed hers. A slave is not complete without a master, isn't that what he'd said?

She had his attention now – all of it.

She opened her mouth and took his cock right to the back of her throat again, so deep she had to control the reflex to gag.

Hawksworth moaned, running his fingers into her long blonde hair and holding her head so she could not move back. She felt his prick pulsing strongly between her lips.

He relaxed his grip. She pulled back to use her tongue on his glans, licking it all over and covering the dome with saliva.

'What a sweet little mouth you have,' he said, almost in a whisper.

She pushed back on him again, then began a regular rhythm, gliding her mouth back and forth, sucking hard as he thrust inward, licking with her tongue around his glans on the outward stroke.

'Yes…' he encouraged. She could see the muscles of his thighs tightening and feel his fingers digging into her scalp.

Andrea increased the tempo. By angling her head back she could get the whole of his cock inside her mouth and feel his glans throbbing against the back of her throat. She wanted to feel the spunk shooting out of him. Last time, she remembered, he'd withdrawn at the last moment. She prayed he'd not do that again.

But that seemed to be precisely what he did have in mind. As she felt his cock beginning to jerk powerfully in her mouth, he grabbed her hair and pulled her head back until his glans was poised at her lips. He held himself there for a second, his erection throbbing, then suddenly appeared to change his mind. He angled his hips and thrust his cock back into her as deep as it would go.

She took her opportunity. Before he could change his mind again she concentrated her tongue on his glans, flicking it as hard as she could against the ridge which, she knew, was the most sensitive part. This produced instant results. Hawksworth's cock twitched against the tight confines of her throat and she felt a jet of hot liquid spurt forth. For a second nothing else happened. He held himself rigid, every muscle in his body locked tight. Then his cock jerked again and the spunk gushed out of him in a stream, cascading down her throat. Andrea desperately tried to swallow it all, but some overflowed and pearled down her chin.

Hawksworth did not move. He stood there naked with his fingers entwined in her hair, allowing his orgasm to wash over him. Andrea felt his cock soften and touched it gently with her tongue, the taste of his spunk filling her mouth.

Eventually he pulled away. He picked up his whisky and took a sip, then pressed a button on the bulkhead by the bar.

'Yes, sir,' Isabel said, opening the door from the forward cabin, apparently unfazed by Hawksworth's nudity. Clearly she was accustomed to such incidents.

'Get Abrahams back on the phone for me, would you?' he said.

'Yes, Mr Hawksworth.'

'Then get her ready.' He nodded towards Andrea but did not look at her.

'Certainly, sir.' Isabel closed the door again.

Hawksworth picked up his trousers and briefs and pulled them back on. He slipped into his shirt.

A moment later the phone rang.

'Yes...' Hawksworth listened, then began talking in French.

The cabin door opened and Isabel returned. She took hold of Andrea's arm and helped her to her feet. 'Come on,' she said. There was a definite glint in her eye.

The stewardess pulled Andrea to the back of the cabin and pushed her through another small door.

'Alone at last,' she said conspiratorially, closing the door.

They were in a small metal-lined cabin, which had obviously been designed to hold cargo. Andrea could see several cases strapped down by nylon webbing.

Screwed into the bulkhead between this and the passenger accommodation was a T-shaped structure covered in white leather, with six white leather straps hanging from the crosspiece. Another strap was dangling from the vertical component just off the floor.

Isabel spun Andrea around and undid the snap-lock that held the cuffs together, releasing her from the bondage. Then the stewardess crouched down beside a small leather case on the floor, by one of the storage units, and opened it.

'Put these on,' she said, straightening up with lithe grace. She handed Andrea a bright red rubber garment, a pair of gloves made from the same material, and a packet of stockings.

The rubber garment was like an old-fashioned full-length girdle, with shoulder straps and short suspenders dangling from the hem. At the front, however, two large holes had been cut in the rubber to expose the wearer's breasts.

Andrea pulled the rubber garment over her head. The inside had been coated with talcum powder to reduce the friction, but it was still difficult to peel the material over her body. Eventually she managed it. The girdle was extremely tight and constricting. It extended right down over her buttocks and lower belly. Her breasts poked through the holes at the front obscenely. She opened the cellophane packet of stockings and shook them out. They were black and sheer with a glossy finish, a fully-fashioned heel and a seam.

'Sit on this,' Isabel said, producing a small metal stool from the far end of the cabin.

The seat of the stool was cold. Andrea raised her legs one by one, and rolled on the stockings, making sure the seams were straight. She clipped them into the suspenders of the rubber girdle.

'Now the gloves.'

Andrea worked them up her arms. They extended well above the elbow. It took a great deal of tugging and manipulating before they were both in place.

Isabel took a pair of red patent leather ankle boots from the case and handed them to Andrea. They had a tapering four-inch heel. 'Put these on too.'

Andrea pulled the boots on.

'Good,' Isabel said, clearly enjoying the delicious sight before her. 'Now stand up.'

Andrea got to her feet again. Isabel took her by the arms and pushed her back against the bulkhead with her shoulders in the centre of the crosspiece of the white leather T. She raised Andrea's left arm at right angles to her body and secured the first of the leather straps around her wrist. The second strap fitted just above the elbow and the third at the top of the arm. The stewardess secured her other arm, then knelt at Andrea's feet and bound her ankles together with the strap at the bottom.

'Better than a seatbelt,' Isabel said, smiling. She raised a hand and stroked Andrea's cheek. 'Look at you... you're so needy, aren't you?' She ran her fingertips down Andrea's throat, along her collarbone and onto the rubber girdle. She flicked both exposed nipples with her fingernail, then moved down under the hem of the girdle, to her mons. Isabel's hand moved inward, parting her labia and finding her clit.

213

Andrea gasped as the finger pressed on her clitoris.

'So needy,' Isabel repeated huskily. She pushed her finger back into Andrea's cunt, then brought it up to her own mouth and sucked on it. 'And so juicy.'

The skirt of Isabel's grey uniform was knee length and quite tight, but the stewardess managed to wriggle it up over her hips. Her flesh-coloured nylons were clipped into a white suspender belt and she wore silky white French knickers. Isabel pushed her hand into the leg of the knickers and Andrea saw her finger searching for her clit. Then Isabel began to fret it from side to side.

The stewardess moved closer. She pressed her cheek against Andrea's and kissed her ear, the shapely contours of her uniform jacket rubbing against Andrea's naked breasts. 'Lovely,' she whispered as she wrapped her free hand around Andrea's neck and seductively writhed against the rubber girdle.

The plane banked to the left and the cabin floor tilted. Isabel clung to Andrea for support. As the plane levelled out again, Isabel gave a tiny cry and moulded her body against the helpless Andrea.

After a moment she pulled away, squatted down on her haunches, and rummaged in the leather case. Even in such a lewd position she oozed sex and class. She extracted a small object, which Andrea could not see properly. But, as she stood up, Andrea saw she was holding what looked like a metal ball-bearing in her hand; but its surface was covered with tiny little spikes.

'Spread your thighs a little,' Isabel ordered.

With her ankles bound together it was difficult to obey, but Andrea managed to open her knees and squirm her thighs apart. Isabel pushed the spiky metal ball between them, right up against her sex.

'Hold it there,' she instructed, her tone becoming more firm.

Andrea closed her thighs again. The spikes of the metal

were sharp and bit into her flesh. She closed her eyes and nibbled her lower lip, trying to ignore the niggling discomfort.

Without a word, Isabel pulled down and straightened her grey skirt over her curvaceous hips and bottom, brushed her fingers through her lustrous hair, and walked into the passenger cabin.

Chapter Eleven

The plane was starting to descend. Andrea could feel the pressure building in her ears.

Isabel's attentions, as well as the master's, had left her unbelievably frustrated. But there was nothing she could do about it. Without the spiky metal ball pressed between her thighs she could have tried to manipulate her clitoris by squeezing her thighs together. This was obviously what the metal ball was there to prevent.

She would have given anything to be able to finger her clitoris. It was alive, dancing against her labia, itching to be relieved. But once again she was denied even this most basic of comforts – which made matters worse, of course. The constant reminders that she was a slave and could not even touch herself only increased her need. 'So needy,' the stewardess had said. And she was absolutely right.

The plane had been in the air for about an hour, Andrea thought, as she heard the clang of the landing gear under the fuselage.

It had long since got dark and Andrea could only glimpse the landing lights on the runway through the single porthole as they came in to land. She had no idea where they might be.

It took about five minutes for the plane to taxi to a halt. Andrea caught a glimpse of a long black limousine, waiting on the side of the tarmac.

She heard a thud of doors being unlatched.

The cargo door opened and she felt a rush of fresh air. It was balmy and scented with flowers. A man in overalls began unloading the luggage; he appeared not to give Andrea a second glance.

Isabel walked in from the passenger cabin.

'Comfortable?' She pushed her hand down between Andrea's thighs. 'Open wide,' she said. Andrea did as she was told and the spiked ball dropped into Isabel's hand. The woman began unbuckling the straps around Andrea's arms. The belt around her ankles followed. As soon as she was free, Isabel used a pair of metal handcuffs to bind Andrea's wrists behind her back.

Isabel helped Andrea down the six steps to the tarmac and led her to the limousine. A driver stood with the rear door open as cases were loaded into the boot. She saw Hawksworth inside on the phone.

The driver closed the door the moment Andrea was inside too.

It was a short drive. Andrea caught sight of a road sign in French at a small roundabout. They were in France! After three or four minutes of winding down country lanes they were driving through the wrought-iron gates of an impressive eighteenth-century chateau.

The car did not stop at the front of the building, where a double flight of stone steps swept up to huge front doors, but drove around to the back. Here, a large conservatory flooded with light had been added to the building. As they approached, Andrea could see that it contained a swimming pool surrounded by a profusion of exotic plants.

The car came to a halt by a door at the rear of the chateau. Hawksworth was still deep in conversation and made no attempt to get out. The driver opened Andrea's door.

'Go with him,' Hawksworth said, putting his hand over the telephone for a second.

The driver led Andrea to the door and rapped with his gloved hand.

Light flooded out into the courtyard as a woman appeared in the doorway. To Andrea's astonishment, she was dressed in an identical costume to her own: a red rubber girdle, rubber gloves, black stockings and red patent leather high heels.

She even wore a steel collar like the one that had been locked around Andrea's neck on the first day. There was only one point of difference – the girl was wearing a red velvet mask over her eyes.

'*Merci, Henri,*' the girl said. The driver walked back to the car.

She held out a mask. 'Put this on,' she said, with a seductive French accent. Then she realised that Andrea's hands were cuffed behind her back, so she put it on Andrea herself.

They walked into the chateau, down a brick-floored and well-worn corridor into a small, surprisingly intimate sitting room.

'*Bon soir.*'

A petit middle-aged woman, with the fairest hair Andrea had ever seen, sat in a light blue armchair. She was wearing a brief white satin slip with a lace bodice. Another corseted girl knelt in front of her; her corset was made of black velvet, with laces running all the way down her back. The blonde's legs were wide apart, one foot on the floor and the other raised in the air, her calf resting on the girl's shoulder. The girl's mouth was pressed to the blonde's sex and her head was bobbing gently. Andrea could see that her naked buttocks were criss-crossed with weals, at least six or seven of them and all, judging by their scarlet colour, applied fairly recently.

A tall grey-haired man in a white cotton robe was sitting on a large sofa in front of a stone fireplace. A girl knelt in front of him too, her costume identical to the clothes Andrea was wearing, right down to the velvet mask. The only difference was that her hands were tied under her chin by a thin nylon line secured to the steel collar around her throat. She was servicing the man in very much the same way Andrea had serviced Hawksworth on the plane.

'Welcome, my dear,' the woman added, idly stroking the black hair of the girl who knelt in front of her. 'You've arrived at just the right moment, as you see.' Her English was

218

impeccable, with hardly a trace of an accent.

'Come over here,' the man said bluntly.

Andrea hesitated. Was she supposed to obey these people as she obeyed Hawksworth?

'Do it.' Hawksworth's voice rang out across the room. He was standing behind her, a stern expression on his face.

Andrea felt uneasy as she moved over to the man.

'Kneel,' the man ordered, his lustful eyes crawling all over her.

She knelt beside the identically dressed girl.

'Share it,' the man snapped, pulling his turgid cock out of the other girl's mouth.

Andrea didn't need to be told twice. Acutely aware of her master's eyes boring into her back, she began to mouth the large cock, its shaft glistening with the other girl's saliva. As she took one side, the first girl planted her mouth on the other, their lips almost touching at they sucked on the rod of flesh. In unison, they began to slide their mouths up and down.

'Hawksworth, how nice to see you,' the blonde welcomed her guest.

'Marie-Claire, it's a delight as always,' he replied.

'She is for training, no?' Marie-Claire nodded towards Andrea.

'I don't think you'll have any difficulties. She has a real talent for it.'

'Then that promises to be fun. Won't you join us? Take your pick.' She gripped the brunette's hair and pulled her head up. 'This one is very skilful, aren't you, Claudine? Though, as you can see for yourself, we have had to take her in hand tonight, haven't we?'

'*Oui, Madame Vuittenez*,' the girl admitted meekly.

'Or there's Simone over there,' the woman continued. 'You won't mind, will you, Pierre?'

'For you, Charles, anything,' the man said conversationally, as though having two beauties kneeling before him with their soft lips caressing his erection was the most normal thing in the world.

'And who is this charming creature?' Hawksworth asked, turning to the girl who'd met Andrea at the back door.

'Sophie, our star pupil,' said Marie-Claire.

'Come here, Sophie.' Hawksworth casually beckoned her over.

The girl walked closer. Andrea could only see her master from the corner of her eye as he bent forward and kissed Sophie on the lips. He had never done that to her.

'For the moment, I am content to watch,' Hawksworth said.

'*Bon*.' Marie-Claire smiled. 'I love being watched. Are you comfortable here, or shall we go upstairs?'

'I'm fine here,' Hawksworth said. He selected an armchair and sat down.

'She's good,' Pierre said, looking at Hawksworth but nodding towards the kneeling Andrea.

'Thank you,' Hawksworth replied.

'Has she been buggered?' he asked bluntly.

'She has indeed, but only by me.'

'Do you mind?'

'My dear man, you're going to have her here for seven days. This is the last lap of her training. You and Marie-Claire have *carte blanche* with all the girls.'

'True.' Pierre stroked both the lovely heads in his lap, as though they were his favourite pets. 'Kneel up on the sofa, girl,' he ordered Andrea.

She instantly did as she was told and mounted the sofa on all fours, helped by Simone.

'Oh...' Marie-Claire suddenly threw her head back and groaned in delight. Claudine's mouth was still on her sex, her tongue working obediently at her clitoris. 'Sophie...' Marie-Claire sighed, 'bring me the nipple clips. If Charles wants a show, will give him one.'

Sophie crossed to a small box on an occasional table. She

took out a thin metal chain, on the end of which were the oval clips Andrea had already experienced.

'Get her nice and wet for me, Simone,' Pierre said.

Simone wriggled beneath Andrea until her head was between Andrea's knees, her face immediately below her sex. Simone wrapped her hands around Andrea's thighs, just above her stocking tops, and pulled her cunt down on to her face. Instantly, Andrea felt the girl's tongue darting between her labia and nudging against her clit. It was such a relief after all her frustrations that she whimpered out loud.

Pierre had risen to his feet and was stripping off his cotton robe. His cock was very smooth, the glans slightly bigger in circumference than the shaft that supported it. He stood by the side of the two girls and cupped Andrea's breasts. The holes in the rubber girdle were small and the constriction had caused the flesh to redden but, until he touched them, Andrea had not realised how sensitive they had become. As he pinched the nipples a huge jolt of pleasure shot through her body.

Already she was feeling the familiar precursors to orgasm though she knew, with Hawksworth's eyes watching every move she made, she was not allowed to come. But Simone's tongue was artful. It seemed to be able to find the spots that produced the greatest pangs of pleasure, and wave after wave of delight was making her sex convulse wildly.

She watched Sophie take the nipple clips to Marie-Claire and pull the shoulder straps of the slip down to bare the blonde's breasts. Her tits were not large but high and round, with small dark nipples. The girl fitted a clip over the woman's right nipple. As the jaws closed, Andrea felt a rush of fellow feeling in her own breasts as she saw Marie-Claire's body tremble. She knew exactly what the Frenchwoman was feeling. The second clip followed, making Marie-Claire gasp.

Pierre's hand wrapped around Andrea's neck, pulling her forward onto his cock. She opened her mouth and sucked it in, her eyes searching out Hawksworth's, remembering how it had felt as he'd come in her mouth not very much earlier. He met her gaze, those deep blue eyes betraying not the least emotion.

'*C'est mouillée?*' Pierre asked.

'*Oui*,' Simone said, her voice muffled on Andrea's sex. '*Ça va.*'

He pulled his cock out of Andrea's mouth and climbed up onto the sofa, kneeling behind her. Andrea felt his erection nudging against her buttocks.

Simone had raised her head and was busy coating Pierre's cock with her saliva, making loud slurping noises as she did so. Then, as Andrea felt Simone's lips return to her labia, Pierre's cock thrust into the opening of her anus.

'No…' she squealed.

But her body betrayed her, her sphincter opening to allow his glans to slip effortlessly inside. The stab of pain was intense, but it changed to pleasure so quickly that her mind had no time to register the discomfort. Already the thrill was radiating throughout her body. Her sex clenched and she felt her clit pulse hungrily as Simone's tongue caressed it.

Everywhere around her was sex. She could see Marie-Claire stretched out across the armchair, her head thrown right back, both legs now resting on Claudine's shoulders, the heels of her white satin slippers digging into the girl's back. Claudine was licking her sex like an ice cream, with broad strokes of her tongue, while Sophie was standing beside the chair with the chain of the nipple clips in her hand, pulling it up so high that the blood drained from the blonde woman's nipples.

Pierre thrust his cock into the depths of Andrea's anus. Another wave of pain flooded over her, followed by a wave of irresistible excitement. Her whole body shuddered. Simone's tongue was working ceaselessly between her legs, bringing her closer and closer. She was on the brink of yet another orgasm. Andrea stared at Hawksworth, trying to beg him with her eyes to give her permission, but he was looking at Marie-Claire.

'No,' she whispered to herself, trying desperately to hold back. She was sure now that all the events of the day had been planned, including what had happened with Diana, with the aim of testing her to the limit.

Behind her, Pierre began pumping harder, the tight tube of her rear lubricated by Simone's saliva. She had never realised that her anus could be as sensitive as her cunt. 'No, please no,' she breathed.

Suddenly Hawksworth's eyes met hers and everything stood still. For a moment she remained in stasis, as he looked at her. Then he nodded, a gesture that had only one interpretation, and she came, her orgasm flooding out of her like water from a dam. She screamed and shuddered, her snug rear passage closing around the rod of flesh that invaded it. Somewhere in the miasma of feeling that convulsed her, she felt Pierre's cock jerking and was aware of a hot wetness deep in her core.

Eventually the feelings ebbed away. She opened her eyes and looked down between her legs. Simone had gobbled Pierre's wilting cock into her mouth and was busy licking it clean of the last drops of his spunk.

Across the room Marie Claire must also have come because Sophie was delicately removing the nipple clips, replacing them with the soothing balm of her tongue. Claudine sprawled on the carpet, discarded, her services no longer required.

'Quite a show,' the master said.

'Glad you enjoyed it,' Marie-Claire sighed. 'Why don't you take one of the girls now?'

'No, I've got to go. I'll be back to pick her up next week. Perhaps then—'

'Go?' Andrea gasped, suddenly feeling extremely alone and vulnerable.

'You know better than to speak without permission, girl!'

223

Hawksworth snapped immediately.

'Where are you going?' she pleaded, ignoring the warning in his tone.

'That's none of your business,' he said sternly. 'Now be quiet and don't embarrass me further!'

'You're not leaving me here?' Suddenly Andrea felt as if she'd been thrown into a cold shower. Her sexual energy had completely drained away. She'd come here with her master. Everything she'd done had been for him. He couldn't merely discard her for a whole week!

Hawksworth got to his feet, his stance threatening. He was clearly angry.

'I can't... I just can't...' she sobbed, shaking her head. Suddenly the rubber corset and the stockings and gloves appeared obscene and faintly ridiculous. She didn't want this. She had done it all for her master. Of course, she had been away from him before, but the prospect of a week in the middle of France, hundreds of miles away from him, was something quite different. She would do anything for him and with him, but this was too much to ask.

'Very well,' he said, his voice calm once again. He moved over to the sofa, took a small key from his pocket, and unlocked the handcuffs. Andrea looked up into his eyes, pleading with him, though she wasn't sure what she wanted him to do. This had been her decision. The expression on his face was one of disinterest... contempt.

He nodded to Marie-Claire, who was also now standing. The blonde walked to Andrea and helped her off the sofa. Without a word, she led her out of the sitting room and down the corridor. She opened a door on the left and guided Andrea inside.

'Take your clothes off,' she said. As soon as Andrea had wriggled out of the rubber garments, Marie-Claire gathered them up and went to the door. She walked out, and Andrea heard a key being turned in the lock.

The room had a small single bed, a straight-back chair and a mirror. Andrea stared at herself. She looked different; the unaccustomed make-up changing the angles of her face, but her eyes were unchanged. Despite everything she'd seen in the last few weeks, they stared back at her with the same intensity as ever.

She noticed, as she brushed her hair with her fingers, that her hands were shaking. In the space of a few minutes her whole world had collapsed. The look on her master's face, the total disinterest he had displayed, had touched her to the quick. But she didn't know what else to do. She had no idea what Marie-Claire's training would involve, but she could go through with it if, at the end of each day, at least she had some hope of being taken to her master. She didn't mind sharing him, or watching him with another woman, but not seeing him at all would be too much to bear.

After no more than ten minutes the door opened again.

Hawksworth entered the tiny room with a plain beige dress folded over his arm. He laid it on the bed next to her. There was also a pair of grey cotton panties, a bra and flat-heeled brown shoes.

'Put those on,' he said quietly, walking back to the door.

'Master,' she said. 'Please don't go.'

'I am no longer your master, Andrea.'

Her heart sank. 'Don't say that.'

'I thought you understood.'

'I can't bear to be without you, master.'

'That is precisely what you have achieved by refusing to be trained here. If you do not wish to obey me then you will be sent back to London and I will never see you again.'

'No,' she whispered.

'Yes. Now get dressed. The plane is returning in an hour. Your old job is waiting for you.'

Andrea was stunned. Of course what he said was true. She could not expect to go back to the manor and have him take up where they had left off. All that was over. She sat on the bed, staring at her knees.

'Such a pity,' he said, as he opened the door.

'Please don't go,' she begged again.

'I have to,' he insisted. 'Do you still not understand that?'

She tried to collect her racing thoughts. She supposed one day she would once more have to face the cold reality of her flat and her job, but the thought of walking into the office on Monday morning was like a slap in the face. She had already begun to speculate about The System and what the master would ask her to do after her training. All that appeared to be over too. 'Please, master...'

'You've let me down, Andrea,' he said, coldly.

'No,' she said firmly, determinedly, rising to her feet, her fists clenched by her sides. 'I'll do it. I'll stay. I'll do anything... Just tell me I can stay.'

A hint of a smile flickered across Hawksworth's face. 'Of course you can stay,' he said. 'But I'll tolerate no more childish behaviour or weakness from you. Do you understand?'

'Oh master!' She threw herself into his arms, a flood of relief overwhelming her.

'Get on your knees,' he ordered.

'Yes, master,' she said, relishing the words again. 'Anything you say.' She didn't care. She didn't care what Marie-Claire did to her, she didn't care how long Hawksworth was away, as long as she could see him again and be his slave. She realised with absolute conviction that that was all she had ever wanted. She knew she should never have tried to assert herself. She was past all that. She had no ability to choose any more; no will of her own. She sank to her knees. Now she belonged to him. What he wanted for her, was all she wanted for herself.

'You'll have to be punished for your silly tantrum,' he said.

'Yes, master... please punish me.'

More exciting titles available from Chimera

1-901388-23-9	Latin Submission	*Barton*
1-901388-19-0	Destroying Angel	*Hastings*
1-901388-26-3	Selina's Submission	*Lewis*
1-901388-29-8	Betty Serves the Master	*Tanner*
1-901388-31-X	A Kept Woman	*Grayson*
1-901388-32-8	Milady's Quest	*Beaufort*
1-901388-33-6	Slave Hunt	*Shannon*
1-901388-34-4*	Shadows of Torment	*McLachlan*
1-901388-35-2*	Star Slave	*Dere*
1-901388-37-9*	Punishment Exercise	*Benedict*
1-901388-38-7*	The CP Sex Files	*Asquith*
1-901388-39-5*	Susie Learns the Hard Way	*Quine*
1-901388-40-9*	Domination Inc.	*Leather*
1-901388-42-5*	Sophie & the Circle of Slavery	*Culber*
1-901388-11-5*	Space Captive	*Hughes*
1-901388-41-7*	Bride of the Revolution	*Amber*
1-901388-44-1*	Vesta – Painworld	*Pope*
1-901388-45-X*	The Slaves of New York	*Hughes*
1-901388-46-8*	Rough Justice	*Hastings*
1-901388-47-6*	Perfect Slave Abroad	*Bell*
1-901388-48-4*	Whip Hands	*Hazel*
1-901388-50-6*	Slave of Darkness	*Lewis*
1-901388-49-2*	Rectory of Correction	*Virosa*
1-901388-51-4*	Savage Bonds	*Beaufort*
1-901388-52-2*	Darkest Fantasies	*Raines*
1-901388-53-0*	Wages of Sin	*Benedict*
1-901388-54-9*	Love Slave	*Wakelin*
1-901388-56-5*	Susie Follows Orders	*Quine*
1-901388-55-7*	Slave to Cabal	*McLachlan*
1-901388-57-3*	Forbidden Fantasies	*Gerrard*
1-901388-58-1*	Chain Reaction	*Pope*
1-901388-60-3*	Sister Murdock's House of Correction	*Angelo*
1-901388-61-1*	Moonspawn	*McLachlan*
1-901388-59-X*	The Bridle Path	*Eden*
1-901388-62-X*	Ruled by the Rod	*Rawlings*
1-901388-63-8*	Of Pain and Delight	*Stone*

1-901388-65-4*	The Collector	Steel
1-901388-66-2*	Prisoners of Passion	Dere
1-901388-67-0*	Sweet Submission	Anderssen
1-901388-69-7*	Rachael's Training	Ward
1-901388-71-9*	Learning to Crawl	Argus
1-901388-36-0*	Out of Her Depth	Challis
1-901388-68-9*	Moonslave	McLachlan
1-901388-72-7*	Nordic Bound	Morgan
1-901388-27-1*	A Strict Seduction	del Rey
1-901388-80-8*	Cauldron of Fear	Pope
1-901388-74-3*	In Too Deep	Beaufort
1-901388-73-5*	Managing Mrs Burton	Aspen
1-901388-75-1*	Lucy	Culber
1-901388-77-8*	The Piano Teacher	Elliot
1-901388-25-5*	Afghan Bound	Morgan
1-901388-76-X*	Sinful Seduction	Benedict
1-901388-70-0*	Babala's Correction	Amber
1-901388-06-9*	Schooling Sylvia	Beaufort
1-901388-78-6*	Thorns	Scott
1-901388-79-4*	Indecent Intent	Amber
1-903931-00-2*	Thorsday Night	Pita
1-903931-01-0*	Teena Thyme	Pope
1-903931-02-9*	Servants of the Cane	Ashton
1-903931-04-5*	Captured by Charybdis	McLachlan
1-903931-03-7*	Forever Chained	Beaufort
1-903931-05-3*	In Service	Challis
1-903931-06-1*	Bridled Lust	Pope
1-903931-07-X*	Stolen Servant	Grayson
1-901388-21-2*	Dr Casswell's Student	Fisher
1-903931-08-8*	Dr Casswell's Plaything	Fisher
1-903931-09-6*	The Carrot and the Stick	Vanner
1-903931-10-X*	Westbury	Rawlings
1-903931-11-8*	The Devil's Surrogate	Pope
1-903931-12-6*	School for Nurses	Ellis
1-903931-13-4*	A Desirable Property	Dere

* * *

All **Chimera** titles are available from your local bookshop or newsagent, or direct from our mail order department. Please send your order with your credit card details, a cheque or postal order (made payable to *Chimera Publishing Ltd*) to: **Chimera Publishing Ltd., Readers' Services, PO Box 152, Waterlooville, Hants, PO8 9FS**. Or call our **24 hour telephone/fax credit card hotline: +44 (0)23 92 783037** (Visa, Mastercard, Switch, JCB and Solo only).

To order, send: Title, author, ISBN number and price for each book ordered, your full name and address, cheque or postal order for the total amount, and include the following for postage and packing:
UK and BFPO: £1.00 for the first book, and 50p for each additional book to a maximum of £3.50.
Overseas and Eire: £2.00 for the first book, £1.00 for the second and 50p for each additional book.

*Titles £5.99. All others £4.99

For a copy of our free catalogue please write to:

Chimera Publishing Ltd
Readers' Services
PO Box 152
Waterlooville
Hants
PO8 9FS

or email us at:
sales@chimerabooks.co.uk

or purchase from our range of superb titles at:
www.chimerabooks.co.uk

Sales and Distribution in the USA and Canada

LPC Group
Client Distribution Services
193 Edwards Drive
Jackson
TN 38301
USA

Sales and Distribution in Australia

Dennis Jones & Associates Pty Ltd
19a Michellan Ct
Bayswater
Victoria
Australia 3153

* * *